The Hidden Legacy

Julie Roberts

Rene
by ir
in p
by

ISBN 9781783757756

Copyright © Julie Roberts 2016

The right of Julie Roberts to be identified as the author
of this work has been asserted by her in accordance with
the Copyright, Designs and Patents Act 1988.

All the characters in this book are fictitious, and any
resemblance to actual persons, living or dead, is purely
coincidental.

Acknowledgements

I would like to thank my editor, Jay Dixon, for her kindness and generous help in preparing my novel for publication.

My thanks also, to everyone who helped with my research. Especially:

Adam Waterton, Librarian, Royal Academy of Arts, regarding the Summer Exhibition 1815.

The staff of The Courtauld Institute of Art, Somerset House, for historic architectural advice.

And the staff of the Hoop and Grapes in Aldgate for their historical legend of a secret tunnel.

To my husband, Tony, who has been my most devoted supporter, from the first word to the last.

CHAPTER ONE

April 1815

This moment was the beginning of her new life.

Meredith stood in front of a building in Ludgate Hill. She owned every brick and room squeezed between a silversmith and a tailor's premises. From today it was her home, her art studio, and gallery. She wanted to dance and clap her hands, though such girlish behaviour would not be appropriate. But it was still a wonder that her beloved guardian, Frederick, had bequeathed it to her.

She stepped close to the bow window, which reflected her green eyes bright with happiness. A light breeze lifted a strand of dark hair as she rubbed her finger over a dust spot. The new easels had emptied her purse, but they had been worth every penny as they displayed her two favourite paintings, a river scene and a portrait of a boy.

The sound of bolts being drawn in the adjoining shops made her heart beat faster. Could she succeed in the art world? Would artists allow an un-sponsored, unprotected woman into their realm of canvas and oils? Enter studios where models were draped in only swathes of scarlet silk?

Going inside, she left the front door open. It presented a more welcoming entrance than a client having to knock. The dusty and dingy room of two weeks ago was now covered with unbleached linen panels. It had transformed the space into a light and airy gallery. In pride of place on the long wall was her painting of Frederick.

She picked up *The Times* and read the advertisement she had placed. It looked small and insignificant amongst so many others.

Artist of experience seeks pupils to tutor in the graces of drawing and painting.

Mondays and Wednesdays – 9am until noon.

Charge 5s.0d per morning.

Sanders Studio, Ludgate Hill.

Should she be sitting when a client arrived? She swept her skirt across a wooden chair and seated herself behind a spindly-legged desk that she had bargained fiercely for with a mean-faced trader at a flea market – but she loved the elegant tone it gave the gallery.

Fifteen minutes passed. She couldn't sit a moment longer and paced the length of the room, counting each step … Thirty minutes! What would she do if no one came? Frederick had, in his will, provided her with an allowance which ought to cover her own expenses. But there was also Mrs Clements to provide for. It had only been proper to invite her to leave Harlington and come to London as her companion and housekeeper. Her tuition money would be essential to pay Mrs Clements' wages. And what about buying her art materials? If she sold a painting she would need to create another to replace it. Her plan to put aside a little money each quarter for emergencies was looking more than fanciful. Clearly being independent meant shouldering a lot of personal and household responsibilities.

Clattering horses' hooves sounded outside the window and Meredith hurried to see what was happening. A well-attired gentleman was lifting a little girl from a coach. A moment later he opened the inner gallery door and together they stepped inside.

Now that she could see him better, he was a very handsome gentleman. His dark hair touched the collar of his jacket and his eyes were the darkest of brown. He removed his hat, favoured a slight bow, and said, 'Good morning. My niece and I have come in answer to an advertisement regarding tuition. Would you please announce to the artist that Mr Fox and Miss Weston are here?'

This was not a good start. He thought she was an assistant? Her hands started to tremble and she clasped them tightly and prayed the dark dress she wore gave her a professional appearance.

She curtsied. 'You address the artist, sir.'

He stepped back, 'You! But you're a ...' he faltered, 'a lady, a very young lady!'

If this was the reaction she was going to get whenever a prospective client walked through the door, interviews would be extremely tedious. But she would not be intimidated by his words; she raised her head an inch and replied, 'I am Miss Meredith Sanders, at your service, sir. I can assure you I am fully qualified to tutor.'

Mr Fox gestured to the window. 'Come closer that I might see better a lady who recommends herself so highly.'

Meredith bit her tongue. How many times had she been warned that her frank speaking would be her downfall? Was she now going to lose this client she so desperately needed?

'I beg your pardon sir, I meant no offence.'

Amusement tinged his voice as he repeated, 'I asked you to come nearer the light.'

The last thing she wanted to do was provoke a disagreement, so she stepped forward and said, 'This is a bright room, sir. However, I am happy to oblige you.'

His gaze started at her feet and moved upwards to her

eyes, his expression revealing nothing of his thoughts. 'Tell me, how many of these paintings can I attribute to you?'

'All of them, sir.' Meredith kept her tone civil and swept her arm in a circle towards both long walls. 'I paint watercolour and oil, portrait and landscape.'

'Um,' was his only comment. 'Do you have a stool for my niece to sit on?'

Meredith indicated a wooden chair in the corner and the child sat down. Miss Weston's behaviour was demure, but there was an expectation in her, an excitement as she leant forward and watched her uncle's every move.

Mr Fox toured the room that was now her gallery, stopping to study first a landscape, then a charcoal sketch and finally the portrait of Frederick.

'Who is this?'

'My …' she hesitated, then the untruth left her lips, 'my late father, who was also my dearest friend.'

'Would you say this is a good likeness?'

Her grief, never far from the surface, returned. 'Oh, yes.' Her voice warmed, as it always did when she spoke of Frederick. 'He had the dearest of natures. Those lines beside his eyes were caused by laughter and his lips tilted up at the corner when he smiled. And he always wore the most brilliant of colours.' She was drawn into the painting, remembering the long summer days in his studio, how he had taught her to mix the oil paints, sketch an outline.

'I am much taken with your talent, Miss Sanders.'

She forced her memories aside, relieved to hear Mr Fox now viewed her with a more appreciative manner. Now that her initial fear had calmed, she could see his face was not so stern, his voice a more gentle tone. And his fine woollen green jacket fitted his broad shoulders to perfection. She let her gaze drift lower to the pale

4

breeches and highly polished boots. Such an outfit could only come from the highest quality shops. A flutter of excitement ran down to her toes.

'Thank you, sir. Your compliment is a great encouragement.'

'How many pupils do you have? I would like Miss Weston to receive your full attention if she were to study here.'

'I have none at the moment, sir. You are my first client.'

Her palms were wet and her pulse raced. She didn't want to babble, but what else could she say to entice him to let his niece attend? 'I would not charge any more for private lessons, should Miss Weston be the only pupil.'

Mr Fox raised his brows. 'Ah. You are out to bargain with me?'

'Bargain with you, sir? I only meant …' Her cheeks burned. Did he think she was trying to increase her fee? Certainly she was in need of the tuition money, but she was not a scheming fraudster. No indeed!

'Sir, may I point out that I am not –'

He interrupted, a frown creasing his forehead. 'Where do you come from? Your accent is unfamiliar.'

Why did he want to know that? Did it matter? She had advertised offering art tuition, not applied to be a governess. But a sharp reply could go against her. Civility was surely the best action. 'I'm from Harlington, sir.'

'You're a country girl, of course. Where do you conduct your lessons?'

A spark of hope rose up. 'I have a studio at the back of this gallery.'

'I would like to see your references, before we proceed any further.'

'I can give you my personal references. My

professional accomplishments are what you see on the walls.'

Meredith took three letters from her desk drawer, one from the Reverend Lyle, a second from Squire Norris, and the last from the Honourable Mrs Kilburn. She handed them to him.

'Each of these persons I have known for the past ten years.'

Mr Fox sat on her visitor's chair and opened the first letter.

What if she were unacceptable? Living under Frederick's protection she had never had the need to be interviewed, never to pay her own way. Her heart beat fast, as her dream of running this establishment, painting and selling her work, lay in what people like Mr Fox decided. To hide her nervousness she sat behind her desk and waited.

Minutes passed as he read, giving no indication by either manner or voice of how he was assessing her. He placed the letters on the desk.

'You have excellent references, Miss Sanders. Yet I have no friends or acquaintances that I could approach to vouch for you. By your own admission, you have come from Harlington, an area I know nothing of.'

This was another dilemma that had not occurred to her, that parents would be unwilling to leave their child in the care of a stranger.

He tapped his fingers on the desk. 'Do you have a companion living with you?'

'Yes, Mrs Clements is both my companion and housekeeper, sir. We have rooms above on two floors.'

'How long have you had her in your employ?'

'Mrs Clements came with me from Harlington. She was my father's housekeeper for twenty years.'

'May I ask you to draw a small sketch of my niece, to give me some assurance of your skill?'

Meredith drew in a breath and held it. He wanted her to draw with him watching? She released her breath, but her throat tightened and her hands suddenly had pins and needles. 'If that is your wish, sir, I will collect my sketch book and charcoal.'

He nodded. 'Do you want my niece to stay where she is?'

'Yes. Is a head and shoulders sufficient?

'That would be quite sufficient, Miss Sanders.' His voice held no malice, no triumph, only the respectful request of a client.

Meredith's legs were trembling and her heartbeat was so loud in her ears she was sure Mr Fox could hear it as she walked into the studio. She closed the door and leant against it. His request was unexpected and frightening, but this was her chance to prove she was an artist, not just a *lady who paints*. She picked up her sketch book and charcoal, and mustered her inner bravado.

Mr Fox had moved her visitor's chair in front of his niece, sitting by the window.

'Thank you, Mr Fox. Now, Miss Weston, just look at one of the paintings on the wall behind me – excellent. This will take a few minutes, so please, keep very still.'

Meredith waited, her charcoal poised over the paper. Behind her she could feel Mr Fox's presence, caught the faint scent on his skin. Yet he was not threatening, instead there was a comfort in him being there. Her fingers relaxed and she studied the child. With quick strokes she drew the contours of her face, her lips, her nose, but it was her eyes sparkling with excitement that brought the sketch alive. Meredith finished the portrait with the tight fair curls peeking from under her cap and her shoulders covered with a lace collar.

Meredith turned and handed him her sketch book. Everything she hoped for now lay in Mr Fox's hand.

He stood silent. Then a smile parted his lips. It

changed his countenance instantly. He glanced towards his niece and she started to rise, but he held up his hand. 'Sit a moment longer, Sarah. Patience is a lesson a young lady must acquire.' His tone was light but firm and the child sighed.

'I know, Uncle Adam.'

This was a different man to the one who had spoken so brusquely when he arrived. Was this a sign he was accepting her? The clock ticked away the minutes matching the thumping of her heartbeat as he studied the charcoal portrait.

'Miss Sanders, I am not a stickler for the high protocol of the gentry, but my niece is under my protection and I must be quite sure that she is brought up to a standard my brother-in-law would expect. Miss Weston is only eight years old, but I think she requires a younger person to be with for part of her education. Her day governess is a mature matron and very strict, a requirement my aunt insists on.'

What did this mean? Could she take this comment as an advantage? Waiting for his answer was a torture. She crossed her fingers, praying he would say yes. He went over to Frederick's portrait and studied it for several moments.

'May I offer a trial period of one month? If all progresses satisfactorily, then I see no reason why you should not continue Miss Weston's art tuition. I would insist, of course, on leaving a maid as her chaperone. Is this acceptable to you?'

Her breath left her in a rush. 'Thank you, Mr Fox. One month's trial and a chaperone are quite in order. Would you like to see the studio, sir?'

'I would indeed.' He turned his attention back to his niece. 'Come, Sarah, let us go and see Miss Sanders' studio.'

The child who had waited with such patience now

jumped up and down, her fair curls bobbing under her white cap. 'Oh, yes please, Uncle Adam.'

Meredith opened the door and stepped aside, allowing them to enter.

'Oh, this is so very nice. And there is paper and charcoal ready for me.' Miss Weston touched one of the four tables and sat down. 'Will I really be the only one?'

'At the moment, yes, but I hope to have other students very soon.'

Meredith's moment of optimism vanished as the child's forehead creased in a frown and Mr Fox started to tour the room much as he had her gallery. The bareness of the room suddenly struck Meredith as a barrier; had he expected a more palatial room for his niece to study in?

Miss Weston's frown cleared and her face brightened as she asked, 'If I'm the only one, could you come to Tallow House? Then I can draw the garden.'

Mr Fox stopped pacing. 'Would you consider coming to Great Ormond Street, Miss Sanders?'

Go to his home! She didn't know anything about him. What if his motives were not honourable? 'I don't know how far …' Her stomach was full of butterflies. She needed time to think, but this was not the time to go weak. 'I'm afraid not, sir. The cost of travelling and the time involved would not make it a viable business proposition for me.'

'Ah. So it *is* money that drives you, Miss Sanders. That I understand. May I make a proposal for your personal tuition of my niece? I will send my coach for you twice a week and provide all the materials you need and a room for a studio. Would double your fee cover the additional travelling time? If you wish to take on a little extra work, I will not object.'

He would not object! This was *her* business. She might be a woman in a man's world, but how dare he

9

give out orders as though she were a servant? The superior manner of the man was ... She opened her mouth to say, 'No. Thank you,' but didn't. Twenty shillings a week, guaranteed, would give her a small income and pay Mrs Clements' wages. It left plenty of time to secure other clients and sell her paintings. And his disinterested approach didn't give the impression of any untoward intentions.

Squaring her shoulders to her full five feet six inches she looked into his dark eyes. 'I think I can agree to that, sir. When would you like Miss Weston to start?'

'Your advertisement read Monday and Wednesday. These are convenient days for me. I will send my coach at eight-thirty so you may start at nine o'clock. You will require paint and brushes and other supplies. My footman will call to collect a list this afternoon.'

In less than an hour, Mr Fox had taken over her professional tuition. And as for Miss Weston, she couldn't think why he had bothered to bring her; other than he was taking away her charcoal drawing.

But she replied, 'Yes, sir, I will agree to that.' Now was not the time to upset the apple cart and lose her only client.

Miss Weston was so excited she couldn't keep still and hopped from foot to foot, her fair curls bouncing with each hop. 'Thank you, Uncle Adam. Oh, I can't wait to paint like Miss Sanders.'

The man who had given her the chance to fulfil her dream stepped into the doorway. 'I have taken up most of your morning, so you may include today in your bill. Shall we say payment bi-weekly?'

Meredith felt she should stand to attention and salute, but his generosity deserved an appreciative reply. 'Thank you, Mr Fox. I'm sure Miss Weston and I will fare well together. I am confident you will see much improvement in her drawing and painting by the end of our trial period.'

She accompanied him through the gallery to the door. 'Thank you for your faith in me, Mr Fox.'

'I hope we will both benefit, Miss Sanders. Good day to you. Come, Sarah, Jackson will take you and Betsey home.'

Meredith saw Mr Fox speak to his coachman and, presumably, Betsey, the nursery maid standing beside the horses. A moment later, Miss Weston and her maid climbed into his coach and the rattle of the horses' harness faded as the coachman steered the two greys towards the city. Mr Fox walked away in the opposite direction to St Pauls.

Mr Fox was arrogant, but underneath this he had displayed kindness to both his niece and her. Wealth, however, did not give him the right to treat her as one of his servants – even though she did need his money.

Bright light blazed through a high window and sunshine filled the studio. The bareness of the walls had not seemed a disadvantage until Mr Fox started his inspection. Seeing it from a client's point of view, she needed a few of her paintings to add colour. And what better way to encourage students than by example – her watercolour landscape, the ruined castle in oil, she had charcoal and pencil drawings. Perhaps she should tell them painting didn't only go on paper and canvas – she had climbed a ladder with a bucket in one hand and a brush in the other and sloshed the whitewash on the walls. She wouldn't mention that her work apron didn't protect her dress, or her face and hands being spotted white.

Mr Fox intrigued her. Who was he? Definitely a gentleman of financial standing; but what business was he engaged in?

She glanced at her clock on the table, it showed eleven o'clock – only an hour left, but there was still time for the doorbell to tinkle again. She really did need one more pupil.

Meredith sat down at a table and stared at the blank sheet of paper. She picked up a charcoal stick and started to sketch Mr Fox: his dark hair, eyes black with sparks of white. His nose was firm and straight and the angular chin gave his face a determined expression. She remembered his indulgent smile to his niece and stroked the charcoal to form his mouth. Her gaze lingered on the parted lips. She wasn't sure her decision to give private lessons was a wise choice. What would have happened if she had asked for two pounds a week? Would Mr Fox have agreed? She most certainly needed to improve her negotiating skills.

At twelve o'clock, Meredith locked the front door. She was both elated and disappointed and just a little frightened that there had been no other client. She couldn't afford another advertisement until Mr Fox made his first payment. But she must be grateful to him, some money was better than none; after all, artists were renowned for being poor.

Meredith climbed the stairs to the first landing and stopped in the doorway of a square room that had been equipped as a kitchen. It overlooked the back yard and would be hot come summer, but today the warmth from the fire was most welcome.

Mrs Clements was a rotund woman and almost filled the space between the sink and table. She was straining water from a pot, the rising steam tinting her face a rosy red. Meredith loved the old lady; she was more than a paid servant, she was her dearest friend.

'Whatever you're cooking, Clemmie, it smells good. I need something nice to cheer me up.'

'Did you not fare well, dear?'

'I have one client and I agreed to go to his home to give private tuition to his niece.'

'Isn't that good?'

'Yes, but I will need to sell a painting before my next allowance.'

'Of course you'll sell one. Now, off you go into the parlour. I'll be five minutes. I have your favourite, boiled ham and bread.'

Meredith went back along the landing into a room with a window overlooking the busy shopping street. She leant her forehead on the glass and watched the stagecoach leave the Belle Sauvage Inn and weave through the carriages that were vying for a place to stop. Doubts about the success of her venture plagued her again. The world of business was run by men; they made the rules. A spark of rebellion surged through her. She had challenged them before when a girl; she could do it now as a woman.

Clemmie came in and she turned round. All the furniture had come from Appleton House: the yellow brocade sofa from her bedchamber, the two brown wing chairs from Frederick's study, and the mahogany table and chairs from the dining room. The red and yellow carpet made it homely.

Inside this building she was safe, locked in a world provided for her by Frederick and because she had called herself Meredith Sanders from the day he found her.

Outside was the world she feared. She was caught between the two places that had haunted her for the past ten years – Newgate Prison and Blackfriars.

CHAPTER TWO

Adam Fox re-read the report he had received from his agent a month ago.

I beg to report that a stevedore has dropped one of our imported crates from Portugal and that it did split open. Inside was a painting wrapped in canvas and bound thickly with fine fabric. The shipping papers record the crate contains cambric cotton. The receiving address is Sanders Studio, Ludgate Hill. During the night the crate disappeared from the warehouse.

He had immediately visited the premises, only to find the door locked. He had peered through the window, expecting to see an artist's studio, but the room was completely empty. Enquiries at several premises proved useless and no one knew where the owner had gone.

Adam tapped his fingers on the leather panel of his desk and read again the advertisement in *The Times* newspaper – the same address as on the import papers. In the space of a few weeks it was now a renovated art studio, gallery, and school owned by the deceased owner's daughter, Miss Sanders, who was promoting herself as his protégé. This coincidence he could not brush aside. Sarah's desire to draw and paint gave him the perfect opportunity to look into what may not have been a careless clerical error.

He slipped the report and the newspaper into the long drawer of his desk and sat pondering what today would be like for his niece. He got up and went to the mantel shelf and picked up the charcoal drawing of Sarah. He touched her curls and smiled. She had been so happy and excited when he had returned home, her chatter full of expectation of her lessons with Miss Sanders. He would have it framed as a keepsake.

He turned to the wall behind his desk and looked at the portrait of his sister, Beatrice. Her death had been sudden and tragic and Victor had been heartbroken. When his brother-in-law pleaded with him to take on the guardianship of Sarah, he had not realised the great responsibility it entailed. Victor, free of his obligation to his daughter, had packed his trunks and sailed away to Europe. In the four years he had been gone, his infrequent letters from foreign ports revealed nothing of his future plans. Adam sighed. He should not judge Victor too harshly when he, himself, had never known the love and comfort of a wife.

His thoughts turned back to Meredith Sanders. He had expected a gentleman artist and had been put to odds with being curtsied to by a young woman. As an art tutor she was far too young and probably had little experience in teaching. But her sample drawing of Sarah did show her talent. Without a doubt she fascinated him – a lady presenting herself as a professional artist in a male-dominated world? He looked out of the window at the newly leafed trees and they reminded him how her emerald-coloured eyes dimmed in the shadows or sparkled in the sunlight. And her gown! He laughed aloud at how she had tried to disguise her shapely figure. He had, perhaps, been a little too severe in his manner, but she had been so proud and independent. Yes, there was something about Miss Sanders he couldn't quite get out of his mind – whether her young innocence was true or false, her fierce bravery was real and the feminine authority quite extraordinary – without a doubt she had the spirit of a filly not yet tamed.

And living in the country, what manner of upbringing

had she received? Certainly in a style that encouraged free speech. A wicked thought passed through his mind; what would it feel like to pull the clips from her dark hair and let it tumble through his fingers ... She was coming today, her first visit to his home. For once he was grateful of Sarah's strong personality. The woman and child were indeed kindred spirits.

He glanced at the mantel clock. Business called; he had no more time to think about the mysterious Miss Sanders.

At nine o'clock Mr Fox's coach stopped at Tallow House in Great Ormond Street.

Meredith surveyed the town house with trepidation. The only grand home she had been in was Harlington Manor. Frederick and she had dined there once a week when he was at home in Appleton House. Both Squire Norris and Frederick had a great passion for playing chess and would spend the evening closeted together battling strategies.

It had been rumoured Mrs Norris had brought a considerable dowry to the marriage. Unfortunately the union had not produced any children and Emily Norris had taken to teaching her the skills of household management and the social graces of society. Now she would put that tuition into practice.

Meredith took a deep breath. This was just another moment when she had to step into the unknown. She accepted the offered help of a footman and stepped out of the coach. Sarah came running through the front door, her face flushed and full of excitement.

'I've been looking through the window for you. Come and see what Uncle Adam has bought for us.' Taking Meredith's hand she pulled her in and towards a central staircase. 'We have a studio room next to my schoolroom. You'll love it, Miss Sanders.'

'Miss Weston! Please. Wait a moment.'

A door opened and a petite woman, dressed in a travelling pelisse, stood in the doorway. 'Miss Sanders. Good morning. I am Miss Thomson, governess to Miss Weston.'

Meredith curtsied, 'Good morning.'

'May I have a moment of your time?' Meredith followed her into the room. 'As you can see, I am about to leave. Mr Fox's coach is taking me to the staging point. My brother's wife has died. He has three small babes.' Her voice broke, and she dabbed her eyes with a handkerchief. 'Mr Fox has left to go to his warehouses at the docks; and Miss Fox does not rise until noon. She has requested I see you before I leave.'

'My condolences, Miss Thomson, I am so very sorry to hear such tragic news.' Meredith wanted to comfort her, tell her she knew how she felt and how the death of a dear one left an inner coldness that only another human can warm away. But such a display from a stranger would be unwelcome.

'Thank you. Miss Fox has kindly consented to help Miss Weston in her reading and arithmetic.' A smile softened her tight lips. 'I have set two new times tables for her to learn. This will cause a great deal of frustration for Miss Fox. Miss Weston is an intelligent child, but she is also very impatient.'

'Please be assured, I will encourage her too.' At least this was one small task she could do for the governess.

'I hope to return within the next few weeks after my brother has come to terms with his grief. And, of course, he must find a housekeeper who is willing to take on the children.' She dabbed at her eyes again. 'I have no need to show you to the studio; Miss Weston has been waiting with great anticipation to do that herself. I asked Mr Simms, the butler, to provide a jug of lemonade on your arrival.'

A jangling of harnesses sounded through the open front door.

'The horses are getting restless. I must go. Good bye, Miss Sanders.'

Meredith bowed her head and stepped aside.

In the hall, Miss Thomson clasped Sarah's hands. 'Be good, child. I will think of you every day.'

Sarah rose up on her toes and kissed her cheek. 'I promise to learn the times tables before you come back. I know Aunt Izzie will insist.'

Miss Thomson touched her cheek where Sarah had kissed her. 'I hope you will, dear.' Then she turned and went out to the waiting coach.

This was not what Meredith had envisaged: Mr Fox not in residence, his aunt indisposed, and her only contact was a distraught governess. She was now an unattended art tutor left to proceed as she saw fit.

'Can I show you our studio now, Miss Sanders?'

The boisterous child of five minutes ago had deflated into a sad little girl sitting on the bottom stair tread. Meredith looked round the circular hallway that was filled with daylight coming through a cupola roof window spreading to every corner of the chequered tiled floor. A small table, with a silver bell and salver on it, were the only decoration against the cream walls.

'I think I should see *someone*, Miss Weston, other than your governess. Oh dear, this is all very strange. So be it, show me the way, Miss Weston.'

Formal manners seemed very lax in this household. She would have to reassess Mrs Norris's teachings.

'Will you not call me Sarah?'

'Your uncle may not approve of that, especially here.' Meredith waved her free hand as she was pulled up the stairs. 'But, when we are alone together, then yes, I will call you Sarah.'

The stairs ended at a circular landing. A door stood

19

open and they entered a room overlooking the rear garden. Meredith drew in a sharp breath and stopped. This was a studio fit for the finest artist in town.

'Isn't it wonderful, Miss Sanders?'

'I am amazed. Your uncle must be expecting great things of you. Is your mother interested in the arts?'

The little girl's happy manner melted away like butter left in the sun. 'Mama died and Papa has gone away. Uncle Adam looks after me now.'

She knelt and took Sarah's small hands into hers. 'I'm so sorry to hear that. We must try very hard to please your uncle and repay him with the best paintings ever. Tell me, what would you like to draw for your lesson today?'

'I want to draw the flowers in the garden. Don't you remember that is why I asked if you would come here? I watch it a lot from my window. Miss Thomson frowns and says I am daydreaming instead of learning my numbers.'

'Then we must make a bargain. When you are in the schoolroom, you pay attention to Miss Thomson. When you are in here, we will dream about all the lovely pictures you will paint.' Meredith squeezed her hands, 'Agreed?'

'Yes. But it will be very hard to do.'

Meredith stood up and looked around the studio: an easel, a table and two chairs; a six-drawer chest, brushes, and a palette of watercolours.

'There's paper and canvases in the long drawers and smocks for us both in the small drawers. Has Uncle Adam forgotten anything?'

'I doubt it.' There was far more here than on her list. 'Shall we begin? First put on your smock and get your sketch book and a pencil.'

Meredith closed her eyes; she needed a few moments to assess this unexpected situation. Most of the equipment would not be required for years. Sarah was a child, not a professional artist. Did Mr Fox think she was going to work miracles? She thought back to her early days with Frederick. Drawing had been her first joy, the flowers in the garden, the meadows and farm animals …

Lost in her reverie, she didn't see Sarah kneeling on the window-seat looking into the garden until she asked, 'How do I draw it, Miss Sanders?'

'Not from a window. We will go down into the garden. You can decide when you find the flower you like most.'

Sarah jumped from the seat and took hold of Meredith's hand. 'I'll show you the way.'

Her excitement had returned and she pulled Meredith out of the room, down the stairs and through a rear corridor out of the house.

Beyond a neat area of flagstones, a stepping-stone path skirted a glossy-leafed holly bush and Meredith saw an enclosed country garden stretching long and narrow before her. Dandelions and daisies floated like jewels in the untamed grass, and a pink flowering cherry tree shaded a seat in the farthest corner. Against the boundary walls a profusion of climbing roses waited to bud and burst into colour. 'Isn't it lovely? Last year Aunt Izzie planted a hollyhock and it grew taller than me.'

Meredith couldn't believe her eyes. Here was a haven of nature's greenery in a London town house garden. And, hopefully, from June onwards there would be a mass of summer flowers.

'Well, I can understand now why you wanted me to come here, Sarah. It is beautiful.'

'There's a seat, but you can't see it from here. Follow me, Miss Sanders.' And she skipped off along the path.

Meredith didn't hurry: she could now see clumps of primroses and glimpses of violets; splashes of meadow saxifrage. The sweet song of a robin came from somewhere near a small glasshouse beside a gate in the rear wall. This was home to her. She missed Appleton House and the countryside, especially the fields and the farm which she had walked to with Clemmie once a week for butter and eggs. A lump filled her throat and she blinked back the tears.

A moment later she found Sarah sitting on a stone bench concentrating on a patch of daffodils and sat down next to her. 'That is very good, Sarah. I can see you are not a complete beginner.'

'Miss Thomson has taught me a little, but Aunt Izzie wants me to excel in watercolour painting. It is one of the refinements required of a lady. Will it take a long time for me to be as accomplished as you? Did you have to practice lots and lots of times? Like when I learn a new multiplication table, I have to repeat them over and over.'

'Yes. With drawing, you have to practice for many years.'

'Umm … that sounds quite hard. But I shall try every day to improve.'

Meredith smiled over the child's bent head. So, Mr Fox had high marriage hopes for his niece. She pointed to the delicate yellow flowers. 'Draw your daffodils as you see them. Some are already open, others are just peeping, and, look, some are still buds.'

'Oh, yes. Will three flowers be enough to make a pretty picture?'

'Of course, and your enthusiasm is most admirable.' Her words of encouragement made Sarah lift her head and smile at her.

'Thank you, Miss Sanders. I shall give this picture to Aunt Izzie when I have painted it.'

After placing her advertisement, she had been apprehensive about teaching others what she had learned. But seeing the child's happiness, Meredith realised Miss Weston was the beginning of her dream.

'One day you will be a very talented artist. Your uncle has chosen wisely in encouraging you to the arts.'

'Oh, it's Great-Aunt Izzie too. Didn't Uncle Adam tell you, she lives with us?'

Meredith closed her eyes and let the early spring sun warm her face. What a beautiful watercolour the country flowers would make against the background of this house when the garden was in summer sunshine, and the brickwork in shade. Time passed, peaceful, soothing, until she heard a male voice calling Sarah's name.

'Uncle Adam, we're here, on the seat. Come and see what I've drawn.'

He came into view and Meredith stared at the man who had come from a warehouse. His dark coat and pale breeches were spotless; his polished boots gleaming without a trace of dust. She felt like a schoolgirl, breathless, waiting for her dashing knight to rescue her from a giant dragon. Then she remembered to stand up and curtsy. 'Good morning, sir.'

'Good afternoon, Miss Sanders. It is past the noon hour. I had not expected to find you still here.'

'Oh, I beg your pardon. Miss Weston and I were so enjoying the garden I have forgotten the hour. I will leave at once.' Meredith turned to her pupil. 'If you have finished your drawing, you can paint it next time I come.'

Sarah jumped off the seat and ran to her uncle. 'Please, Uncle Adam, can Miss Sanders come back sooner? I don't want to wait until next week.'

'I'm sure Miss Sanders has other commitments. You will have to be patient. However, perhaps Miss Sanders will consent to stay and eat with us.' He cocked a quizzical eyebrow in Meredith's direction. 'It would be a good opportunity to meet my aunt. Will you stay?'

His voice was warm, the question asked in a different

tone to the one he had used when they first met. It threw Meredith into a quandary. But as she had only met Miss Thomson on her arrival, here was a chance to meet his relative and household.

'Thank you, I would like to stay.'

As she walked along the path, Meredith was very conscious of their social differences. He made no attempt to speak and she wondered if he did not consider her worthy of conversation.

When they reached the flagstones, Mr Fox, without warning, stopped. 'Thank you, Miss Sanders, for coming here. Sarah is a very lonely child. My niece has been much happier since meeting you.'

His features were serious, but Meredith sensed a moment of friendliness from him. Her nervousness eased, but her mouth was very dry as she answered, 'I am delighted. We have enjoyed our lesson together this morning. Miss Weston shows a promising talent for art.' She looked down at the ground, finding his presence overly close.

'I'm glad you were here when I arrived.'

He held out his arm and she put her fingers on his sleeve. She had entered a world completely different to any she had known before.

Miss Isobel Fox sat in a winged chair. A small woman with a likeness of features to her nephew, except her fine white hair gave a feminine grace. She held a small glass of liquid.

Meredith curtsied as Adam Fox introduced her. 'It is a pleasure to meet you, Miss Fox.'

'So, you're the girl who has fired my niece to such furore? I trust you will not disappoint me. I expect great things of Sarah by the time she leaves the schoolroom.' A note of authority tinged her voice. This was a person Meredith would not want to oppose.

'I'm sure she will, ma'am, if what I saw her draw this

morning can be nurtured in the right direction.'

'Good. That is what I want to see before I die. The gong has already sounded, it is time to eat. Help me up, boy; this wretched leg of mine is paining me again.'

Adam Fox held an ebony cane out to her and placed his hand under her elbow, saying, 'A little less sherry, Izzie, might be the cure.'

Broth soup with cubes of pasty made a pleasant meal and Meredith was sure her time at Tallow House would be a happy one. Clearly, Mr Fox indulged his niece, referring several times to making visits to art exhibitions and trips into the country.

'Miss Sanders, would you consider accompanying us on these visits?'

Meredith's cheeks burned with embarrassment and the impropriety of such a suggestion. 'It is most generous of you, sir, but I have not yet organised my other commitments.' She had that feeling again of being persuaded in a subtle way to his wishes. It all sounded very desirable, but days out seeking pleasure would not earn her money to fill her larder. 'Thank you for a delightful lunch.'

Adam Fox stood up. 'I'll call my coach.'

Meredith rose from the table and curtsied to Miss Fox.

In return she received a nod, 'Miss Sanders.' Then the old lady picked up her sherry glass that had been refilled.

On her way back to Ludgate Hill, Meredith wondered what was making her feel so happy. Her morning with Sarah had been enjoyable, the child was pleasant, the garden enchanting. She told herself to be honest: Mr Fox had a lot to do with it.

CHAPTER THREE

At Ludgate Hill, Meredith found the street door unlocked. Inside, Mrs Clements stood at the bottom of the stairs like a sentry on guard. 'There's a client waiting in the gallery. I didn't like to leave her alone.'

'Someone is here to look at the paintings? Oh, Clemmie, will this be my first sale? What is she like?'

Mrs Clements pursed her lips, released them, and said. 'Not what I would have expected. Would you like me to stay here, just in case …?'

'No, you go upstairs. This may take some time.' Meredith patted her hand, 'Perhaps a tray of tea; it's a little early to be offering wine.' She opened the gallery door and went in.

The giant of a woman who turned to her had dark skin and lips so thick they gave the impression of being permanently pouted. Her hair was blacker than coal and styled high under a feathered hat. She made no attempt to move from the spot where she had been looking at the portrait of Frederick.

'It is a remarkable likeness.' Her voice was soft and flowing. 'You are Miss Sanders?'

'Yes. Good afternoon, ma'am.'

The rustle of crimson silk and cotton filled the gallery as the woman's full skirts swished across the floor. 'My visiting card; I did not wish to leave it with your servant.'

Meredith read her name: Madame Roseanna Lightfoot, Art Exporter and Importer, Jamaica.

'How may I help you, Madame Lightfoot?'

The woman ignored Meredith's question. Instead, she walked over to a painting and stood assessing the watercolour landscape of Harlington, with its white clouds in a blue sky, dark woodland high on a hill with a stream flowing down into a meadow of summer flowers.

'You have Frederick's touch of reality. He has taught you well. However, I have not come to buy, but to collect the original Turner painting. Frederick's untimely death has caused a tiresome delay, it must be returned at once. I have the copy.' She turned again to look at his portrait. 'He had the touch of the Master himself and it will pass as Turner's own hand to the colonials.'

Meredith went hot and couldn't think; her mind was empty. What was Madame Lightfoot talking about? What painting? What Turner? The woman was a lunatic. As she walked towards her, she seemed to grow larger. She stopped so close Meredith was forced to step back.

'You have good play-acting skills, Miss Sanders. I am not fooled by your innocent shocked look. Where is it?'

Meredith took a deep breath to restore her composure. 'Would you please explain yourself? Frederick was not a forger. He loved his work. You have it all wrong.'

'Impossible! He never failed to tell me how talented you are. His passion for your work was astounding. He praised you constantly as the daughter of kindness in his aging years. Of course he would want you to succeed him. Why do you think he left you this home, this studio? To continue his life's work – the heiress of his talent.'

Madame Lightfoot's ranting ceased. She sighed and her eyes glinted like pale opals. 'Now, let us continue without this pantomime of lies.'

'I cannot help you. I was never consulted or

instructed on Frederick's professional business. His trips away from Harlington were frequent, sometimes lasting several weeks. My role in his life was as a daughter, a companion, to discuss and research our artistry.

'He was not a nobleman, but certainly of good birth. Rightly or wrongly, I assumed his wealth came from his paintings or other legitimate business dealings.' With each word the horror of what she said grew. Frederick had been a dishonest man! A rogue!

Roseanna Lightfoot grasped her shoulders. The face that had been calm became distorted and ugly, 'Liar. Liar! You know where it is. Turner's painting must be back at Somerset House by the end of next week. It is part of the Royal Academy's Summer Exhibition.'

The dark woman pushed Meredith. 'You are his successor. This is why he left you all this!' She went over to his portrait. 'Isn't that so, Frederick?' With no answer from the painting, she swung round again to Meredith. 'Don't try to cheat me, Miss Sanders, or you'll be *very* sorry.' In a blur of crimson she stormed out, leaving only the bang of the gallery door quivering on its hinges behind her. Meredith was in no doubt she would be back.

Whatever was happening? Meredith looked at Frederick's face. There was nothing showing in his eyes of deception. He had been her mentor, her friend. She didn't believe the woman, yet there was sureness in her manner. Behind her, the sound of rattling china announced Mrs Clements and tea, but she could not look away from the portrait.

Clemmie placed the tray on the desk and filled a cup. 'No sale, dear. Never mind, there will be others. How did your morning go?'

Panic and fear ran through her veins and her stomach ached as she held herself rigid. Releasing a breath, her body reacted in the reverse, and she started to shake.

Frederick copied famous paintings to sell as originals. He had been a criminal! A touch on her arm made her turn.

'Drink your tea while it's still hot, dear. You're shaking, Meredith. What *has* that woman done?'

'Do you know what Frederick did when he came to London?'

'No, dear, I was his housekeeper and he kept it so. Meredith, you look quite pale.'

'I'm all right, thank you, Clemmie. It was just something that woman said. I *will* sell a painting soon.' She sipped the tea until the cup was empty and put it back on the tray. 'There, your tea has revived me.' Meredith could never tell Clemmie what Madame Lightfoot had said of Frederick.

Mrs Clements sighed. 'Poor Mr Sanders, that storm on the way home did him in. Chilled to the bone he was. The old rarely get over the fever.' She sniffed and picked up the tray. 'Will you stay here?'

'Yes. Perhaps another client will come.'

Shocked and filled with disbelief, Meredith hugged herself. Was it true? Could it *really* be true? She needed something normal, not visions of Frederick in the dock before a magistrate. What could she do to clear her mind? She went to the desk drawer and took out the sketch of Mr Fox. Sitting down she picked up a charcoal stick and added lines beside his eyes, drew his neck and added a neck-cloth. She stopped; this was becoming a portrait. She added another thing she had seen that day – his ears – they hugged his head, just showing beneath the dark hair.

The gallery door opened and Adam Fox was standing there in the flesh.

'Ah, you are here. That is excellent. I wanted to engage you in a business proposition, Miss Sanders. Is this a convenient time?'

There he was again, using that commanding manner that should annoy her. Flustered that he may have seen her drawing him, she pulled open the drawer and slid the sheet inside.

To divert him and hide her embarrassment she smiled and answered. 'Yes, Mr Fox, it is convenient, sir.'

'Excellent.' He stepped forward. 'Would you consider taking on a commission for a portrait of Sarah? My brother-in-law will come home one day and I should like him to have some memento of his daughter's childhood.'

She wanted a distraction, but this request was the last thing she expected. Her head was now full of indecision. What if she said yes and then couldn't do it? So what was she doing in London? Had she not come for just this opportunity? How else was she to get her work publicised? Secure a patron for her art?

Without any forethought, she blurted out, 'But I am an unknown. Why ask me?'

'I have seen your work. Your small sketch you did at our first meeting has had me pondering on such a commission.' He waved his arm at the walls. 'Secondly, Sarah is a child and I should be reluctant to subject her to either some young flamboyant gentleman or an elderly fuss-pot. I should also be obliged to have a maid with her at all times. No, I have decided, you are the one.'

Evidently, he had made up his mind before coming to see her. Meredith tried to imagine how he would react if it didn't meet his expectations. But Frederick had assessed she was ready; his written words in his will had encouraged her to come here, to Ludgate Hill.

She swallowed down her panic. As before, this was not the time to present a portrayal of a weak, nervous woman.

'It would be a great pleasure to paint Miss Weston. I

31

would use oils, of course.' His features softened. This was the man she liked; the man who made her heart beat faster.

'When can you start? Would tomorrow be convenient?'

Taken by surprise, she exclaimed, 'No! I mean –'

'Of course, we must agree a fee. What would that be, Miss Sanders?'

Good fortune such as this was her dream come true. It would solve all her money problems until her next allowance arrived. But how much should she charge?

'I don't know, sir. I have never taken on a sitting before. I think I would have to take some advice on this, but I'm sure we can come to an agreement.'

'Excellent. Would two guineas be sufficient to secure your commitment?'

Meredith didn't understand his urgency. She was being pressured again. He was rolling her along like a ball and she had to stop him.

'Mr Fox, you are most generous. Two guineas will suffice until you have seen the finished portrait and are satisfied. Then we will discuss a fee.' She drew herself up, her back straight. She would not be treated as if in need of his charity. 'I will begin tomorrow morning. Please ask your niece to choose her prettiest dress.'

Mr Fox had left the gallery an hour ago, but Meredith remained sitting at her desk looking at nothing in particular, although her mind was racing. It darted from the good fortune of her commission to the horror of what the dark-skinned woman had said about Frederick. This thought sent her to stand in front of his portrait. 'Is it true?' she asked his image. 'Were you split as two people? Playing my father Frederick at Appleton House and a criminal here in London?'

With this dawning truth came questions she had no

answers for. There was no Turner painting in this house. She and Clemmie had cleaned and sorted out every room. Madame Lightfoot had said she wanted it back by the end of next week – that was only ten days from now. But she didn't know anything. So how was she to find the painting? Or was this a trick – was the woman a charlatan, someone who preyed on gullible women. Would her next demand be money?

The meaning of her menacing words came to mind: *Something sinister would happen to her.*

Meredith thought of the unsavoury characters who roamed the streets – men who smelled of unwashed bodies and dirty clothes. Men who carried knives, sharpened to slice a throat for a promised penny. Should she go back to Harlington? But the woman would know where Frederick had lived when he wasn't here. So where else could she go?

CHAPTER FOUR

Meredith couldn't sleep. Frederick's villainy kept spinning round in her head. The woman had been so angry; explosive was a better way of describing her.

A Turner had been stolen! Well, borrowed in a way, for Madame Lightfoot had said it must be returned, which could only mean its disappearance would soon be discovered. What mattered most to her was Frederick's good name and reputation; he may have vowed only to be her friend all those years ago, but he had become far more than that; she had loved him as a father.

Meredith plumped up the pillow, closed her eyes, and tried to clear her mind but Frederick was there and wouldn't go away. The air in the bedchamber was stuffy, even though the window was open. A habit she had continued from that first night at Appleton House – an escape route if things had not been quite as Frederick had promised. That a stranger could take her into his home hadn't seemed real and she had feared her fate would end up no different than if her father had married her off to Warder Snipes.

Meredith felt she was being dragged back to her past life but she didn't want to think about her real family.

Meredith opened her eyes. What had awakened her? Mingled with the darkness was a smell of ale and then the bedcovers moved as a figure bent over her. She screamed. A hand clamped over her mouth.

'If you make a sound, I'll kill yer.' He took his hand away.

The intruder was a man – a small man and he held the covers tightly so that she couldn't move. His smell was suffocating and she turned her face aside.

'Who are you? What do you want?'

His unshaven cheek scraped her neck and his wet lips touched her ear as he whispered, 'I can get in 'ere to yer anytime I like, Miss Sanders. I have a message for yer, "Find the painting."' He coughed, the phlegm gurgling in his throat; when the spasm passed he laughed. 'As a little bonus for me trouble, I could climb in beside yer. But not this time ... if we meet again, who knows?' His weight lifted from the bed, the door clicked shut, and he was gone.

How had he got into the house so quietly, how had he unlocked the outside doors? His breath had been like poison, his bony fingers icy cold. Worst of all was his croaking voice and those awful words; she had no doubt who had sent him, *Madame Lightfoot.* Meredith was paralysed with fear, then reaction set in and she shivered. Her teeth started to chatter, she had no control over her body. All she wanted was to hide from the smell of the man, hide from his words – *next time he would lay with her*; she pulled the covers over her head.

She needed Clemmie. Could she tell her about this man? If she began, she would have to confess Frederick's past. No, she must deal with this herself. But she had no idea where the painting was or how to go about finding it. The minutes passed. She got up and listened at the door, but could hear nothing. She opened it just an inch then wider until she could see out. The landing had no window and was pitch black; what if he was waiting to touch her mouth with his wet lips, pull her nightgown from her body and touch her skin? Meredith stepped back and closed the door. A cold wind blew the curtains into the room and she rushed to close and lock the window. She clutched her nightgown to her neck; he couldn't have gained entry this way; she was on the second floor. She got back into bed and pulled the counterpane over her head again. Gradually she relaxed and turned on her side, drew her knees up, still clutching the covers, safe inside her burrow, safe from the ferret as she waited for any sound to tell her he was coming back – a creak from the stairs, the rattle of her door handle? The silence was as terrifying. She peeped outside to look at her clock on the bedside cabinet. Three o'clock. Again at four o'clock. Finally, she drifted into a troubled sleep of shadowy images, but only the face of Madame Lightfoot showed clearly in her dream.

A voice awakened her. 'Meredith? What are you doing under the bedclothes?'

She was hot and tangled in a mass of rumpled sheet and blanket. Her nightgown was twisted around her like a corkscrew. What was she to say to Clemmie? What plausible lie sounded real?

'Just trying to keep out the morning sounds. Rattling carts are no substitute for the birds.'

Did she sound normal? She pushed the covers aside and looked at her housekeeper. There was nothing in Clemmie's expression that gave rise to any trouble. *How did he get in?* She would have a good look at the windows and doors later. Right now, she needed her cup of tea and give no indication of how she really felt. Clemmie must never know what happened last night.

Two hours later, Mr Fox's coach set her down at Tallow House. The front door was opened by Mr Simms. 'Good morning, Miss Sanders.'

'Good morning.'

Sarah was waiting in the hall. 'Good morning, Miss Weston. You are indeed wearing a pretty dress for your portrait. The morning light is perfect. Shall we get started right away?'

'Yes, please. Before I grow up any more and Papa will not recognise me.'

The child's matter-of-fact manner surprised Meredith. Did she not miss her father? Or had Mr Fox taken over the role so easily she only missed him on special occasions, such as now when she would sit for her portrait? She wasn't sure how to handle this very grown-up child and thought it best to let the comment pass.

'Then let us hurry before you grow another inch.' They ran up the stairs hand in hand, both eager to start, but for a different reason. This commission could be her first step to establishing a name for herself and her studio.

Meredith selected a canvas from the chest's drawer. How strange that there was one the correct size. Had Mr Fox forethought this commission? How could he have, unless he could see into the future? What a ridiculous thought she reprimanded herself as she set up the easel.

Sarah sat on the window seat with a rag doll on her lap, her blue dress the exact colour of her eyes and the sunlight heightening her fair hair. 'I want you to sit very still, Sarah. It won't be easy, but I need to make sure I get your proportions correct. Can you do that for me?'

'Oh, yes. I can be very still. Dilly and I want Papa to see me just the way I really am.' Her smile matched the pleasure in her eyes. 'Uncle Adam is such a nice man. Do you not think so, Miss Sanders?'

Meredith held her pencil poised ready, but lowered it. 'Yes, he is. You are very fortunate to have such a thoughtful uncle.' She stared at the blank canvas, wondering again why Mr Fox had insisted that she paint his niece.

Thirty minutes later, Sarah's voice broke her concentration. 'Am I sitting still enough, Miss Sanders? My back and neck are aching now.'

'Can you manage a few more minutes?' Meredith studied Sarah's mouth and the soft fullness of her lips. She stood back to assess her work on the easel. There was something missing; the breathing, living subject had a sparkle. It had been there that first day in her gallery, a bubbling child encouraged by Mr Fox to express herself with confidence.

'That will suffice for today. We can spend the rest of the morning in the garden.'

'Oh, yes please. I'll take my sketch book down and draw another flower.'

'You go on. I'll put the canvas away and follow you shortly.'

Sarah ran out of the door, her aches and pains forgotten. Meredith relaxed, aware now that she too had a pain in her shoulders and neck. The first sitting had gone well. But when she applied the oils, could she bring out Sarah's childishness and not make her too mature? Experience told her the portrait would never look perfect until she had brushed her last stroke. That aside, she was not comfortable with the thought of prying eyes seeing her work, assessing her ability. She removed the canvas from the easel, wrapped it in a cloth, and leant it against the wall. Not hidden, but it made her feel better. With her own sketch book and charcoal in hand she left to find Sarah.

Meredith declined to stay at Tallow House for lunch. She did not want such a personal situation to become a habit. This would not be good for her professional relationship that she wished to maintain with Mr Fox. Sarah was a delightful child, but somewhat strong willed and Meredith did not think Miss Fox would approve such an informal arrangement.

Meredith left Clemmie darning her stockings and went down to the gallery. The quiet room should have soothed her, but instead made her think about the risks she was facing. No clients were coming; no enquiries about her tuition. She went to the window and took Frederick's last letter to her from her pocket. In the afternoon light she opened the folded paper.

I have taught you all I can. It is time for you to go to London and let the people see your talent.

Dearest girl, have faith in yourself …

She had visualised wealthy clients browsing her paintings, discussing with them their views on oils versus watercolours, demurely smiling as they made an offer. But the reality was that no one had come, except Mr Fox.

Her allowance of one hundred pounds a year would never cover her living costs in London. Mr Fox's commission money would help, but once that was spent, what then? On top of this was the horror of the missing Turner. She paced the boards; time was slipping by.

She locked the street door. There was only one room that had not been thoroughly sorted, the attic that Frederick had used as a study. She had shied away from going through his personal papers, but could there be a clue there to his secret life?

Meredith climbed the narrow stairs to the dark-panelled attic. The small window let in little daylight to brighten the knotted wood floor that supported only a desk and chair strategically placed on a square mat. It would be impossible to work without a candle on a dull day but the afternoon was sunny and sitting down at the desk she took the first sheet of paper off a spiked holder.

After thirty minutes Meredith yawned, bored with reading receipts for brushes, canvases and pigments. Some were years old, while others were dated just before he died. Obviously Frederick did not have the clerks' meticulous mind for order and filing. There were three drawers each side of the desk and she pulled open the top right-hand one to find it bulging with more receipts. The second drawer was the same, the third drawer was locked. Where was the key? The opposite three were the same – full of papers. Meredith pulled hard on the locked drawer, but there was nowhere other than the desk for the key to be. She pulled handfuls of receipts out and piled them on the desktop. In the bottom left drawer she touched a key – it fitted the locked drawer and turned on a well-oiled mechanism. Inside was another key, except this one was a door key – the number six scorched into the leather tag. She ran her hand inside the drawer and pulled out several receipts that were not for artists' materials. These receipts were for the rental of a room at The Grapes Inn, Aldgate.

Aldgate was some distance from Ludgate Hill. Why would Frederick rent a room when he had the gallery and the rooms above? *Why?* Only one answer came to mind. This could be where he did his unlawful artistry.

She would have to go to this inn, but how could she get to Aldgate? She could walk, take a hackney, but the area would bring her nearer to Blackfriars, nearer to where she had vowed never to return. This brought as much fear as the man who had sneaked into her bedchamber last night.

Footsteps sounded on the wooden stairs. She swept the papers back into the drawer and put the key in her dress pocket. A moment later Clemmie came in. 'Mr Fox sends his respects and requests a few moments of your time. I have asked him to wait in the gallery.'

What did he want? What possible reason could he have to call? 'Tell him I shall be down directly. I need to wash my hands.'

'Is everything all right? He isn't becoming a nuisance, is he? I can tell him you are indisposed.' Clemmie straightened and her plump figure took on the stance of a boulder that would be hard to move.

'Everything is quite in order. I expect he wishes to discuss Miss Weston's sitting. I'll come down.'

When she entered the gallery, Mr Fox was looking at the watercolour landscape Madame Lightfoot had praised. He turned and bowed. Meredith curtsied and waited for him to speak.

'Is that the countryside you have been living in, Miss Sanders?'

'Yes. I could see that from the garden of Appleton House. There is so much space and light there, so different from the city. I have not yet become accustomed to the crowded streets and constant noise.'

'I hope soon to buy a property in the country; Sarah should not be in London during the summer months. Would you recommend Harlington?'

Meredith went to the painting. She would like to be there now, safe in the home she loved, never knowing Frederick's dark secret. But that was not possible. She had given up the tenancy when she left.

'Yes, I would.' She sensed his presence close behind her.

'Would you sell that to me?'

Meredith wanted to say no. It belonged to her past that she didn't want to let go. So why had she put it in the gallery to sell? How ridiculous to get sentimental over a painting someone wanted to buy. Could it be because he was intruding into her life, again! The price was three guineas and that, together with her teaching fee, would cover her expenditure until her midsummer allowance. She stepped sideways and turned to him.

'Of course, they are all for sale.' Her abrupt words sounded rude.

'Thank you.' His reply was as abrupt.

'Do you wish to take it now?'

'Yes. I came to pay your advance fee for Sarah's portrait. She was so excited and told me how much she enjoyed her sitting. It seems you have found a special place in her heart, Miss Sanders. I thank you for that.'

His praise was unexpected and lifted her spirits. She badly needed some good news after the discovery of the mystery key.

'Miss Weston is a lovely child, Mr Fox. I hope I can do justice to her loving and happy nature.'

She lifted her painting off the wall and placed it on the desk. Sitting down she took a sheet of paper, ink and quill from the drawer. This was her first bill of sale for one of her paintings. Not to just any person, but to Mr Fox. She hoped he didn't notice her hand shaking as he put his gold coins into a little basket on the desk. When the ink dried she handed him the folded sheet.

'Thank you, Mr Fox. You are my first client. This is a memorable moment.'

She felt compelled to look at him and his dark eyes looked directly into hers as he said, 'And a memorable moment for me, Miss Sanders. I shall hang your painting in my study. If I am asked who the artist is, I shall say, Miss Sanders of Ludgate Hill.'

His words made her cheeks hot and to avoid answering she said, 'I have a question I should like to ask, if I may?' And before she lost her nerve, 'Do you know a place called The Grapes Inn at Aldgate?'

Mr Fox frowned and without answering, walked over to look out of the window. With his hands clasped behind his back he asked. 'Why do you want to know?'

Meredith's skin tingled. She should not have said anything. What a fool! But who else could she ask? It seemed a simple question; all she wanted was a yes or no.

'I'm sorry I troubled you, Mr Fox. Thank you for your patronage. Will you please tell Miss Weston I will come tomorrow for another sitting? The light is perfect at the moment. Good day to you, sir.'

Mr Fox did not move. 'I asked why you wanted to know. It is not an establishment suitable for a lady. Nor a gentleman either.'

She had made a mistake. Why had she opened her mouth and let out words she would not give him an answer to?

'It is of no matter, I am just curious, I must have heard the name somewhere.'

Mr Fox turned and walked over to her. 'Curious? Why should you be curious about a tavern inn? I'm sure you have not been in the company of any such person who would frequent such a place. Please, answer my question.'

She went and locked the door. This conversation needed to be kept secret. 'Would you come into my studio?'

He raised his eyebrows. 'If you so wish, Miss Sanders.'

Meredith led the way and closed the door. Her mouth was dry and when she tried to speak no words came out. She coughed politely behind her hand and tried again.

'I find myself at a great disadvantage, sir. I know very little about you, but you are the only person I feel able to approach. There is a very personal matter that I wish to speak of. I must ask for your sworn oath that you will not repeat our conversation.' There, she had put her trust in a stranger, although in some ways her employer.

Adam Fox walked towards her and stopped close enough to take her hand. 'I swear not to repeat this conversation. But I am intrigued as to what a lady of your standing can have in common with The Grapes Inn.' He raised her hand and kissed her fingers. 'You have my oath, Miss Sanders.'

Meredith stepped back, needing space from this man who was about to hear her most dreadful secret. 'As you know I was brought up in the country. Frederick was an artist of immense talent; my achievements are to his credit. I will not allow one wrong word said against him.' Her throat tightened, this was all so very difficult to tell him. 'He travelled to London often and would be away for long periods of time. Mrs Clements and I never travelled with him. He left his entire estate to me, including these premises.' She paused, waiting for a response, but Mr Fox made no comment and she continued, 'On Wednesday afternoon a Madame Lightfoot came to the gallery ...' She stopped.

'You keep referring to your father by his given name? Why?' His voice was sharp, his mouth a line of disapproval.

Should she be honest, but that would involve her telling him about her real past. She kept to her lie. 'He preferred it.' Meredith's heart beat faster; lies were not what she wanted to tell Mr Fox. Oh dear, everything was becoming so complicated.

'Please, go on, Miss Sanders. So far your life story has been interesting. This all seems hardly worth subterfuge.' He waved his arm towards the closed door. 'What other mystery in your life do you wish to divulge?'

'Madame Lightfoot implied that Frederick was a forger of paintings. That he had hidden an original Turner, borrowed, sort of, from the Royal Academy. It must be returned to her by the end of next week.' There, she had told him.

'And where does The Grapes Inn come into this?' Mr Fox did not move or give any indication of his thoughts. But his eyes never left her.

'I have found a key locked in his desk for a room at The Grapes Inn, Aldgate.'

'Ah. So we are back there now. If I am not mistaken, copying other artists' work is not a crime. In fact, it is practised by many aspiring artists.'

'Yes. This is so. But Madame Lightfoot did not give that impression – she said he was copying it in secret. It has been taken without the Academy's knowledge and the copy is to be sold as an original. Therefore, is it not forgery?'

Now the truth was out; she had put Frederick's name at risk. Could she be charged by the magistrate as having his ill-gotten gains?

She expected an outcry of rage from him, but he remained silent. What was she to say now? The only movement of his mouth was that he clenched his jaw.

Mr Fox sat down on a table. 'Well, Miss Sanders, is there more? Have you told me everything? I cannot assess the situation unless you have.'

Her moment of decision had arrived – keep quiet or tell him about last night. Locking her fingers together she looked down, humiliated. Shame surged through her. But if she didn't tell him, and it came out later, he might not trust her about anything else she told him. 'Not all, sir.'

He crossed his arms. 'Then continue, Miss Sanders, with your tale of woe.' An edge of anger had now come into his voice.

'Last night …' Perspiration wetted her forehead, blackness filled her vision, and she fainted.

She opened her eyes. Mr Fox knelt beside her on the floor, his arm supporting her shoulders and he was fanning her face with his receipt.

'Lie still, you're as white as this paper.' He fanned her face for a few moments longer, then said. 'Try to sit up,' and eased her to a sitting position.

'Thank you, sir. I am perfectly all right now.'

'All right, is it? Pray tell me what monstrosity happened here last night?' His voice was calm, a total contrast to the thunderous look on his face. He stood up and offered his hand.

Meredith ignored those strong fingers; he had touched her quite enough and she struggled to rise with as much dignity as her predicament allowed.

'You're quite the independent lady, Miss Sanders. Please, sit down on a stool while I call Mrs Clements –'

'No!' Her outburst stopped his flow of words. 'Clemmie knows nothing about this matter. She is not to be involved.'

'That may not be possible. Given the enormity of your father's crime and the little time you have to return the stolen masterpiece –'

Meredith interrupted again, 'No, Mr Fox. This is my problem, I will deal with it.'

'On your own, I think not. Now complete your story before I tire of all this and return home.'

The last fifteen minutes had clearly shown she could not face this alone. She had to put her trust in Mr Fox.

'Very well, sir. Last night a man entered this house and came to my bedchamber …' She paused; she really didn't want to tell him. 'He threatened me, saying that he could get in here at any time. He had a message, "find the painting". He also said he would climb in beside me if he came again.' She choked on the last word; the thought was unbearable and she couldn't look at Mr Fox.

His strong hands pulled her close, his arms wrapping round her like a shawl, the warmth of his body easing away her fears and she cried – all her pent-up emotions flowing away with her tears. He was so solid, someone she could lean on, depend upon. She wanted to stay where she was forever.

But that was not to be. He pushed away and held her at arm's length. 'You cannot stay here. You will come home with me.'

'No. I will *not*. It is improper for me to live under your roof, even if it is for my protection. I thank you for your consideration.'

'Madam! Have you no sense in your head?'

'Sir! I know what I am to do. I shall go to The Grapes Inn and search for room six. If the painting is not there, maybe there will be a clue, a diary, a …' She trailed off. How could she go to an inn on her own?

Mr Fox raised his hand. 'Miss Sanders, I have known you only a few days, but I cannot believe you are capable of any underhand dealings. If you are, you have hoodwinked me and I shall, indeed, feel a complete fool if you are found to be of a criminal persuasion. But I am putting my faith in you being a person who has been caught up in a most scandalous scheme by someone you dearly loved. I will go to The Grapes Inn. Alone.'

Meredith stared at him. She couldn't think, couldn't reason, but she did make one decision. 'Thank you. I am persuaded that your trust is something I shall hold dearly. But I cannot allow you to do this for me alone. I will come with you. I have to know what Frederick was doing and why. He wasn't lacking money, his estate proves that. Oh …' Another thought had struggled into her consciousness. 'Is that what I have inherited?'

'That is not a problem we have to worry about now. Our priority is the painting. We cannot go as we are. Our manner and dress will instantly block any questions we need to ask. How are you as an actress, Miss Sanders?'

'An actress? I don't understand?'

'You need to be some kind of tavern girl and I'll be a river man. We will require the appropriate clothes, I know of a second-hand stall that will do us well.'

'Is that really necessary?' He was rolling her along like the winter wind.

Mr Fox raised his eyebrows and Meredith now recognised it as something he did when he was becoming impatient. 'Believe me, it is *very* necessary. And you need to lose your lady's voice. It may be wiser for you not to speak and leave the talking to me. We need to have false names.'

'False names, but why, this is making a simple task into a melodrama, sir. I simply want to go and look at the room and find an answer to the lost painting.'

'Don't you think the innkeeper will be suspicious if two well-dressed people, especially one a lady of your position, start asking questions about his inn? Mr Sanders would not go there fashionably dressed. I can assure you I am far more familiar with the types who frequent The Grapes Inn. They are men who work in my warehouses, Miss Sanders. Now, let us get back to our preparations.'

Meredith made no reply. It seemed wiser to go along with his plan.

'I shall be Dello Murphy, and you?'

She hesitated, and then said, 'I'm Merry, sir, a girl who frequents the taverns.'

'Merry, is that short for Meredith?'

'It could be, I suppose. Will it do?'

'Yes, it is most fitting.'

CHAPTER FIVE

His reflection in the mirror pleased him: a black jacket, wrinkled cotton shirt that had once been white, canvas trousers smelling strongly of tar, and a pair of battered boots.

'Very good, Fox. It's been a long time since those childhood play-days.'

His jocular words did not match his stern face. Doubt her or trust her? These words had plagued him all the while he searched for the tavern clothes. He had much to lose if he was being dragged into a scheme of crime, especially as his trade was Import/Export of any goods he could negotiate. If the Customs men found any mismatched goods to the declared import papers, he could be accused of being in collusion with an illegal act, even smuggling. Any untoward investigation could mean his business would suffer, including the possibility his loyal clients would take their business elsewhere. And if he were charged with a felony, it would take a great deal of persuasion to get a verdict of not guilty in a magistrates' court.

Fox poured a small glass of brandy and sat in his chair by the fireplace. There was without doubt one element of this scenario he could not let go – even if the discrepancy his agent had found was a genuine clerical error – he needed to seek out the truth. He was now in a position to assess Miss Sanders, who had shown her dependence on him and by going along with her scheme he could now watch and wait. Yet she had portrayed such innocence and he truly hoped she was not involved with her father's villainy.

He wondered how she was coping, and her given name slipped past his lips. 'Meredith.' So formal; somehow the name Merry suited her better, but he was not yet able to call her either; social manners forbade such familiarity. He laughed out loud. They were about to embark on a clandestine venture, alone, with no chaperone and he was worried about names! But if this escapade should become known, her reputation would be ruined.

Why hadn't he *insisted* that he go alone? Because he knew, after only an acquaintance of a few days, she would follow her own mind. This way, he had her under his protection – physically – albeit against all propriety.

He returned his empty glass to the table and blew out the candles. The room went pitch black, not even a slit of light showing under the door. He went behind the closed curtains, opened the sash window and stepped out onto a narrow ledge above the garden. Within his arm's length a tree towered beyond the roof. He had wanted to have it cut down, but Aunt Izzie had persuaded him otherwise. Now he thanked her stubbornness for there was no way he could have walked out through the front door without the risk of being seen by the household. After dinner he had given the impression he was retiring for the night with a bottle of brandy and the business accounts.

He reached out to a stout branch and tested the bough with his foot, heaved forward and started descending bough to bough. Boyhood memories had played a trick on him – he was no longer the child who could scamper around woodlands playing hide-and-seek like an agile monkey. As he continued to descend the leaves that were beginning to bud on the thin twigs whipped against his face. Then his foot touched the top rung of a ladder he had propped against the lower trunk earlier and a few seconds later he reached firm ground. He hurried along the path, passing the stone bench, to the gate at the bottom of the garden.

Adam paused and looked up at the moon in a starlit sky. Once he stepped into the alley beyond, he placed his own reputation, business, and his family's future on a young woman's plea for help. He ran his hand over his disguise. Only time would tell if he had made the correct decision.

At the end of the alley he got into the hackney carriage that waited for him.

Meredith remained in the gallery mulling over what she had agreed to – but she finally had to admit this was the only way she could get into the Grapes Inn. Two hours later a woman delivered a package containing her disguise. She locked the front door and went to her bedchamber.

The garments were like the clothes her mother had worn: washed out cotton, ragged hem, the once pretty lace border around the scooped neck torn and hanging loose. She couldn't put them on, the memory was too painful. Yet, if she didn't do this, Frederick would be the one to suffer. Death did not mean he wouldn't be branded a thief and a forger. The events that were happening were beyond her control. She was being pulled into a web that was weaving her past and future together; she was becoming a criminal herself.

A soft tap on her door made her push the clothing under her pillow. She rolled on to the bed, took a book from the bedside cabinet, posing a scene of calm contentment.

'Come in,' she called.

Clemmie bustled in. 'That is just what you need, Meredith, a little reading and then an early night. I've brought your supper on a tray, is there anything else you need?'

'Nothing else, thank you, Clemmie. You're quite right, this is just what I need.' She feigned a yawn. 'I will soon have the candle doused and be asleep.'

'Then I will retire too. City life is far more hectic than in the country.'

'Clemmie, do you regret leaving Harlington? I should have given you the choice; I just assumed you would come here with me. If you want to go back –'

'Of course I don't, Meredith. Please don't think that. I only meant … well, there are so many people and the carriages rush by without a thought of us poor folk walking. But the markets provide us with fresh produce each day. It just takes me longer to walk there and back to buy it.'

'Then I must go with you on the days I do not go to Tallow House.'

'Oh, I'm not complaining. Sleep well, dear, good night.'

Meredith felt a pang of guilt as Clemmie closed the door. She was allowing Frederick's past to overshadow everything else in her life.

She locked her door. Now was the time to change and become Merry, the tavern wench. She unbuttoned her gown, stepped out, and laid it on the bed. Taking the clothes from under the pillow she fingered the threadbare red dress and grey shawl; both would offer little warmth on a cold night. Even the shoes were shabby; she would feel every flint and cobble.

She slipped her arms under the red skirt and into the bodice. The smell of body odour made her retch and she held her breath – she was a child again, poor and dirty – She sighed and held her hand over her nose and mouth. But she had no time for self-pity and pushed her bare feet into the shoes. As she pulled out the pins her hair tumbled into dark curls and she ran her fingers through the thick strands to create a tangled mass; combs were a luxury for waterfront girls.

A stranger stood reflected in the long mirror. This is what she would have been had she not run away – Frederick had been her salvation – her repayment tonight was to meet Mr Fox. She blew out the candles. The landing was as dark as last night; the stairs seemed more steep than usual, but she made it to the front door.

Outside was a hackney carriage. The door opened and a stranger alighted and held out his hand.

'Mr Fox?'

The reply was low and lilting. 'It be Dello Murphy, ma'am, protector of Merry.'

His unexpected Irish accent and jovial manner coaxed her response. 'Cor, Dello, abou' time, it's mighty naughty for a tavern girl to be ridin' in a coach with a gentleman.' Her words came out so easily; what was happening?

Meredith sat opposite Mr Fox, his disguise as alien as her own. In the enclosed space she could smell the worn leather seat pads and cigar smoke clinging to the inside lining. Mr Fox's breath came across to her, clean, and she could see his face as they passed by lighted buildings. Only now did it come to her that the intimacy of their ride could place her in a very delicate position if she were exposed as a lady of means. But she did not voice her concerns. The coach stopped and they alighted outside the inn.

Mr Fox whispered close to her ear. 'Play-acting time,' and draped his arm around her shoulders, steering her into the tavern room.

First the noise hit Meredith; then the smell of ale; then the men sat at the tables. The years rolled back to when she had been sent to similar inns to find her father. Everything was overpowering and she turned into Mr Fox. He tightened his grip on her shoulder.

'I'm here, Merry. There is an unoccupied table in the corner.'

She drew a breath and looked at his face, saw him smile and raise his eyebrows. That look spoke volumes, saying: *you wanted to come with me, Madame Adventurer.*

He was challenging her. She tilted her chin. 'I am quite all right now, sir. Let us continue with our ruse.'

The tavern was crowded. Tradesmen were lifting mugs to their lips swallowing thirstily, their clothes only a notch above the sailors in their ragged jerkins and canvas trousers. Burning tobacco smoke swirled in a fog around the blackened beams and thinned out over the yellow stained ceiling.

Meredith followed Mr Fox between the tables, his arms waving here and there as though he were familiar with all, his hips swinging to avoid the clientele.

Mr Fox was good. He had asked for play-acting, so that's what she would give. She slipped the shawl seductively from her shoulders and feigned a smile to her lips. When they reached the empty table she sat down on a stool offering the best view of the room.

Adam moved his seat close and his body heat warmed away her cold fear. She leant towards him. 'Who are those gentlemen?' She pointed a finger towards a few well-dressed young men of means.

'It is better you don't know, Miss Sanders.'

'I disagree, sir. Please, explain. Your tone is somewhat disapproving, I think.'

His eyes met hers, dark and stern. 'So be it. They are dandies, gentlemen of breeding, and their tavern wenches who will persuade them to lose their guineas in the dice games played later.'

The girls were young and pretty, but their powdered faces and painted lips turned them into harlots who bedded and fondled for money. One of the dandies pulled a girl down onto his knees, pushed the dress off her shoulder, and ran his fingers down into the bodice. Seductively, the girl wrapped her arms around his neck.

Meredith gazed in utter horror, yet fascinated. This was her past world – a place she had thought never to return to. She shouldn't be here. What had she been thinking when she questioned Mr Fox about Aldgate? She didn't have to be told what those girls were – they were what she could have become – working for money to pleasure any gentleman able to pay the landlord's price. Maybe she would have been lower, fit only for the sailors.

Now was not the time to sink into the pit of darkness she had climbed from. So she asked, 'How do we find out about room six?'

'An opportunity will arise, from an unexpected quarter, no doubt. It's a busy night for the innkeeper; that's good. We can move around without too much curiosity. You have the key?'

'Of course, do you think I would come without it?' Forgetting her role-part her words carried clearly beyond their table. 'Ouch!' She felt his boot stamp down on her toes.

'By 'eavens, girly, how long have ye been practisin' them posh words?'

How stupid of her and, to avoid his eyes, she looked down at her hands.

A serving woman put two mugs of ale on their table, and leant towards Mr Fox.

'Anything else, luv? My name's Sal and I can git yer anything.' She slid round the table and sat on his knee. 'I'm free in fifteen minutes. Give yer gal the slip, she's not yer type, I can give yer ten times the pleasure than that skinny mouse.' She breathed in and her bodice tightened. 'I haven't seen yer 'ere before. I can show yer the ropes, so to speak.'

'Well now, Sal, that could be sometin' I might like. What room number be ye upstairs?'

She put her lips to his ear, 'Five,' and nibbled his earlobe, 'one to four is always reserved for the dandies. You've not enough silver in yer pocket for those girlies, laddie.'

'I thought there were six rooms 'ere? Who has that one?'

Sal ran a finger down his cheek and onto his lips. 'Askin' questions around 'ere, laddie, yer might end up in the alley with a knife in yer back. Six is in the cellar. It's a private rent.'

Mr Fox may only be play-acting, but the woman's behaviour was insulting. All Meredith's past instincts came to the surface. She stood up and gave the serving woman a shove, sending her sprawling on the floor.

'Git yer hands off what's mine. I found 'im first and I'll be the one to give 'im a good time.' Sal was back on her feet in a flash and charged towards her.

Adam Fox stepped between them. 'Please, girlies. I know the Irish 'ave the leprechaun magic, but Sal, sweetheart, I'll be back tomoro'. You can show me your charms then.' He took a coin from his pocket, slipped it inside her bodice, and gave her a wink.

She straightened her dress and picked up the tray. ''Til tomoro', laddie.' She swaggered triumphantly away to tend her other customers.

'Sit down, Merry. Drink some ale and then smile and put your arms round my neck. Those who were curious enough to pay attention to that little scene will think it strange if you don't play up to me.'

Meredith picked up the mug and sipped, sipped some more, and more and more to delay her next move. Finally she put it down, turned her head and smiled at him.

'Ohhhhh, Dello! Yer don't want that gutter gal, when yer can 'ave pretty me.'

She put her arms around Mr Fox's neck and pulled him close, aware of his warm skin, the rank odour of the clothes. His eyes were as black as the darkest night and his lips were parted. She moved her head just enough to let her lips touch his. They were soft and she felt the desire to press harder, just a little harder to make it into a kiss ... His hands drew her even closer, his lips responding to hers. When he drew away, his voice was low, wistful, 'Oh, Merry, me girl, you have a wicked streak of an actress in you.' Play-acting, it may have been, but she would have liked to try it again.

He lifted his tankard from the table. 'We must wait for a diversion before we can go below, which won't be long. There seems to be some heated words between those two men over by the door.'

Meredith looked across the room to where he nodded. One man was big and burly, with hair that had once been black and was now streaked with grey. His voice was loud and he was leaning forward with his hands on the table.

'You owe me a guinea, Piper. Them chairs was perfect when I delivered 'em to yer. Pay up, man, or I'll take it from yer with me fists.'

The man named Piper stood up. He was a small man: a caricature of a squirrel in clothing. Dark ginger hair ran from his head down his face into a pointed beard, his dark eyes darted from side to side. He was no match for the big man, who grasped a handful of his crimson jacket and lifted him off his feet. The two antagonists glared at each other as roars of, 'Pay him, pay him,' filled the tavern room.

Mr Fox stood up. This was the distraction they needed. Meredith followed him to a door with the word CELLAR scotched into the wood. It opened with ease and he stepped inside onto a landing. A faint glow of light showed a flight of stone steps. He beckoned her in and closed the door.

'Follow me down. Be careful, the steps look well worn.'

At the bottom three arched pillars supported a narrow corridor. A single lighted lantern revealed moss growing on the brick walls, and the floor smelt of damp earth. There were several doors; one had a chalked six at the top.

Meredith delved into her pocket and gave him the key. 'Be mindful, sir, we don't know what is in this room.'

'I am grateful for your concern, Miss Sanders, but I do not expect to find Frederick Sanders' ghost.' He unlocked the door and pushed it open. The room beyond was nothing more than a gaping black hole. He unhooked the lantern hanging from the first arched pillar and went into the room.

In the circle of light Meredith could see a table with a single candlestick. Mr Fox was lighting the wick from a taper. 'I'll put the lantern back before it's missed. We don't want to attract undue attention.' A minute later, he closed and locked the door.

'Now we can see what is going on here.' He raised the candlestick above his head and sniffed. 'There is a smell of paint,' he sniffed again, 'also an underlying whiff of linseed.'

He put his hand under her elbow and guided her round the room. The walls were bare, the only sign of an artists' studio was a wooden easel.

'Unfortunately, this is not what we expected, Miss Sanders. There is no painting, real or false. But there is something strange; the smell of paint lingers far too fresh, someone has been using this room recently. I am thinking that this is, perhaps, a communal studio. In which case, we are in danger of being discovered at any moment.'

'You make it sound frightening, Mr Fox. We are here, after all, to find the painting, or at least a clue as to its whereabouts. I cannot go until we find some evidence to follow up.' All her hopes had been here, in this room. Where else could she look?

'We have established the room exists and that it's used as a studio. Now I am going to take you back to Ludgate Hill, and the safety of your bedchamber.'

'No! Time is running out. I need to find the painting. Don't you understand the seriousness? A Turner painting! Not just an unknown like me. A masterpiece! It is known by all his associates and followers at the Royal Academy. The minute they discover it is missing, the Bow Street men will be summoned.'

Mr Fox's lips set in a firm line. 'I understand how you feel. My own expectations were high that this room would clear up all your troubles. But it does not, and this is no place for you. I will have no argument.'

'Sir, I am the one who is in charge here. I am –'

He pulled her to him and kissed her fair and square on the lips. Not a lingering passionate kiss; but hard and demanding. When he released her his voice held the command of a general. 'No, Meredith. I am in charge while you are with me.'

The determination in his eyes flared her temper. 'You're a despicable man. You have no right to kiss me as if I am a common tavern wench. I should not have told you about Frederick; I should have come here alone.'

A battle of words was forestalled by the sound of voices in the corridor. Mr Fox raised his hand for silence. A door opened and closed.

'It is definitely time to go.'

Meredith stood close to Mr Fox as he unlocked the street door.

'Thank you for coming with me tonight. The Grapes Inn was not a place I could have gone on my own.'

'Umph! Is that an apology, Miss Sanders?'

'Yes, I suppose it is. We don't seem to have achieved much, except finding the room and the smell of paint. I don't know where to go from here.'

'I have a few ideas, but before I mention them, I need to make some enquiries. Will you stay tomorrow, after Sarah's sitting?'

'There is so little time left to find the painting. Eating pasties with your aunt will take an hour that I could spend searching.'

'And where will you search?' His words had an underlying sigh of impatience.

Meredith didn't know. She had been so sure of finding the painting in the tavern room. 'Very well, I will stay and wait to hear your findings.'

He had been right about everything. He was a man who knew the ways of London, knew how to protect her. Tonight would have been a disaster without his help. In the darkness she felt vulnerable, but not alone anymore.

'Good. Now creep in and get some sleep.'

She slipped into the hallway and relocked the door. Without a lighted candle the stairway was frightening and endless. When she climbed the second flight the top tread creaked. Not daring to breathe she stared at Clemmie's door waiting for it to open – it did not – and she hurried into her own bedchamber. Only when she locked her door and took off the 'tavern girl' clothes did she breath freely again. Ignoring the smell, she hid the dress and shawl at the back of a drawer.

Filling the wash bowl with cold water, Meredith scrubbed her face and neck with a rough cloth. She wanted to cleanse herself of the Aldgate smell and the clinging, sickly ale. A feeling of inner dirtiness rose up inside her and she stripped off her underclothes, scrubbed her body until it tingled, her only thought to wash away her past. But memories of Blackfriars flooded their way into her mind: the basement room, her family, the dank smell and the darkness. All so like The Grapes Inn. She hadn't seen or heard any, but she knew there were rats down there.

Slipping on her nightgown she got into bed, pulled the covers over her head to escape her memories. In their place, Dello Murphy merged into Mr Fox. He had played his part so well, had excited her; his devilish face and dark eyebrows transforming him into a rogue, a man of the streets and alleys. Was that where he was now, following up his ideas? She should have gone with him, not let him bring her back like a timid maiden. Tomorrow she would tell him so; any more ideas and she would be going too.

CHAPTER SIX

Meredith admired her young subject as she stroked her brush of white oil paint into highlights in the fair hair on her canvas.

'A few more minutes, Miss Weston, then we can go into the garden.'

'Thank you, Miss Sanders; my neck is really hurting now. I hope Papa comes home soon so I don't have to sit for another painting. Well, not for a long time.'

'Do you get letters from your papa?'

'No. Uncle Adam does and he tells me what he says. He always sends his love to me.'

Meredith thought how sad that Sarah's father didn't send a separate note to his daughter. Maybe he didn't realise she was growing up; that she could read and write now.

'And that love is a very precious gift, Sarah. You could keep your sketch book as a special present for him.'

Meredith watched her expression. Real pleasure lit up Sarah's eyes and a smile parted her lips. It was the look Meredith had been longing to see to bring her portrait to life and she quickly changed her brush and added that happiness.

'I am finished for today. You may go down into the garden now.'

The child needed no second bidding as she ran through the door, her footsteps echoing back from the stairs.

As Meredith cleaned her brushes her thoughts

returned to Sarah. She seemed to have an ideal life, but buried under that lay the solitude of an only child – loved dearly by Mr Fox and her great-aunt, but ignored by her father. She could understand his grief, but not to write even an occasional personal note? She now left the canvas on the easel since she had started painting knowing it could be viewed by anyone if they came into the room, but that was unlikely since a plaque had been put on the door, Miss Sanders' Studio. Only one person could have given that instruction, Mr Fox, and she appreciated this thoughtfulness for her privacy. Was this getting her too close to the Fox family? It so, this would not do. She needed Mr Fox's help but it must not go beyond that.

Meredith found Sarah sitting on the stone seat absorbed in making a flower-chain in colours of white, ruby and amethyst. This part of the garden had become their favourite place. Meredith waited, studying the movement of Sarah's fingernail as she slit the stem and carefully threaded a new flower through. These little personal moments could be used to improve her portrait. Often, Sarah's bored expression did little to give inspiration at her sittings.

Meredith waited while Miss Fox sampled the soup.

'Very nice, but tell Cook just a few more herbs next time.' The footman murmured a reply and left the dining room.

The chair that she had hoped would be occupied by Mr Fox remained empty. Where was he? Meredith couldn't ask, it would be impolite, but the frustration of not knowing was like an itch that wouldn't go away. Every minute she sat eating, she could be searching.

Miss Fox's voice interrupted her thoughts. 'How is the portrait coming along? Have you progressed enough for me to have a look yet?'

Meredith's heart missed a beat. She had not thought anyone would ask to see her uncompleted work. 'No!' Her sharp reply caused Miss Fox to raise her eyebrows. 'I beg your pardon, but it is much too early for that. Miss Weston is only a child and long sittings are not advisable. I do not wish it viewed until I have finished.' Her answer was prim and ungracious, but she was not sure how she would respond to criticism. With every brush stroke she wondered if she had taken on a too-ambitious task.

'As you wish, Miss Sanders, I hope I am still breathing when it is finished.'

Miss Fox's remark was also sharp and could have a double meaning. Did she think her too slow or that she expected to die within the next few weeks?

'I'm sure you will be here to see not only this portrait of Miss Weston, but her coming-out one as well. You are a picture of health.'

Miss Fox halted the spoon to her lips and laughed. 'You have the right social graces, Miss Sanders, I like you more each time I see you.'

'Thank you.' After their moment of discord the compliment was unexpected.

By the time Meredith had finished eating, the empty chair had become an instrument of torture. Her head ached and the tension in her neck and shoulders were excruciating. He had promised – well, almost – to be here. What had gone wrong? Was he lying injured somewhere? The tavern woman had said there was much danger in asking questions. The door opened and her moment of relief turned instantly to disappointment, as the footman announced the carriage was waiting to take her home.

Meredith paced the length of the gallery, only the missing Turner filling her mind. The door opened and this time her disappointment turned to anger. Instead of Mr Fox, a girl dressed in the grey clothes of a maid curtsied and said, 'Miss Sanders, this is for you.' She handed over a note and left.

Breaking the seal Meredith opened the sheet. There were two words – *Eight Days* – there was no need for more. The dark-skinned woman knew how to put fear into her. Violence wasn't necessary; she could do it so subtly by her presence, the dirty man, and now two words.

Where was Mr Fox? She couldn't wait for him. She must go back to The Grapes Inn and that cellar room. There must be something they had missed. She locked the street door. At the top of the stairs she listened to Clemmie snoring in her kitchen chair. She had taken to having a little nap in the afternoon since coming to London. Again, Meredith wondered about the wisdom of bringing Clemmie to the city.

She hurried into the sitting room and wrote a note saying she had gone out to buy new brushes and propped it against a vase on the dining table.

The second-hand dress smelt so foul she couldn't wear it. She searched amongst her gowns and took out the work dress she wore when helping Clemmie with household chores. The dyed cotton was definitely the sort of thing a servant would wear and be in keeping with the inn. She put on the shoes from last night and loosened her hair. The person in the mirror was a halfway representation of Merry, the riverfront girl, and she hid her disguise under a lightweight cloak. The key, several coins, and half-used candles she put into a drawstring bag.

Meredith crept down the stairs; Clemmie's snores and whistles came and went in regular breaths. As she escaped into the bustle of people and carriages in Ludgate Hill, she stopped to collect her thoughts. They told her she didn't know how to get to The Grapes Inn.

A passenger alighted from a hackney carriage at the Belle Sauvage and she hurried across the road and smiled confidently at the coachman. 'To The Grapes Inn, Aldgate, please.'

'To Aldgate, miss? Are you sure? Ain't no place for the likes of you.'

The bravado in her bedchamber began to wane. And she got in before she changed her mind. 'Yes. Please take me there.' The ride was slower than last night, the roads now busy with traders, barrow boys and horse-drawn carts. But she didn't feel threatened; this area was from her past, she was well aware how these people lived and survived. Nevertheless, she shivered as the hackney halted in front of the inn.

The tavern room still smelt of ale and tobacco, but now the only noise came from a group of men sat drinking at a table. There was no sign of the serving woman or the other 'ladies'. One of the men stood up and staggered towards her, swayed against a chair which he threw aside. His slurred words were directed at her. 'Lookin' for someone, dearie? Will I do?'

'Come back 'ere, fool. She ain't your sort,' called one of his companions.

'I'm anyone's sort, even the hoity ones. They likes a bit of rough, like me.' He was drunk and Meredith backed away, but he kept coming towards her.

'I'm here to meet someone, sir. Please return to your friends. Is the innkeeper here?' Her breath, coming in quick gasps, matched the beat of her heart. The man stopped within two steps of her; she could smell the ale on his breath, see his rotten teeth.

'He's out the back. Come an' have a drink.'

Meredith stood her ground. 'Then I'll wait.'

A draft of air touched her face and Sal came in. She put a basket on the counter and turned. 'Sit down, Hawk.

I know what yer thinking. Connie will be 'ere soon.' He didn't move. 'Jack Tar, come an' git Hawk before he falls down.'

Sal pushed Meredith. 'Git out. This ain't a place for ladies' maids.'

What had she been thinking? She had seen last night what this tavern was. But she managed to say, 'Thank you,' to Sal and fled. Outside she ran round the side of the inn and leant against the wall. She was trembling so much her legs couldn't hold her up and she slithered down the rough bricks onto the dirt road – she was back to her beginnings. Except she'd run away from all this and had no intention of letting the likes of Hawk turn her from the reason she had come here. The inn must have a back entrance and looking along the wall she saw a door set into the brickwork.

She got up and tried the rusty latch which lifted easily. Inside was a yard, stacked three high with casks of ale and an entrance door was open. She hurried through into a passage and on her right was a flight of steps leading down to the cellar. After two treads the steps angled left and daylight was lost, but as last night, a single lantern glowed in the corridor. Unfortunately, she could not reach it to light her candles.

Meredith unlocked the door to room six and walked into the blackness holding her hands forward, searching for the table. When she bumped against it she stepped back, rubbing her thigh. The flint box proved tiresome, but she got the candle lit and closed the door. She emptied the candle stumps out of her bag and set about taking the flame to them. The added light didn't reveal any new clues. The smell of linseed still lingered, but this was impossible if there was no paint. It didn't make any sense. She picked up the single candlestick and walked slowly around. When she reached the back wall a draft of air fanned the flame and she moved the candle closer, tracing the flickering light as she lifted the candlestick higher. She stepped further along and felt a second draft – this must surely be an opening – where was the handle? Was this the clue she was looking for?

Occupied with her task she was only aware that the cellar door had opened when the candles flickered on the table.

'And who might ye be?' The deep voice filled the room.

She dropped the candlestick and the flame went out. She had forgotten to lock the door. Now she was found out – with another drunken man barring her way of escape. His hands grasped her shoulders and swung her to face him.

'Let go of me.' Meredith pulled away from him. 'Get out. You have no right to come in here.'

He stepped back a pace. 'I could say the same to you.'

His voice was not slurred and he didn't smell. He towered over her, large and muscular, but his clothes were clean. The lights from the table played on his face and she recognized him as one of the men who had provided the diversion in the tavern room last night; then a second recognition.

The lines on his face made him look older and his hair was greying, but it was the scar on his forehead she couldn't take her gaze from – the scar she had given him when he had threatened her mother with an axe. The last time she had seen him was the evening before her twelfth birthday in Newgate prison. Her father! The man she had run away from!

He mustn't find out who she was. The excitement of finding the hidden door vanished, and fear raced to take its place. He picked up a candle from the table and bent towards her.

'I'm sorry I frightened yer. My name's Woody, I

work here. Come up to the tavern and have a tot of brandy.'

'No!' In the daylight he would surely recognise her.

'I think yer should, missie, yer don't look too good. Come.' He put his big hand around her arm and pulled her forward.

Meredith cringed from him, 'No! I won't go.'

'It's for yer own good. Come.'

She tried to pull away from him. The table tipped and the flames stretched into elongated cones of fire. Two of the candle stumps had not waxed to the table and fell on to the floor, one so close to her dress hem a brown scorch mark darkened and flared. Meredith screamed.

From the doorway a black silhouette sprang forward; her assailant toppled over as he was pushed aside. When her rescuer turned on his heel, she recognised Mr Fox. He stripped off his jacket and smothered her burning hem.

'What be going on 'ere? Are ye all right, girly?'

'I don't know … I mean, yes. What are you doing here?'

Her father got up from the floor looking thunderous and lunged at his attacker and both men fell to the ground with a thud. Fox was younger, more nimble and was up while his opponent panted for breath.

'He wasn't hurting me, sir. There's a lot to explain –'

She was cut off by a roar from her father who was now standing.

'Sir, please. My friend did not mean to hurt you. Please, accept his apology.'

Mr Fox, standing behind her, exploded with a roar of his own. 'I can do me own fightin', without any apologies comin' from a colleen 'alf me size. Should they be necessary; which they aren't.'

Meredith moved between them. 'I thank you both for your help. Fighting over me is quite worthless.' Raising her hands, one at each antagonist, she continued sweetly. 'Perhaps a tot of brandy, in the tavern, is a fair reward for both of my gallant defenders.' She lowered her eyes to the floor, clasped her hands, hoping she looked the picture of a demure damsel in distress.

'Very well, missie.' Woody looked across to Mr Fox, 'You be paying, of course.'

Adam's body relaxed and she breathed a sigh of relief. 'May I have a few words with you, sir?'

'That you may, madam.' Fox waved at his opponent. 'Go upstairs and find a table.'

The man nodded. 'I didn't mean yer any harm, missie.'

Mr Fox picked up the candlestick and drawstring bag from the floor and blew out the candles. 'I'm sorry –'

He cut off her apology. 'Are you completely mad? Coming here alone, to a tavern, to this room where anything could have happened to you.' Taking hold of her arm he led her out into the corridor and locked the door.

'Mr Fox, why didn't you come to Tallow House as you promised? You know my time is running out.'

'Miss Sanders, I do have a business to attend, and unfortunately, that had to take my full attention today. Captains do not wait while I run backwards and forwards to Tallow House, with I will add, no new information to give you. I am here now, to try and find some clue, no matter how small, to help you. And just in time, it seems, to stop you burning to death.'

For the first time, Meredith saw a side to Mr Fox she had not yet encountered – a man capable of decisive decision.

'I'm sorry, I thought I could –'

'And, by doing this escapade …' He waved his arm in a speechless gesture. 'I'll take you back to Ludgate Hill.'

'You cannot. That man is waiting for you.'

'I know where he is. I'll come back later.' He turned towards the tavern room steps.

'I didn't come in that way, there's a backyard.' Meredith pointed in the opposite direction.

'And how did you find out about that?'

She had no intention of telling him about the scene in the tavern room. 'I consider it improper for me to go into such a place alone, so I looked for another entrance.'

Mr Fox's stern expression changed to a smile. 'Perhaps Dello Murphy will forgive you your mad impulse, just this once, Miss Sanders. Please, lead the way out.'

Beside the busy road, Meredith stopped. 'Your chivalry is of the highest regard, sir, but I managed to get myself here, I can see myself back.' She didn't want Mr Fox to waste time escorting her, when he could be seeking information they so desperately needed. 'Please, Mr Fox, I shall be quite safe.'

A hackney carriage stopped a few yards away. 'If I put you in that coach will you promise to go straight home?' He waved to the coachman and the horses moved forward.

'Yes. But will you come and tell me what you've found out?'

As he closed the coach door she sensed his indecision in leaving her. 'I will not do anything else, I promise. Just hurry and see if you can find out more about that room.'

'Very well, Miss Sanders. We need information and this man may be able to give us our first clue.' He stepped back and the coach drew away.

During the journey she thought about Mr Fox fighting her battles. She had a past he must not know about – the paternal father whom she had not seen in ten years and was petrified to acknowledge. Mr Fox would despise her for lying. And more important, he might think she had deceived him about Frederick and Madame Lightfoot. A confession would not help her find the painting.

CHAPTER SEVEN

Satisfied Meredith was safely on her way home, Adam Fox returned to the tavern. He sized up the angry man before him and recognised the challenger of the quarrel last night.

'Now me hearty man, what be all that shenanigans below?' Adam asked as he sat down.

'I just went in to 'elp the girl and she acted like I was a thievin' footpad.'

'The girly didn't invite yer in, then?

'Well … no. I saw a light. I 'elps a bit with the tenants.'

'Tenants yer say. How many use room six?'

'Dunno. They comes and goes. Arty sorts, looks like they could do with a good feed.' He laughed at his own words. 'Thin as them brushes they use.'

'What say we 'ave a jug of ale to drown our little girly's tantrum?'

'Thank 'ee. The innkeeper stocks a good cask of ale. Yer packed a good fist to me jaw'

Adam ordered a quart jug and waited, not speaking until the order was placed on the table. He filled the man's tankard to the brim, his own only half. He raised his tankard. ''ere's to a new beginning. I could use some 'elp with a little bit of business I have the good fortune to be tenderin' for.'

'Now, what sort of business would that be? I ain't into the smuggling. I'm a good carpenter; wood carving an' furniture, simple, nothing fancy.'

Adam studied the man: he was middle aged; well fed and big shoulders bulged under his shirt – a waterfront man. He would hold up well in a fight.

'Tell me … what be yer name, man?'

'Ah, me name. Let's just keep it to Woody. That's me name around 'ere.'

'Tell me about room six?'

'Not much to tell. Like I said, they be arty sorts. Reeks of paint, but ne're seen a picture. They brings in stuff, ne're seen anything go out. But see, I ain't here all the time.' He drank until the tankard was empty and put it back in the middle of the table. 'That be a fine ale, a pity to let it go flat.'

Fox refilled the tankard and watched him drink it in one go. When Woody banged it back on the table he asked, 'Have yer ever seen an elderly man?'

'Perhaps.' He pushed his mug forward. 'Thirsty work, thinking.'

'Mebbe another jug'll help?' He signalled to the innkeeper and when it arrived refilled the man's tankard.

'A funny dressed man used to come, like yer say, middlin' old, older than me. He reminded me of a joker, always wore bright colours. I haven't seen him for some time.'

''ave yer ever seen a big dark-skinned woman?'

'Don't think so. If she comes at night, I wouldn't see her.' He banged his mug on the table again and gave a loud laugh. 'Plenty of them dark beauties come in with our gentlemen customers. Yer want me to get yer one?' Woody helped himself to the last of the ale.

Adam knew he had got all the information he was going to get today. He got up and slapped the man on the shoulder. 'See yer soon, Woody.' He put a silver coin on the table. 'Pay the 'keeper and the rest is yers fer seein' who comes and goes to room six fer me.' He sauntered past the counter and left through the tavern door.

He had promised Meredith to go directly to see her, but to arrive in his Dello Murphy outfit could cause much concern. Instead he went to his warehouse office, where he had changed that afternoon. When he reached the building, the painted brick name of Fox and Son, Importers and Exporters, stabbed at him. When his Irish grandfather had arrived in Liverpool from Dublin, he had just one guinea in his pocket. He had set about buying and selling and within a few weeks his guinea turned into six pounds. Two years later he owned a warehouse in London, met Molly Gunn, and married her. A year later, the warehouse sign read, Fox and Son. That had remained a truth until the death of his father a few years ago.

He should have the name repainted – A. Fox, Importer and Exporter – but keeping the original made him feel there was still a bond to the man who had loved and taught him his trade. He often sat at his desk having imaginary discussions with him – asking his advice, answering with his own decision. He had travelled far and wide, wheeling and dealing with merchants to establish a sound business. So far, he had increased tonnage, negotiated good prices and invested some of the profit in steam machinery. Now he was ready to expand further. Life had been going well until the complication of Meredith Sanders. She was impulsive, strong-willed, and nothing like any other woman he had ever met. A fluttering fan and a dropped handkerchief wasn't her way of attracting attention.

He climbed the outside steps that led directly into his office. He liked the uncluttered room, with only a heavy desk and chair set on the simple wooden floor. The only decoration was on a brick wall: a framed painting of a schooner in full sail, racing over the waves.

The persona Dello Murphy disappeared into the private washroom. Fifteen minutes later, Adam Fox walked out suitably attired as a man of means. He sat at his desk and let his thoughts wander in and out of the mystery that had developed concerning Frederick Sanders – a man he knew nothing about except from the adoring words of his daughter. The unexpected appearance of Madame Lightfoot set a far more sinister cloak of evil on the man. What had started out as an import documentation query was now drawing him into a felony that could have serious criminal consequences for him. He was not only putting his business at risk, but his family's good name. He did not move amongst the elite of society, but his aunt and Sarah would be shunned by the circles they did have friends and acquaintances in. The more he analysed his thoughts, the more he realised the outcome could have immense social barriers raised against him. He had promised Victor that he would care for Sarah in all aspects of her upbringing. Izzie was a frail old lady now, and he could not have her remaining days tainted by his actions.

He drew a sheet of paper from his desk drawer, picked up his quill, dipped it into the ink pot and made a list.

1. Is a Turner really missing from the Royal Academy?
2. There has been no theft reported in *The Times*.
3. Who is Madame Lightfoot?
4. The midnight intruder must be part of the scheme.
5. Would the next move be a demand for money?
6. What would the consequences be to Miss Sanders if he went to the constables?

But he had agreed to help Meredith and would not go back on his word. He had set himself a fine line to walk along – search for the truth, and protect his family. He must be careful not to fall into the wrong side. He would wait for Woody's report and Madame Lightfoot's next demand. He stood up, adjusted his neck cloth, pocketed his list and left.

The gallery bell tingled when he stepped inside. Adam saw no one and instantly felt concern. Was Meredith not back? Surely she was not still in Aldgate? He turned to go to her private rooms when the door of the studio opened and she waited in the doorway. First he felt relief, then chagrin. Had she been hiding? Who from, him? He wanted to scold her daring madness of that afternoon, and at the same time protect her from all that was spiralling towards her. She looked pale and tired. He had an overpowering desire to take her in his arms, hold her and tell her everything would be all right. Tell her he had made a little progress at the tavern; that the odd-job man was going to keep an eye on the room. He wanted to kiss her sad eyes, her beautiful mouth – breathe in her sweet scent. Take her home with him, where he could protect her. He was speechless for a moment.

'Good afternoon, sir.'

She didn't move into the gallery, so he walked towards her and saw the strain of her dilemma showing on her face. 'Are you all right, Miss Sanders?'

'Yes, thank you, although this afternoon was surely a traumatic affair.'

'What the hell were you doing there?' Her off-handed manner amazed him. 'Do you realise how dangerous … have you not a grain of intelligence in that head of yours?' The restraint of trying to keep calm, hide his worry, failed and he closed the gap between them and pulled her into his arms and kissed her fully on the lips, not caring whether she saw him as an accomplice, client, or lover.

Her reaction was fire and ice. She melted into him

and returned his kiss, then pushed him away, her words clear as frozen water. 'Don't ever, do that again! I am a lady, not Sal from the tavern, who you found so easy to please.'

Adam didn't recognise her at that moment. She had gone rigid, her arms held straight at her sides, hands balled into fists. Her dark blue dress had long sleeves and the bodice buttoned to her neck. She had combed her hair flat across her head and pinned it into a bun. The transformation was unacceptable.

'What have you done to yourself? What has happened to you? Did that man touch you?'

'No, he did not.'

'Then why have you attired yourself in such a way?'

'I am a lady. Not a woman from the waterfront.'

'Meredith, please. I did not mean to degrade you. I am worried about you –'

She raised her hand for silence. 'Mr Fox, I do not expect you to be my bodyguard. However, I do appreciate your help and I *do have a grain of intelligence* to accept it! Mrs Clements has gone out, but I think, under the circumstances, as my partner in this criminal venture, we can take tea together in my sitting-room.'

Mr Fox formally bowed. 'Thank you. Tea would be most appreciated.' He would agree to anything, to bring her back to her beautiful and spirited self. She locked the street door and he followed her up the stairs to the first floor.

The room was a pleasant surprise with a window overlooking the street. Observing protocol, he made no attempt to sit down until invited. This seemed a courtesy he was not to be offered as Meredith waited in the doorway.

'May I sit down?' He waved his hand towards one of the armchairs.

'My apologies, sir, please be seated. I will make the tea.'

What had happened to make her so frosty? Surely, the escapade into Aldgate had not offended her senses so much that she now felt compelled to become a sour spinster? No, there was something else wrong, but at the moment, it would be unwise to pursue the subject. He sat down and waited.

Meredith came back a few minutes later and set the tray on a low table by the other matching chair. Her hand trembled as she poured the tea into the cups. He leant forward, taking the tea she offered. 'Thank you, Miss Sanders.' She did not look at him.

He was stunned at the strength of his feelings for her. They had lost their camaraderie somewhere along the way this afternoon. Had he misjudged her independent manner, was it just a maiden's bravado? He was so lost in his thoughts he did not fully hear her when she spoke.

'... I carried a candle round the walls and there is a draft from an opening.'

'I beg your pardon, am I to understand that there is a hidden door in room six?'

'Yes. But there is no handle or lever of any kind. I was a fool not to have locked the door then I would not have been interrupted by that man. But I don't think he intended to harm me, in fact, he seemed concerned. He was trying to persuade me to go up to the tavern room, when you came rushing in through the doorway.'

'I came rushing in! Is that all I get for tackling your assailant and saving you from death by fire?'

'Sir, I did not mean it like that. I am indebted to you, for I was terrified when the flames began to flare up my dress. You were, indeed, my saviour this afternoon.'

She was turning him upside-down and inside-out: one moment melting in his arms, then an ice-maiden, now a demure lady.

She clasped her hands in her lap. 'I must go back tonight.'

'We will go back.'

'If you will accompany me, I will accept your offer, Mr Fox. The Grapes Inn is a place I should not like to visit again on my own.'

'I would not expect you to frequent an establishment like that.' He stared at her and saw colour spread over her cheeks. 'I will collect you the same time as last night. I am most grateful that you discovered the back entrance.' He put the china back on the tray, the tea untouched. 'Good afternoon, Miss Sanders.'

Meredith stood up. 'Good afternoon, Mr Fox. I will show you out.'

The hackney clattered to a stop close to The Grapes Inn and Adam helped Meredith out. He instructed the coachman to return in one hour.

Opening the back gate Adam led Meredith across the yard and down into the cellar, the lighted lantern still hanging from its hook. He took a key from a pocket and opened the door of room six.

'Where did you get that key? I thought I had the only one.'

'It's a little trick known as copying into dough, Miss Sanders. I did it last night.'

'Oh, how clever!' There was a slight sarcasm to her tone. 'Where did you get it made?'

Mr Fox ignored her question. He didn't think she would approve of his ways and means at the moment, considering her prim countenance that afternoon. He guided her in and lit several candles. Then he closed and locked the door.

'The paint smell is stronger tonight.'

He sniffed. 'I'm not sure. You probably have a more sensitive nose for it than I. Where is this hidden door?'

Meredith went to the back wall and ran her hand along. 'Here, I can feel the draft again.' She moved on and stopped. 'And again, here.'

Picking up two lighted candles he gave one to Meredith. 'Run it up as far as your arm will reach and then down to the floor. I will try to find a latch.' He took a thin stick from his jacket pocket and slipped it into the crack and ran it up and down. Two bricks from the bottom it stopped. 'I think this is where we open it.' Nothing happened when he put pressure on the stick, or when he tried pressure from below the steel rod. Prodding the bricks, the bottom one moved in and the camouflaged door slid forward and sideways. 'A magician's trick, no doubt, but we have an entrance.'

Meredith stepped back. He expected fear to be on her face, but instead there was a radiant sparkle to her eyes and an excitement in her voice.

'Halleluiah! Oh, Adam, we are getting somewhere at last. This is what we have been hoping for. Quickly, let us go inside.'

In the midst of her excitement, Adam heard his name slip from her lips. It sounded strange, yet beautiful. He wanted to say so, but feared she would return to the prim matron of that afternoon and held back his words. Instead he barred her way with his arm.

'Not so fast, ma'am, I don't fancy being trapped inside without knowing how to get out.' He pushed his foot against the brick and the false door slid back into place. 'Excellent, it opens and closes from this room. I will go in to see if it can be closed and opened from inside. If it cannot, you are on this side to let me out.'

'You cannot do that. What if it doesn't open from your side and I cannot get it open from this side? You will be trapped. I'll go inside.'

'No. Nothing will go wrong. We will test the mechanism again. This time you operate the brick.'

Meredith pushed the side of her foot against the brick and the door opened. 'There you are, perfect. Now close it.' Without too much weight applied, she closed it.

Adam opened the door again, held his candle high, and stepped into the hidden room. He could definitely smell new paint now. As he swung his light in an arc, he saw four unframed paintings were hanging from nails on the wall. He was not a follower of the arts, but he had to assume they were all copies of famous artists' work. He went to one: a landscape of red poppies scattered like drops of blood in a cornfield with distant hills under a cloudless sky. It could be in England or France – there was no signature. He stepped to the next, a portrait. The world of artists was a long way from the ships and dockland warehouses he did business in each day.

'Are you there? Mr Fox, answer me.'

'I'm here. I'll try and close the door now. Stay where you are.'

He might have known she would not obey him. Her candle held high, she came in.

'Oooooh! Paintings.' She went to the one at the end of the row.

'Meredith, – Miss Sanders – will you please go back? I need to test the latch.'

'Just a moment, is this the one?'

'I wouldn't know. What did Madame Lightfoot say?'

'She just said the Turner, as if I knew which one. But I don't.'

'First, we test the latch; then we study the paintings. Outside, please, Miss Sanders!'

This time she obeyed.

Adam ran the candle light along the bottom of the opening. There was a lever; he pushed it down and the door slid back into place. With only the one candle, the room dimmed and it became difficult to see the paintings. A long time ago he had been in the hold of a ship when the cover had been pulled shut. The darkness had been complete: a cloying, suffocating cloth of black with only his own breathing to fill the void. He had that same feeling now. He pushed the lever up and the door opened and he stepped quickly out into the outer room.

'It works all right.' Meredith sounded as excited as a child opening a present.

'Perfectly. Whoever did that work, knew his trade.'

'What do we do now? The originals are not in there.'

'One must assume they are back where they belong: hanging in our public galleries, or on the walls of the great houses of our honourable lords.'

'But not the Turner painting Frederick was using. We are no better off than before. I still have to find the original.'

He was not listening to her, but to the sounds in the corridor. The voices were coming closer and the footsteps had stopped outside room six. Seconds later, a key was being inserted into the lock. He pushed Meredith through the false doorway, with one huge intake of breath he blew out the candles and followed her into the secret room. He pushed the lever and the door closed.

The slit gave only a view of the outside door and then only silhouettes. Two people came in, a large canvas balanced between them. One had a lantern and he put it on the table.

'It looks like there've been visitors already. The shipment must be soon. Open the door, so we can get out of here, I don't want to bump into Lightfoot. Rumour has it she's not happy, something to do with one of her regulars dying.'

Adam pulled Meredith beyond the sliding door and pressed her against the wall. He turned to her and hoped his dark clothes would be enough to hide them. If they were discovered he could pretend to be another artist taking advantage of the secret room for a bit of skirt lifting. The door opened. A faint light filled the doorway and someone came in. Meredith moved slightly and he tightened his hold on her shoulders. He was responsible for her safety and this was the second time she had been in danger today. Why did he let her do it? Because her independent ways mirrored his own. He was a man of the docklands, a place he had worked all his adult life. His father had made him an apprentice, made him learn his trade from the warehouse men, endure the cuffs and knocks from burly dockhands and sea captains. Only then did he work beside his father, negotiating cargos and experiencing how to run an export/import business – a man of his own making, independent and worldly. He had not worked it out yet, but something had made Meredith a woman of spirit. Together they would beat Madame Lightfoot.

There was a sound of shuffling feet, then a grunt. 'That's my last for this trip. The money is good, but the risk bad. The Bow Street men are growing in numbers. I hear they pay well for information; perhaps I'm on the wrong side.'

The accomplice gave a harsh laugh. 'That's as may be, but watch out for Cuba John. He's a mean man with a sharp knife.'

The light faded as the door closed.

Meredith relaxed in his arms. 'Be calm. I want to look into the other room.' Through the slit he saw the outer door close. 'They've gone, we can leave now.' Her hand touched his sleeve, and taking hold of her fingers he tried to rub some warmth into them. 'It's all right. We're safe.'

'Safe! I have never felt so *unsafe* in my whole life. Now I must look properly at the Turner. I think it may be the one that Frederick painted.'

With a new candle lit, she stood in front of the

painting. 'It's the one. I recognise it from a sketch that was in Frederick's portfolio. Below the sketch were test colours. So, here is the forgery, but where is the original? We seem to be solving this crime backwards.'

'It seems that way. We should go now; one near discovery is enough for tonight.'

The hackney was waiting, although he had been longer than the promised hour. Adam helped Meredith inside as the coachman woke from his dozing.

'Away, man and extra pay for waiting.'

CHAPTER EIGHT

Madame Lightfoot stepped from a coach and walked to the back entrance of The Grapes Inn. Cuba John stepped from the shadow of a wall and opened the gate for her. Without a word of acknowledgement, she raised her skirts and crossed the yard to the lighted passageway leading into the tavern. Descending the steps she opened the door to room six and stepped back. Cuba entered and soon a candle flared.

Everything she wore was a flagrant snub to the clientele of the inn and the Aldgate district. Dressed in a flamboyant green silk gown and matching high-collared cloak she entered and locked the door. Her hands covered with cotton gloves and her face hidden by a leather mask, nothing of her dark skin could be seen.

'Get the cloth and other items.' Her tone was harsh and she waved her hand in a dismissive manner.

The man scurried like a rat to the corner behind the door and pulled a wooden chest into the circle of light. He took out a blue cloth and two six-branch candelabra. While he set the table, Madame Lightfoot opened the door to the secret room. One by one she brought the paintings out and hung them on nails fixed in the wall. The room was transformed into an art gallery, with the Turner in pride of place on the easel.

She breathed one word, 'Beautiful,' but it told all. 'We shall strike a good bargain, this night, Cuba. Go to the gate, our guest will be arriving very soon.'

He grinned and went over to the easel. 'And a fair share for me?'

'Get away,' she shouted, 'your breath is like poison to such a masterpiece. Oh, I shall miss Frederick so very much. He was a genius. But what has he done with the original? That girl is like a fish bone in my throat. But I will not be put in jeopardy; she will do my bidding.'

'Would you like me to visit her again? Later, before the dawn; I made her a pretty little offer last time.'

'Keep your evil thoughts and dirty hands off her. The Bow Street men are the last people I want asking questions. Go to the gate, you know he doesn't like to be kept waiting. I want him in a pliable mood. These canvases are exceptionally good. I want the guineas to match.'

Cuba John left, leaving the door unlocked.

The room was hot and Madame Lightfoot pulled the mask off and dabbed her forehead. Footsteps sounded in the corridor and she replaced the mask. A short man in a monk's habit entered, his tonsure circled by wispy grey hair. He stopped by the table. 'Good evening.'

'Good evening. I trust you are well.'

'I am always well, *madame.*'

'Then let us get on with our negotiations. I have five for you tonight on the walls plus the one on the easel.' She signalled to Cuba John. 'Hold one of the candelabra high and follow us.'

The monk went to the first painting. He stepped close and swivelled his head in a circle, seeming to look at every inch of the work. He took several steps back and studied it for a long time. 'A fair canvas, madame, it would not, however, fool a Master. But then, those who will buy, the colonials, can be convinced easily enough. They are nothing but peasants who have made good from their criminal pasts, who couldn't tell a Rembrandt from any governess's paltry attempts.'

Madame Lightfoot inclined her head. 'Quite so, but they get better as we proceed.'

He moved on to the next.

Each painting was inspected as the first. This made for slow progress and Cuba needed to keep changing hands to hold the light high. Finally they came to the Turner.

'This is the exception I told you about, Frederick's "Turner", it is, in my opinion, his finest.'

'You speak as though it is his last.'

'Yes, it is. He died recently. I fear he is irreplaceable.'

'So be it, but I bless his soul, let it rest in peace with our God.'

'Thank you.' And she bowed her head in reverence.

The monk scrutinised and studied the work far longer than he had the others. He tilted the canvas and looked at the back, nodded and walked away and looked again at one he had already viewed. He circled the room with his hands behind his back until he stopped in front of the easel.

'It's almost perfect. Just a few errors, but it will pass, admirably, for an original. It will be hung with pride in one of our distant colonies. A pity he is gone.'

A sigh came from behind the mask. 'I am honoured to be of service to our foreign brethren. I would like to price this one separately. I know this is not our usual way of dealing, but you must appreciate, I have taken quite a risk in getting this particular painting ... or shall we say ... original?'

'Of course, I am most willing to oblige.'

She sat on the chair. 'Put the candelabrum back on the table, Cuba. Go and get yourself a tankard.' She threw a coin onto the table and waited for the man to leave.

The monk leant against the closed door and turned the key. 'Our privacy must always come first, madame.' He walked back and stopped at the table. 'What is your price?'

She took a sheet of paper from her reticule and handed it to him.

He did not open it. 'I believe I will see a very high figure. You know I will have to bargain with you, let us not waste our time and patience in vulgar haggling; my usual price, plus ten percent.'

'Plus twenty percent, sir'

'My client would not go above twelve percent.'

'I'm afraid not. I can sell elsewhere and you know it.'

'You drive a hard bargain. My final offer is fifteen percent and that surpasses the value of that one painting.'

She nodded her head in acceptance. 'One painting you will trick some untutored ass to believe he has a masterpiece painted by the very hand of Turner. Oh, no. You have a very valuable item for sale.'

'I will have the money delivered by hand in the usual way. The delivery date will be notified in *The Times*, as before. Good night, madame.'

'Thank you for a satisfactory evening. Good night.' There was a gloating tone to her voice. '*Bon voyage.*'

The monk unlocked the door and left without responding.

She circled the room and twirled; her gown and cloak billowing like a bell. 'I did it. I won. I would have settled for twelve, you foolish man.' She sat down on the chair, leant back, and took off the mask. She threw back her head and laughed until a tap on the door ended her triumphant call.

In the corridor a big man held a tray with a tankard and jug of ale on it. 'Just bin asked to bring this to yer, ma'am.' She held the door half-open, just enough to see. 'I didn't order any refreshments.'

'No, ma'am. Your man did.' He stepped forward. 'Shall I put it on the table?'

Madame Lightfoot blocked his way. 'I'll take it.' As she held out her hands the door opened further, letting the man see inside. 'You may go. Ask my man to come back, *now*.' She placed the tray on the table and then closed the door with a bang, shouting. 'You are an idiot, Cuba!' Her hands shook as she poured the ale and downed the full tankard until empty.

Sitting down she drummed her fingers on the table. When the door handle turned and Cuba John came in she stood up.

'The paintings must be stored in the secret room until the sailing date. What have you been up to? Don't bother to answer; you have half of it down your jacket. Unhook the paintings with great care, I'll store them away. I wish to be gone before that serving lout comes down here again. Leave the tray outside.'

With the room restored to its bare, dark state, they left the tavern through the back yard.

CHAPTER NINE

Meredith bathed her face and chose a blue cotton and muslin dress to wear.

She had not seen Adam since he had left her on Friday night after their discovery of the paintings in the hidden room. Nor had she been to Tallow House on Saturday. Miss Fox had requested she forego a sitting with Sarah, saying the child was being taken to visit friends for the day.

It had proved to be a day of agony. A day lost when she should have been searching … but where? What had seemed a step forward was, in fact, no step at all. Room six was a dead end. To fill her time she had helped Clemmie with a few household chores and gone with her to the market.

And why was Adam shunning her? Was he having second thoughts? Had the discovery of the secret room, the paintings and the risks involved, gone beyond the line he was prepared to cross?

If this worry wasn't enough, since the first light of day another intruder had forced his way into her mind – her father. She had let her fear of him blot out the rest of her family – especially her mother. What terrible thoughts had gone through her mind that June morning when she woke and found her daughter gone? She would have searched the streets when she didn't go back, asked their neighbours and the river-folk; even strangers. Meredith knew her mother would not have given up until she was sure every corner of Blackfriars had been searched. Did she go to Newgate prison and ask her husband if he knew anything? Would he have pretended shock about her being gone?

Meredith's disbelief that her father could sell her into marriage had never left her. She had paced her bedchamber at Appleton House a hundred times wondering what would happen if she returned one day. Were they still living in Blackfriars?

Ten years rolled back: she was creeping out of that basement room to run away from Warder Snipes. She could have hidden somewhere close, waited until her father saw reason; that there must be another way to get out of Newgate. He had obviously found it, or he would have been dead long ago. The urge to know what had happened grew stronger, but it would mean going back to her past – back to where she had vowed never to return.

She turned and looked at her room: the canopied bed with the thick feather mattress, the washstand and flowered bowl, the chair Frederick had given her to curl up in after he taught her to read. The wardrobe had been a special gift on her seventeenth birthday. She touched the curtains that helped to keep out the night and the noises of the street – a home of luxury compared to Thames Street. How could she go back? She was mad to even think of it. A tap on the door ended her agonising thoughts. Clemmie came in with a tray laden with toast, preserve and a pot of tea.

'I heard you moving about. It's still very early, but I thought you would like to breakfast now. Is everything all right?'

'Not really, I have a headache. Thank you for the tray, I'm sure something to eat will help chase away this malaise.' Meredith didn't move away from the window. Her thoughts weighed heavy and she let Clemmie pour her tea. 'Thank you. I'll be down shortly.'

Clemmie hovered, seeming reluctant to leave and

Meredith babbled on. 'Miss Weston's portrait is coming on very well. I feel so much more confident now that I am using the oils on the canvas.'

Still the old retainer didn't leave, and finally she said, 'Remember that I told you about Mrs Morgan, that nice lady I met at the market last week, the one who is cook to a Mrs Silverton? It's her afternoon off and she has asked me to go and help her sew a new dress. She hasn't had anything new for five years and she wants to wear it for her granddaughter's christening.'

'Goodness, Clemmie, you don't have to ask me for a few hours off. Go and enjoy your afternoon. Just because we are in London, doesn't mean that you have to be here every minute. At Appleton House, you were part of our family, and it's the same here.' The pain in her head increased to such an extent that she thought it would explode. She moved and sat on the chair. 'Would you pass my tea, please?'

'Tired, that's what you are, Meredith. You are a lady taking on work – for that's what it is – a man's work. Ladies sew, read and paint for pleasure. I'm sure Frederick didn't intend for you to become an *employed* person. I speak out of turn, but you have not been the same girl since you took on this *assignment*.'

Meredith thought about the meaning of the word – assignment? Clemmie meant her painting Sarah's portrait. She attributed the word to the criminal activities she had been undertaking these past few days – and nights. Meredith drank her tea and made no reply until she put the cup down on the small table next to her chair. 'Thank you, Clemmie. I know you are concerned, but I am perfectly all right and I have been commissioned to paint a portrait. I am not employed in the usual meaning of the word. It gives me too much pleasure for that.' She raised her hand as the other woman started to speak. 'I shall rest until we go to St. Martin's for the Reverend's morning service. Then this afternoon, go and enjoy Mrs Morgan's company.'

Meredith, with Clemmie at her side, listened to the Reverend Jones' Welsh tones deliver the Parable of the Prodigal Son with passion and thunder to a congregation sat spellbound, drinking in every word. To Meredith, the sermon fitted her thoughts too closely to give her any comfort. Moments later the organ's glorious music for the last hymn filled the church and Meredith tucked her memories back where they belonged, deep within her soul.

Clemmie closed the street door with a rosy blush to her cheeks. Meredith hadn't seen her so elated since they arrived in Ludgate Hill. The housekeeper's new friend, Mrs Morgan, had given her someone to visit of her own station and Meredith hoped it would blossom into a compatible friendship.

The quietness of the sitting room did little to calm her fear of Madame Lightfoot. She needed something to chase away her thoughts and went down to the studio. Frederick would have used this room, but she had not found a palette or brush. As she thought back, there had been no linseed smell. His death had been so very sudden that she had expected to find a collection of finished canvases to sell and unfinished work in here. But it had all been as bare as a pauper's pantry, not even a splash of paint on a floorboard. She hadn't known the real Frederick at all, but she had dearly loved the one she knew.

His easel stood beside her table and she placed a new canvas on it. Nothing came into her mind except Mr Fox. She fetched her sketch of him from the desk drawer. His strong features, dark eyes and hair would be a challenge to capture on canvas in oils. A longing to have the real vibrant man close surged through her. Every day she was relying upon him more. If Frederick's guilt became public knowledge, she would take full responsibility and deny Mr Fox knew anything about the crime. This decision made her more agitated than ever and returning to the easel she picked up a charcoal stick and drew the first lines of his face.

Monday: was it only a week since she had first met Adam? It seemed a lifetime ago and as she mixed blue and black pigments with linseed oil she wondered what her fate would be come next Monday?

Satisfied with her oil paint she studied Miss Weston and brushed shadow into the folds of the blue dress on her canvas. The portrait was coming along well. She had captured the child's smile and sparkling eyes, there was a glow of happiness about her. Did it come from knowing her father would see this when he returned?

'Are you all right, Sarah?'

'I think so. I am a little thirsty, Miss Sanders. Could we stop for a rest?'

'Of course we can, dear. There's a jug of lemonade on the table, let us both enjoy a break for a few moments.'

'Is it time for me to have a look yet? I can't wait to show Uncle Adam. I know you have done the most wonderful painting of me, even before I look at it.'

'Such flattery, but no one is going to see it until I have finished – not even *you*.'

'*Please*. Just one little peep?'

'No, Miss Weston.' Although her reply was firm, Meredith really longed to show someone. In the past she would have shown Frederick and listened to his advice. But now she was on her own, making her own decisions. This is what he had wanted for her.

Meredith poured two glasses of lemonade and gave

Sarah one. 'Would you like to go into the garden for a few minutes? It's such a lovely day and we have done a good morning's work.'

'Can we take our lemonade?'

'Yes. But be very careful going down the stairs. I don't want your housekeeper complaining about spilt liquids to be cleaned up.'

Meredith followed Sarah down the stairs into the garden. They sat on the stone seat and she wondered if Mr Fox would come, as he had that first day, authoritative and taking charge. Why had he taken it upon himself to become her knight errant? Why had she become dependent on him in her quest to find the Turner painting? It wasn't just the insecurity, her lack of knowledge; he knew what to do. There was something that drew her to him. She wasn't sure what, except it was a powerful attraction she didn't want to deny.

Could one fall in love within a week? Even at first sight? How would she feel if she never saw him again? Her thoughts stopped – she would only be half a person. Within a few days he had made her want to be beside him, be in his arms; her cheeks burned with such a scandalous desire. She glanced at Sarah, but the child was busy drawing a snail that was travelling slowly across a stepping-stone.

Footsteps sounded along the path – *Adam?* Flustered and breathless, she dampened her wicked thoughts into submission.

A moment later, only the maid appeared. 'Miss Fox asks if you will be staying to lunch, Miss Sanders.'

'Thank you, yes. Will it be at the usual time?'

'Yes, ma'am.' The girl curtsied and returned to the house.

This was the life she had grown used to: being waited on, good food, intelligent company. No, she couldn't go back, not even just to look. Her father was in employment, so he could look after his family. She would content herself with that knowledge.

Sarah stood up. 'Do you want to paint me anymore?'

'Yes. I have been invited to stay to lunch, so let us make use of the extra time.' Concentration on something more productive than her father would clear her mind, and taking Sarah's hand they walked back to the house.

Miss Fox was in her chair holding a glass of sherry. Meredith had come to realise the old lady had a great liking for her pre-lunch *aperitif*, which extended into the meal and beyond. During her sittings with Sarah she had learned that Miss Fox suffered terrible pains in her legs. A glass of sherry helped her sleep in the afternoon and she also partook of a small glass at bedtime.

'As always, Miss Sanders, it is a pleasure to have your company. Can I offer you a glass of lemonade?'

'No, thank you. I will wait until we are seated in the dining room.' She may have said yes, if it had been a glass of sherry.

'How is the portrait coming along? I think by now a little peep would not be an unreasonable request.'

Miss Fox said this with a smile, which made Meredith's resolution to refuse easier to say. 'Mr Fox has put a great deal of faith in my capabilities. This is my first commission and I would like to complete it before it is placed before you for judgement. I understand your eagerness, but I would like to wait until the final presentation. A few more sittings and you can all see it.'

'If that is your wish, then I will curb my curiosity until you have finished. I must admit, the idea of a professional woman artist thrills me far more than embroidering a motif on a handkerchief.'

'Perhaps I could show you how to paint, in oils, a flower from your garden.'

'Thank you, dear. I take your kind offer to heart, but

we will see. I only go into the garden now on a warm summer day.'

Simms arrived to help Miss Fox from her chair and into the dining room. Meredith was disappointed to see there were only two places laid. She had put all her faith in him being here to tell her of any progress he had made since their last meeting.

As she finished drinking her lemonade, Meredith could not hold back the question. 'Mr Fox has not joined us today?'

'My nephew is very busy. The export business is expanding fast and he has much work to do. This past week we have seen almost nothing of him – morning, noon or night.'

The conversation had taken a turn that made Meredith feel guilty. She was claiming Mr Fox's time, not his business. To lighten the mood, she offered, 'If you would like, I can stay another hour to occupy Miss Weston's time. It is a perfect afternoon to sit in the garden and she can finish her picture of a snail.'

Miss Fox squeezed Meredith's hand. 'Thank you, dear. Miss Thomson is a great loss until she returns to us. I shall instruct Simms to bring the coach later. Off you go, I need my rest now.'

Meredith had grown very fond of the old lady. She must be aware that time was slipping by much too fast if she was ever to see her nephew-in-law again. Sarah wasn't the only one who wanted him to come home. She stood up and curtsied, 'To my task, Miss Fox.'

It really was no hardship to spend extra time in the wild garden. She longed to see the countryside with its fields that spread for miles to the distant horizons. Hear the chirpings of the thrushes and blue tits, and the voices of the farm workers carried on the breeze. She particularly missed her walks with Clemmie by the stream and to the market each week in Harlington, where she knew everyone and could stop and chatter, hear the gossip.

Suddenly, Sarah called, 'Uncle Adam,' and ran back along the path.

Mr Fox lifted his niece high and gave her a kiss on the forehead and sat her in the crook of his arm. 'Is Miss Sanders still here?'

'Yes. Aunt Izzie said she could stay a little longer. I like her being with me. She's sitting on the seat. Is she waiting for you?'

'No. She is not waiting for me. Her offer is for you. She has a very kind heart.' He put her down and took her hand. 'Let's go and see her.'

Meredith stood up. 'Good afternoon, sir.'

'Good afternoon, Miss Sanders. Thank you for keeping Sarah happy with her drawing. I trust it has not intruded on your other commitments?'

Good lord. Had her motive really been to wait and see him? Of course not! But her heart did beat a little faster when she heard his voice. Soon she wouldn't be able to even think without him being in her mind. This definitely had to stop.

'No. Your garden is such a pleasant reminder of Appleton House and the afternoons I spent wandering amongst the tall grasses and flowers.' Why was she so uneasy with him when they had secrets bonding them together? What did he really think of her? He had implied she was reckless; she had connections to a criminal, and treated him with utter disrespect. And why did he continue to let her associate with his family? Miss Fox would be horrified if she knew the truth. To escape she muttered, 'The coach will be here shortly, please excuse me. I have to collect my gloves from the studio.'

'I will accompany you home.'

His smile gave no hint of any liaison between them and she scolded herself for letting him twist her emotions into knots. 'Thank you, Mr Fox. I will be five minutes.' She stooped down to speak with Sarah. 'I will see you the day after tomorrow. You can then paint your drawings from this afternoon. I would love to see this bright colour on paper.'

'Would you really like that, Miss Sanders? Then I will work very hard to have it ready for you.' The child wound her arms around Meredith's neck and hugged her. 'You are the best teacher. Uncle Adam must let you stay forever.'

Meredith was overwhelmed by such a demonstrative embrace and endearing words. All she could reply was, 'Thank you.'

'I think I also owe Miss Sanders my gratitude.' Mr Fox held out his hand. 'May I help you up?'

Meredith didn't want to accept his hand, feel his skin. He made her body go hot and have butterflies in her stomach. Ignoring his help she tried to get up but caught her shoe in the hem of her gown and toppled sideways. Next moment she was in his arms.

'Not quite the help I intended,' he whispered close to her ear, 'although most enjoyable, Meredith. This intimacy surely allows us now to call each other by our given names?' He put her down and bowed.

Why, when she was with him, did she end up in a pickle? She glanced at Sarah, expecting a horrified expression; instead she was clapping her hands with glee.

'I think not, sir. It is inappropriate. We are only acquaintances and certainly not in front of the child.' To cover her embarrassment she nodded and marched up the path and into the house.

Meredith stormed into the studio and picked up her gloves and reticule. To release the tension that was inside her, she said aloud. 'Oh! The wretched man,' but his warm breath and words had done more than she was prepared to admit and more calmly murmured, 'Meredith, indeed.' Hurrying down the stairs, she acknowledged she needed him to go with her if she were to know what he had been up to. Yet to sit so close, perhaps his knees touching hers, made her flustered again. She couldn't do it – but it might cause unwanted speculation if she refused. 'Indeed, he is a wretched man.'

On the journey to Ludgate Hill, Meredith waited for Mr Fox to speak, but he sat mute and stared through the window. What was so interesting about passing houses and horse-drawn carts? And his interest in her had disappeared like a magician's puff of smoke. This was supposed to be her opportunity to talk with him about any developments. He was rudely ignoring her.

'Sir, can we discuss any news you have about our … little adventure.'

He now looked at her. 'Our *little* adventure? Is this what you think the last few days have been? Madam, it may be to you, a country maid with no knowledge of this city's vice. But let me tell you, this is a *big criminal adventure* your benefactor has left you in his legacy. He would have done well to have dispensed with the *artistic* package long ago. Life has a way of ending on a whim and not of our own making.'

'Frederick would do nothing to harm me. The fever took him. He was not to know that the rain would cause his lungs to fail.'

'That was my point, Meredith.'

'Sir, Miss Sanders, if you please.'

He gave an exasperated sigh. 'No. I am your friend and confidant and I shall call you Meredith and you will call me Adam – in private, of course.' His face brightened and he smiled. 'You really don't mind, do you?'

Oh, why did she blush so when he was near? But she

didn't mind, not really, in fact, not at all. The constant formalities between them were tiresome when they were alone, but that was the problem, they shouldn't be alone together. The city had far too many strict rules of proprietary. Life had been so much simpler in the country. 'Very well, sir.' She gave in because there was no good reason to fight him anymore.

'Adam. Say it, Meredith.' He took her gloved hand in his strong fingers.

She wetted her lips; this was a step nearer to the intimacy she feared. 'Adam?' His name left her lips in little more than a whisper, but it rang in her ears like chiming bells.

He raised her hand to his lips, saying, 'Adam and Meredith.'

She heard his words and they sounded like they belonged together, joined in harmony, joined in … she looked at him, what was happening to her?

Adam tilted his head and looked out of the window. 'I have a meeting with Woody this afternoon at The Grapes Inn. I must go and become Dello Murphy again.'

'But you haven't told me anything you have discovered?'

'There isn't really anything of importance to tell you, but maybe later.'

'Please, be careful, I didn't mean to make you angry. I do know how dangerous this is.' Her hand was still in his and she reluctantly withdrew it. 'Please, don't do anything to cause those drunken men to harm you.'

Adam touched her cheek with his finger and ran it down to tilt her chin. 'Thank you for your concern. I will be careful.'

The coach stopped. Adam tapped the roof and the coachman opened the door. He got out and offered his hand to her. 'Goodbye, Meredith.'

Adam pushed a silver coin over the table to Woody. 'So, the dark woman does come below. That be a very interestin' bit of news'

'I've only seen her 'ere this once, and only 'cause her man got careless.'

'And that be what I'm paying 'ee for. Keeping yer eyes open and yer ears lisenin' for what's goin'on in number six.' Adam put a few extra pennies on the table, 'ave a mug of the 'keeper's finest ale and I'll see yer soon.'

He left the tavern room and hurried round to the back entrance, down the steps, and into room six. It amazed him how so many people could come and go without being noticed.

Lighting only one candle he opened the secret door to the hidden room. The paintings were still hanging there. He put himself in the position of Madame Lightfoot; there was danger in keeping goods stored without a buyer, so she must have one awaiting this delivery. She must realise that her situation was threatened, to the extent of imprisonment, if the Turner was not found. The danger to Meredith increased hourly, for Lightfoot would not hesitate to implicate Frederick Sanders to save herself in this criminal ruse.

Meredith waited until Clemmie left to go to a small market that only opened on Monday afternoons. Adam was meeting her father in Aldgate. Now she had agreed to call him Adam, she let his name float around her mind forming his face, his smile, and those dark eyes gentle just for her. But they were for Meredith, the lady; not Merry from Blackfriars.

With both her protectors occupied, this was an opportunity to go back to her past. After all her deliberations and decisions not to go, she wouldn't rest until she did.

She changed into her own work dress again and left the gallery within fifteen minutes. Her heart thumped like a drum beating the rhythm of the soldiers' steps as she walked up Ludgate Street to St Paul's Cathedral. Turning round she looked back. From here on she would be stepping back into her past. Did she want to do this? The answer was a complicated muddle of emotions – a desire to see and the fear of knowing what was left of her home. She walked towards the river.

The roads and lanes had not changed in ten years; they were still the well-worn cobbles. Meredith didn't hurry; she wanted to remember how dismal and cramped life was for the families in the narrow houses, more so in the cellar rooms. Everywhere was so familiar: children knelt sharing a chunk of bread; two small girls sat in a doorway holding hands. Her heart ached; every one of them unwashed, their hair matted, and without exception, torn and dirty clothes. Turning a corner Meredith stopped. Two ruffians were tugging furiously over a cabbage – such an everyday occurrence that no one interfered to stop them. The desolation drained her energy and she wanted to sit down on the cobbles as she had when she lived here. Poverty was still the way of life in Blackfriars.

She turned into another alley. Instantly, hardened mud and deep wheel ruts became difficult to walk along in her fashionable boots; boots she could be killed for if someone was desperate for money. The hovels on either side were little more than huts, held together by its neighbour either side. At least they had not lived quite like this. A harrowing thought burst into her mind: while she lived in luxury, could her family have been forced into a place like this? Time had made her forget the squalor, the choking smells of open drains and the wretchedness of these people.

She didn't have to go on, there was no obligation, but

she would be a coward to turn and run as she had before. Her mission now was to find her family – their fate, good or bad.

Although not hungry, her insides rumbled, almost as though it wanted to feel that gnawing pain again. Hawkers called out, selling pies and milk, spoons and knives. Traders pushed vegetable and fruit carts. She remembered stealing an apple from a cart and how frightened she had been.

A breeze cooled her face as she walked into Thames Street. The road stretched out before her. She was twelve again. She could smell the river, the houses unchanged, all of them in need of fresh paint. The people looked more tired, bedraggled and poor – why had progress passed them by? Did no one care? She had been lucky, no not lucky, she had escaped and fate had found her Frederick.

Meredith saw a young woman sat on the ground, her dress top pushed aside, feeding her baby and trying to cuddle three other children to her. They had that thin, hungry look and it made their dark eyes seem large in their pale, drawn faces. The clothes they wore would have been cast off as rags in Harlington. She wrenched open her reticule, her eyes filling with tears as her fingers fumbled to find her purse. Pity and sorrow raced through her as she put a shilling into the girl's palm and closed the bony fingers tight around it. Running from Warder Snipes had been the right thing to do.

The house was there and the basement room. Nothing had changed: the bricks were black from the soot of chimneys, the door was unpainted, the windows needed washing – she pulled her thoughts to a stop. This was not an area where people cleaned, it was only a place to live, somewhere to eat and sleep. They did not have the fresh country air, the meadows to run in and the farms to buy their food. This was Blackfriars, where one survived and didn't think of a future.

Meredith stood looking at the house. This is what she had come for, just to see. But now she was here, she wanted to go inside – make sure they were there. What good would it do? She had abandoned her family, hadn't cared what happened to them. Why open the wound of guilt wider? Because she had to know, had to see they were all right. Before she could change her mind, Meredith crossed the road and went down the steps. She raised her hand and knocked. Pure undiluted fear raced through her. The door opened and a girl stood in the doorway.

'Yar. What do yer want?'

What could she say? She swallowed hard. 'Hello. I'm … are you the tenant's daughter?'

'Why?' The girl sounded cautious. 'If it's Pa yer want, he's out.'

I know that, I want to know about my family.

'I'm doing a list of families in Thames Street. It's for the … um, St Martin's Church Foundation.'

'Never 'eard of them. Pa says I'm not to talk to strangers.'

She went to close the door, but Meredith put her hand out to stop it closing. 'I'm to give sixpence if you tell me who lives here.' Oh, how the lies now flowed out of her mouth. 'Can I come in?'

Meredith tried to see inside, but the girl slid out and closed the door. 'No. But we can sit on the steps. Sixpence yer say. I'll have it first before I tell yer.'

They sat down side by side. Meredith's misery grew with each breath. The girl's eyes were the colour of her own and her face was so like their mother's. They were still here, still living in the same place. Still eating and sleeping amongst the rats and cockroaches. She should be appalled they hadn't managed to get out of this basement, but selfishly, she was glad, because it meant she had found them.

Suddenly, she had no control over her body and every limb, every part of her, felt weak and it was difficult to breathe. She pulled a handkerchief from her pocket and dabbed her eyes.

The girl held out her hand. 'First yer sixpence, I said.'

Meredith took the silver coin from her purse and handed it over. 'There is your father and you and who else?'

'Like I said, there's only me and Pa.'

The words sent a hammer blow into her heart. There were only two of them out of six. 'Where is your mother?' The shock crawled through her, her brain ceased to function. She forced herself to ask, 'Do you not have any brothers and sisters?'

The girl shrugged. Her breasts were only just beginning to show through the dress top. She could not be any older than when Meredith had run away. 'What is your name?'

'Tilly. Ma died.'

This was little Matilda! Her mother was dead! Meredith wouldn't believe that – the girl was lying, 'When?'

'A long time, I was only little. Pa tells me about her sometimes.'

Mama was really dead – buried beneath the ground; she could never touch her hand, tell her she was sorry. Meredith was unable to put words together, but she had to know the whole story. 'What about your brothers and sisters?'

'Lily got married and left. Me brothers left and 'ave gone to sea. It's just me and Pa, like I said.'

'Is your sister living in Blackfriars? Do you have letters from your brothers?'

'Why do yer want to know all that?' The girl's mouth closed into a firm line.

'Just to …' Meredith couldn't think of an excuse. 'Um … for the records, that's all. There is nothing for your father to worry about.' Tilly bit her lip and Meredith wanted to hug her. She did exactly the same thing when she was worried.

'Lily lives in the country. Me brothers don't know how to write.'

'You don't remember another sister?'

'No. Ma never had any more babies after me.'

Merry was forgotten. She was not remembered at all. Pa never thought she was worth a mention. 'Thank you. I must go now. Goodbye.' Meredith stood and ran up the steps. She didn't look back, she couldn't, and this wasn't how it should have been.

Her legs found new strength and she raced through the alleys, instinct guiding her back. She didn't stop running until she reached St Martin's church in Ludgate Hill. The door was open, the Reverend Jones welcomed the good and the bad at all times.

Kneeling in a pew, Meredith bowed her head. Nothing had gone according to her dream. In all her vows of not returning to Blackfriars, this had never included her mother. She had always wanted to see her again. That was why she had gone today, so she could tell her why she had run away and to wash the guilt from her soul.

But she was too late! Clasping her fingers together she prayed, 'Please, Mama, forgive me.'

CHAPTER TEN

Madame Lightfoot lifted *The Times* from her breakfast tray. She scanned the sheet and a smile touched her lips, 'Tonight, my beauties.' As she continued to read, deep lines creased her forehead and her lips curled back across her teeth like a growling dog. She spat out her words like venom. 'The Royal Academy announces their Summer Exhibition ...' She tore the paper into pieces and threw it across the bed. 'If the girl doesn't find the Turner, everything is lost.' Her anger exploded with the tray flying across the bedchamber floor.

'Sally Ann,' she shouted. 'I'm going out. Prepare my simple grey gown.'

In the shadow of the Tower of London, River Lane housed small dilapidated hovels. Madame Lightfoot's dishevelled appearance and threadbare cloak fitted well with her surroundings as she walked amongst the pitiful souls who slept and begged every day in the gutters. Their hacking coughs, spitting, and whispers followed her until she unlocked the door of number thirteen.

Stepping inside she closed and bolted the heavily reinforced door. A shutter covered a small window and this made the room dim, only the bare whitewashed walls reflected its size. Not a single piece of furniture stood on the scrubbed floor.

A sigh left her lips. 'Hello, Mama, is your spirit here today?' She closed her eyes and waited. 'No, Mama? My receptiveness is at odds with you. We will talk another time.'

She went to the back wall and lifted her arm to the ceiling, touched an unmarked spot. Part of the wall moved out and she descended a flight of steps. Her large hands used a flint and she lit a candle on a table.

The cellar expanded from a dark hole into a large room, the dirt floor embedded with flagstones. Perfectly centred, an easel was placed opposite a winged leather chair. Several small tables were placed around the room, each with a six-branch candelabrum. Lightfoot lit them all.

She sat in the chair and tapped her fingernails on the leather arms. Her head fell back and she closed her eyes. Softly and slowly a rhythmic chant left her lips. Her native tongue speeded up with the repeated rhyme, over and over, her fingernails tapping in time. Her chanting stopped. She opened her eyes and slammed both hands on the chair arms.

'I curse you, Frederick Sanders. You will not rest until this task is complete.'

Reflected in the candlelight were oil paintings, delicate watercolours, and charcoal sketches. Each one painted by a French, Dutch, or Italian master. All in exquisite gold frames hanging on the walls. She smiled and a sigh left her lips. 'Oh, my beauties, you outshine a thousand monuments.' She rose from the chair, picked up a candelabrum, and toured the cellar. She replaced the flaming lights, then lifted a small oil painting from the wall and put it on the easel.

Sitting again, she spoke to the painting. 'You're not for sale, Rachel Ruysch. Oh, how I admire your talent. My mama coaxed me, loved me, but I didn't have the gift. You! To be blessed with a father who encouraged such freedom as you wished. You were a woman painting against the odds of rejection. I could never succeed, but Frederick has taught the girl well. With a little unfriendly persuasion, Miss Sanders could continue his work.'

She sat for a long time, her smile still lighting her eyes. 'Oh yes, Miss Sanders, find the Turner. I want you to work for me.' She put the painting back on the wall, extinguished the candles, and climbed the steps back into her secret hovel.

Madame Lightfoot alighted from a hackney. She waited in the dark until the sound of the horse's hooves died away. A few steps brought her to a door and she went inside. Three-quarters of the way along a narrow passage was a flight of steps. She lifted her skirts and ascended up them to an upper landing. She opened the door on her left. The room was large and furnished with a sofa and chairs in rich golden brocades. A cherry wood dining set completed the arrangement. She stepped onto an exquisite crimson carpet decorated with symmetric lines and swirling symbols. Hiding the window, silk drapes the colour of woodland primroses shimmered in the candlelight.

She was again the woman of wealth. Her hair re-dressed, wearing a dark green velvet cloak over a pink gown. She pulled at the fingers of her gloves.

A young servant girl curtsied. She had the same dark skin and hurried forward to take her mistress' cloak. 'Good evenin', madame, your suppa is ready.'

'Good. But first I will ready myself to retire. I am hungry tonight, Sally-Ann, but I can wait a little longer. Then you may go to bed.'

Two hours later she pushed away a fine china plate, picked up a gold goblet, and slowly swirled the red wine inside. Raising the goblet high, she toasted aloud. 'To the triangle of fate: Turner, Frederick, and Meredith Sanders.'

CHAPTER ELEVEN

Meredith looked down on to the busy road of Ludgate Hill. She was glad she didn't have to go to Tallow House today. Her head was in no state to concentrate on Sarah's portrait. She was a sweet child, but her chatter would have been difficult to cope with against the hammering headache Meredith had succumbed to yesterday after coming out of St Martin's church.

Clemmie came into the room with a tray. 'A cup of tea will help to revive you, dear. Your face is so white, you look like a ghost. Of course, I've never seen a ghost, only stories from my mother.'

Mother to daughter! In that cramped basement there had been no time or place for her mother to tell her stories. Except, sometimes, on hot summer nights, when she crept from her bed and sat on the basement steps, her mother came and sat beside her, held her hands and rubbed a hard-skinned thumb across her palm. In the cool of the dawn she would tell her stories about when she had been a young girl.

Meredith's throat tightened, choking tears threatening to spill down her cheeks. Clemmie's voice came through her agony. 'I've brought a few biscuits. Would you like one?'

Meredith wasn't hungry, but Clemmie looked so concerned. 'Yes, please. Shall we be naughty and sit on the sofa and forget about chores and dusting?'

'Oh, I think I can give that up for today. Come and rest.'

The politeness of sipping tea and nibbling biscuits

made her feel like a tightly wound clock spring. She had to speak about yesterday to someone. And her only confidante that she could tell was sat beside her.

'Clemmie, when I came to Appleton House and Frederick said I was staying, what did you think?'

'That's a strange question to be asking after all this time. Frederick only said that you were a young lady who needed somewhere to live and that you would be of help to me in the house. When I asked your name he said from then on you would be called Meredith Sanders. It really wasn't for me to question.'

'I'm sorry I never told you my story. I think in the beginning I was frightened my father would come looking for me. Then as you both accepted me as part of the household, I didn't want anything to spoil it.'

'What has made you think of it now?'

'Coming back here; to this part of London, near to Blackfriars. Oh, Clemmie, I went there yesterday, to find my mother, and she is … oh, how could I have been so wicked? Now she is dead. Frederick is dead. I am so alone …' She couldn't stop the tears now. They ran down her face and she pulled a handkerchief from her pocket and covered her face.

'Oh, Meredith.' Clemmie moved closer and pulled her into the circle of her arms. 'You have me and I have you.'

'There's more. I need to tell you why I ran away.'

Clemmie frowned. Her eyes took on a troubled look. 'Very well, dear, I'm listening.'

'That day I was twelve …' Meredith relived it as though it were yesterday. 'My father was in the debtors' cells at Newgate prison. We all lived in one basement room. My mother washed and ironed for the dock men and sailors. I scrubbed tavern floors and my brothers mucked out horse stalls. The rent took most of our money each week, so we could never save enough to release my father.'

Meredith paused; the next part was so painful she didn't want to recall it.

'Mid-summer day was my twelfth birthday. My father had struck a bargain with Warder Snipes – marriage to me for his debt payment and release money from Newgate. I had always been an obedient daughter, but this was asking too much of me. So I ran away. I walked all day until the sun was low in the sky. I saw a barn and inside I met Frederick.'

Meredith's heart was hammering and her throat seemed to close up. 'May I have another cup of tea, please, Clemmie?' Without a word being spoken she was given her tea.

'I was very frightened of him. Especially when he took a knife from his bag; but he was only going to cut me a piece of bread and cheese. The next morning he offered me a home, saying he had a housekeeper and I could be his longed-for daughter. And here we are now … I never meant to hurt my mother but I had to make a choice – marriage and drudgery to a man older than my father or freedom.' As she finished, her hands were shaking.

The old lady took them into her warm ones and rubbed them until they were still. 'Oh, Meredith, it is all such a tragedy. Do you feel better for telling me?'

'Yes, I do.' She had bared her soul to Clemmie, and whispered, 'Thank you for taking me into your life and heart.'

'You were there from the moment I set eyes on you, poor little waif that you were. Do you know, from that day, I came alive? You filled the part of my heart that I had saved for a daughter. But I was never blessed with one. So you see, Meredith, we both had a role to play in each other's lives.'

Meredith smiled, a fleeting memory crossing her

mind. 'Do you remember our baking lessons? Those flat puddings I made and how Frederick pretended to love them?'

'Yes, I do, dear. Those little memories often come to me when I'm in the kitchen.'

'Clemmie, I have to do something for Tilly. I cannot leave her there, in that basement. I must bring her here. I can turn the attic into a bedchamber. She could help you, as I did at Appleton. Yes, and Tilly could run the errands so you don't get so tired.' After the shock of hearing her mother was dead, Meredith had not considered how she could help Tilly escape from Blackfriars. 'You wouldn't mind her here, would you?'

Mrs Clements patted her hand. 'No, I wouldn't mind. But you just can't snatch the poor mite from her home.'

'Why not? I am not rich, but I can provide better for her here in Ludgate Hill.' Meredith stood up, feeling betrayed; surely Clemmie was not defending her father?

'This has all been so upsetting for you. But, think this through, Meredith. Your sister doesn't even remember you. Your father must, after all these years, think you are gone forever. And, of course, Tilly may refuse your offer. You cannot consider such a proposal until you, yourself, make a decision on whether you wish to acknowledge your family again.'

The words spoken seemed harsh to Meredith, but Clemmie was right. She wanted Tilly to do what she had done – run away – and whether she agreed or not, Clemmie saw the dilemma more clearly.

'Yes. I need to think this through. But I want to give Tilly the chance to leave Blackfriars.'

'Are you happy here, in London, Meredith?'

That question had crossed her mind several times, but Meredith squared her shoulders and replied, 'I am being overly anxious. Frederick left me a home so that I can become recognised. I know I'm a woman, but whatever the outcome, I must try. There, I have finally told you everything and I feel so much better.'

'Is that all that's worrying you? I will be frank, since your association with Mr Fox you have not been quite yourself.'

Adam Fox was not the reason she was having nightmares. Madame Lightfoot was the one who loomed large and menacing in her dreams. And no miracle was about to happen, unless Frederick told her where to look from his grave.

To pacify Clemmie, she answered, 'It is a little unnerving, and strange, to be responsible for a commission. But I have great faith in what I'm doing. Miss Weston is the perfect subject.'

As a cue to end her confessions a loud knock sounded on the front door.

Meredith had a flutter of butterflies. 'That may be a client! I'll go down immediately.' She patted Clemmie's hand. 'You sit here and finish your tea and have that lonely biscuit, because if I sell a painting, we shall have more than enough money for our needs.'

It was not a client, only the maid of her adversary who curtsied, handed over another note, and left.

Meredith opened the sheet and read: *I have some good news. Meet me at St Paul's steps at three o'clock.* Had Madame Lightfoot found it? Then why not come here and tell her? Why the mysterious meeting at St Paul's? But as long as the Turner had been found, did it matter?

Full of optimism, Meredith hurried back upstairs. She would tell Clemmie a maid had delivered a note requesting she attend a client, at her home, with a portfolio of her paintings.

Ludgate Hill was a cacophony of people, carriages, coaches, and gentlemen on horseback. They filled every bit of vacant space and trader's voices shouted out their wares. And above all this was the jangling of horse harnesses as a stagecoach thundered out of the inn's courtyard. Amongst this mayhem, Meredith walked towards St Paul's a few minutes before three o'clock. It still puzzled her why Madame Lightfoot wanted to meet in such a public place.

She stopped when she reached the church and glanced around; was she to wait at the bottom or top steps? The note had not said … A hand gripped her elbow and she smelt that unforgettable breath. She tried to turn but he stood just to her right and behind.

'Pity we're before the holy church.' His rasping voice was close to her ear. 'Maybe another time; I know where to come.'

Meredith didn't understand why this man was here, why he was leading her away from the steps towards a coach.

'The Madame, she doesn't like being kept waiting.' He opened the door and as she went to climb in he pushed her; only a large strong hand saved her from falling to the floor.

'Get in, Cuba John; you've the manners of a pig,' hissed Lightfoot's voice from inside.

Meredith saw in the daylight the man who had invaded her bedchamber. Now she had a name to put to him, Cuba John. He was smaller than she had thought him that night in the dark; he was certainly skeletal. His skull was almost bald with wisps of hair hanging like black string to his shoulders. His eyes were his most fearsome feature, the lids drooping over pale grey irises in pools of blood.

The coach moved off and Meredith sat on the seat opposite the dark-skinned woman. She was not dressed in her finery today. Her gown was grey cotton under a black cloak, her hat matronly with a small brim and grey ribbons. To restore some sort of decorum, Meredith pulled her dress back into order and challenged her opponent, saying, 'This is an unusual occasion. Could you not have just come to the gallery to tell me you have found the Turner?'

'It is not found.' Her tone was harsh, her face like stone with not a hint of welcome in her eyes. 'Your time has run out. Give me the Turner or …'

The unspoken threat hammered into Meredith. 'I don't have it; I don't know where it is. It's in a hiding place that has gone with Frederick to his grave. That is the truth.'

'Truth, Miss Sanders! You are his successor! Don't try and tell me otherwise. Why would he bother with a girl, if you were not exceptional? We are not permitted, not even encouraged to enter the world of artists. We are expected to embroider, paint in our little books the flowers of the garden, the birds in the trees.' She was shouting at Meredith, but amongst the weaving coaches and thudding hooves no one could hear. 'I will make you pay for this.' She laughed, her mouth wide, the inside of her thick lips showing pink. 'Who knows, maybe you will be joining Frederick sooner than you expect. Then he can tell you his secret.'

Meredith stared at her. *She really had gone mad.* Then a sack was put over her head.

The sack was gone. Meredith lay on a dirt floor and couldn't move with her hands tied behind her back; her ankles too. A draft cut across her cheek and she could smell paint. There were the sounds of voices, distant and muffled. She was lying on her side with her arm trapped under her and every part of her body hurt.

The pain in her arm worsened. She pulled her knees up but it didn't help. There was only one thing to do. She shouted, 'Help. Can you hear me? Help me, please. I'm in here.' How stupid she sounded, when she didn't know where. But that didn't stop her shouting again.

Nothing happened. Then a noise and the door slid sideways. She was in the hidden room at The Grapes Inn.

Cuba John came in and picked her up. She cringed from him and he laughed. 'Not the great lady now.'

'Put her on the chair, but don't untie her.' The voice was Madame Lightfoot's and it still held that harsh, angry tone.

Sitting up was less painful, but with her hands behind her back, she couldn't sit comfortably and had to lean forward. 'May I have a drink?' Her voice was as harsh as Lightfoot's.

'Go and get a pitcher, Cuba, and a tankard of his best ale for me. Don't go getting anything for yourself. You understand?' Cuba John scowled, but said nothing. He unlocked the door and left.

Meredith looked at her captor standing in front of the easel. She could see the painting – the Turner forgery.

'If it wasn't that the deal is done, I could put this back into the Academy. But the Monk is not a man to be crossed. I fear the habit disguise suits his needs; underneath he is a ruthless rogue.'

'What are you going to do with me? Your man ... you wouldn't let him ...' Meredith couldn't get the words out. She prayed the dark woman had some pity in her soul.

Pity did not seem to be one of Madame Lightfoot's traits. 'If he asks me for you, he can have you. But under all that bravado, he is a weakling. I doubt he has the courage to touch someone like you.'

The door opened and the dirty, smelly Cuba John came back in carrying a tray.

'Untie her hands, but not her feet. Give her some ale.' She picked up her tankard and drank thirstily, each swallow making her throat move.

Meredith was not so quick. With the release of the cord her numb hands couldn't pick up the mug. She rubbed them, but when the pins and needles started they were so painful she doubled over, cradling them, but nothing helped until it slowly eased. Lifting the mug with trembling fingers she drank, but little passed her lips, most splashed down her bodice.

'Please, tell me what you're going to do with me?' Meredith glanced at Cuba John. She feared him more than she had Warder Snipes.

'I have a surprise, which will take you far away from here. You've become a problem. The magistrate might find you an easy witness to get the truth from. Your resistance to me and Cuba is one thing, but the Bow Street men are not particularly fussy how they obtain their proof. I've had a good business in London. It's time to move on, as Mama used to say.'

Meredith looked into the hidden room and saw the walls were now bare. 'Have you sold the other paintings?'

'Answers will not help you, Miss Sanders. It's time to go. Cuba, untie her feet, we must be away.'

Madame Lightfoot slipped a canvas bag over the forged Turner and lifted it from the easel. 'Carry this with the greatest of care. Even the slightest damage, Cuba, and your coins of gold will be thrown into the river.'

Instead of turning to the door, Cuba went into the hidden room. Seconds later, the sound of another grinding mechanism revealed a dark passage. Lightfoot pinched out the flame of a candle waxed to the table. She picked up the other lighted candlestick and beckoned Meredith forward.

The hackney coach stopped and Adam paid off the

coachman. The street door was not locked and he went into the gallery. The room was empty and so was the studio. Where was Meredith? Why hadn't she locked the studio door? In fact, the whole house was an open opportunity to a thief. He stood by the window, looking out at the crowd and a moment of uneasiness ran through him. He caught the sound of movement above and hurried up the stairs. In the kitchen, Mrs Clements was unpacking her basket. He tapped lightly on the half-open door and pushed it wider.

'Good afternoon, Mrs Clements. I apologise for coming to your private rooms unannounced, but the gallery is unattended.'

'Goodness me, you've given me such a fright, Mr Fox. Unattended! Miss Meredith must be in her room. Please, come into the parlour. I will call her at once.'

He walked round the room and admired again the warm tones that reflected Meredith's nature. His musing was broken by the hurried footsteps coming down from the upper floor, but it wasn't Meredith who came through the doorway, but a flustered Mrs Clements.

'She's not there, sir. When I left for the market, Miss Meredith was preparing to go to a client's house. But surely, she should be back by now. Are you certain she's not in the gallery?'

'I am more than certain, Mrs Clements. Who is this client?'

'I don't know. She had a note delivered by a maid.'

'This is a strange arrangement. Why didn't she take you? Surely she must know that it's not proper to go alone.' His frustration was rising again; what was she doing now! He only had to let her out of his sight for a few hours and she was off … but where? 'Will you look for the note up here and I will go down to the gallery.'

Adam searched the desk top – nothing – he pulled open the drawer and his worry was momentarily wiped away by a sketch of his own face looking back at him. She had captured his eyes, mouth, and hair with a likeness which brought a burning flush to his cheeks. Is this how she saw him? Had she drawn him with only the curiosity of an artist or from a flutter in her heart? Did it mean that there was a little love there too? A desire, deep inside him, hoped this was true, because he too had feelings for her beyond friendship. But where was she? He lifted the drawing and saw the note. It wasn't about a commission for a painting, but an instruction to meet at three o'clock and it could only be from Madame Lightfoot. And that could only mean Meredith was in danger.

He called to Mrs Clements from the bottom of the stairs. 'I have found the note. I will go at once to look for her.' He didn't wait to hear a reply, but ran out of the door looking for a hackney. Why ask to meet at St Paul's to conduct negotiations about the Turner? There was something drastically wrong. The only common ground he could think of was The Grapes Inn. He prayed that's where she would be.

CHAPTER TWELVE

The tunnel door closed. Meredith was now at the mercy of Madame Lightfoot. What was she going to do with her? Murder her? Throw her body in the river? Or give her to a brothel? The word alone horrified her, but to be sold into one ... her skin tingled and she shuddered ... to be owned and forced to ... Meredith couldn't think beyond that. She was in the hands of not only an art thief but a monster with no morals.

The lie she had told Clemmie meant no one knew where to find her. She should have sent a message to Adam, but there hadn't been time; the note had said three o'clock. She was on her own and it was her responsibility to find a way of escape.

Her eyes adjusted to the dim candlelight. In front of her the dark woman led the way through an arched brick tunnel the height of a grown man, with an unpleasant smell rising from the dry mud floor. Behind her, Cuba John carried the painting.

'Where does this come out?' Meredith could feel the ground sloping downwards and from the candlelight the tunnel was cut straight as an arrow.

'It matters little to you where it ends. You're my,' she paused and her laughter filled the space around them, '... my guest?

'You can't do this. I would give you the Turner, but I don't know where it is. That's the truth. Why won't you believe me?'

'Perhaps I do now. But you've become a threat to me.'

Meredith could now see a wetness coating the walls and beneath her feet the ground had become soft. It slowed their pace and she began to wonder who had built the tunnel? It must be hundreds of years old. Obviously, the innkeeper was unaware of its existence. She tried to judge the distance from the inn, but couldn't.

Fear held her nerve. Screaming hysterics would only enrage Madame Lightfoot. And the thought of Cuba John's hands on her kept her running to keep up with the candlelight.

Water started to drip from the roof, wetting her hair. Slimy green fungi appeared on the walls. How much further were they going? If the woman in front of her succeeded in her plans … she was disappearing without any clues left behind.

The tunnel ended at a wooden door. Lightfoot took a key from her pocket and opened it. Meredith followed and stepped into the room beyond. The other paintings from The Grapes Inn were propped against the walls. So this was how they were moved.

Cuba John set his package down and closed the door.

Meredith couldn't tell if this was a house, an inn, or a warehouse. The room was without furnishings, the whitewashed walls bare and the floor scrubbed clean and dustless. Only one door led into other parts of the building. Escape was looking impossible.

'Go to your room, Cuba. I'll call you when you're needed.'

'Would you like me to take the *young lady*? Give you a last moment with your *treasures*.' His gaze slid from Meredith to Madame Lightfoot. '*Alone*?'

'So, you fancy a little tumble with her, do you?'

'Well, there wasn't a chance to go back and I did sort of promise.' His whining voice sounded like a spoilt child. But he was never that. His skin was now grey; his bloodshot eyes had become glazed and staring. Even his lips had gone the colour of parchment. Every bit of strength drained from her. But win or lose, she would fight him to the inevitable end. She had never been so frightened in all her life.

Madame Lightfoot picked up a painting and set it on an easel in the centre of the room. 'Get out. I've a better use for her than what you want.' His face contorted into a grotesque mask of sneering hate. Without a word he left, using the inner door.

Lightfoot locked the door after him. 'You have artistic work to do, Miss Sanders. These paintings need packing. At least I shall get something out of you before we part.'

Meredith licked her lips and asked. 'Do you have anything to drink?'

'Help yourself. It's in that crate by the wall.'

Inside were a closed pitcher and a pewter mug. Meredith lifted the top and smelt the ale. It looked drinkable and she filled the mug and drank it all.

Madame Lightfoot pointed to a pile of canvas bags. 'Each cover has been made to the exact size of its painting. Sort them out and don't try to dally thinking you will hinder my timetable. Cuba John may look like death, but he has incredible strength in those bones. One call is all he needs. Do you understand me?'

There was no mistaking her threat and Meredith nodded. The task was not difficult and she soon had a bag before each painting.

'Encase each one and sew it up. Not your fancy stitches, tack along twice, overlapping the first. I must say you are more efficient than Sally-Ann.'

Meredith made no reply, only nodding at each command. To anger the dark woman now would only put her life in danger. Did this make her a partner to whatever evil scheme this villainous woman was party to? With meek compliance Meredith took a ball of thick thread and a large needle from the crate. She knelt on the floor and the rough planks snagged her gown. As she eased the portrait of the child into its bag a splinter pierced the plump skin below her thumb. She didn't cry out as she pulled the slither of wood out and then watched in horror as drops of blood spotted the canvas.

'Watch what you're doing! Has that gone through?' Lightfoot's voice bellowed across the room like a roaring bull.

'No, no, I'm sure it hasn't. The canvas is very thick.' Meredith leant away as the dark woman raised her hand to hit her. 'It's stopped!' She sucked the wound and held it up for inspection.

Her knees hurt and she found sitting cross-legged more comfortable, but the paintings were awkward to hold as she leant forward to sew. Without a thimble, the needle dug into her finger and she used her gown to protect it. In contrast, Madame Lightfoot seemed to tackle the packing with little pain or trouble and between them all but the Turner were soon finished.

'Excellent.' She glanced at a small clock attached to the top of the easel. 'There's time to have one last look at a ... shall we call it, a flawless masterpiece?' Almost reverently, she set Frederick's 'Turner' on the easel.

Meredith went and stood before the painted canvas. How had she enticed Frederick to commit the sin of forgery? Copying was an acceptable practice, but to sell it as an original, even to the colonials ... there was no answer. Frederick had died with so many secrets locked in his soul.

With a sigh, Lightfoot put the painting into its bag and stitched it closed. 'Goodbye, Sanders, you always made me my biggest profit.' There could be no more revealing moment to her character than now. Money!

She unlocked the inner door and called to Cuba John.

Adam Fox walked into The Grapes Inn with his heart pounding and his eyes searching for Woody. The man was clearing away tankards from a table in the corner and he moved quickly over to him.

'Woody, I need to speak with you urgently.' There was no pretence of an Irish brogue. 'Sit down. I'll order a tankard in a minute.'

'What be …' Woody paused, 'the trouble? And where did ye get that outfit from? And ye sound like some gentleman, where's yer Irish tongue gone?' He didn't sit as told and his face took on a red tinge of anger.

'It's a long story, Woody. At the moment I want to know if you have seen the young lady here this afternoon. Maybe accompanied by a dark woman?'

'Oh! So she's a *lady* now. What's happened to the servant girl?'

'Has she been here? Her name is Mered …' Adam stopped. 'There are matters that do not concern you. All I need to know is, has she been here?'

'I want to know who she is. No name. No answer. Yer've asked for me help, which I have to admit, I did take a wee wage for, so …?'

Adam had no time to haggle with an odd-job man. Did it really matter? Just a name didn't give away who she really was. 'It's Merry.' His frustration made him raise his voice with each word. 'Did she come here *today*?'

The change in Woody was unexpected. He sat down on the stool with a heavy thud. 'Did I hear ye right? Merry?'

Adam realised there was something amiss. The red face had turned white and the man's hands were shaking. This wasn't being caused by his drinking, for the man was as sober as a magistrate. 'What is it?'

'Could it be? Is she *my* Merry?'

'I don't understand what you're babbling about.' Adam sat down opposite him. He tried to keep calm, but felt more like shaking the man. 'Explain yourself. I have no time to waste nursing you in a womanly swoon.'

'My daughter, Merry, ran away years ago.'

'Don't be ridiculous, man.'

'But she could be. I've tortured meself for years. I'm to blame.' Woody's eyes watered. 'Is it her?'

'No. But that isn't the problem now. I have to find her. She's in terrible danger. I ask you again, has she been here?'

'Danger? What do you mean? Yer saying she's gone?'

'Not of her own free will. I think she's been kidnapped.'

Adam didn't want to acknowledge what was unfolding. But one fact beat within him as strong as a lion. His life would be like an empty shell without her.

'I 'aven't seen her. I came 'ere at four o'clock fer the afternoon work.'

'There's a back entrance. Have you been down to the cellar?'

'No.'

'Then that's where I'll start.'

'I'm comin' too. Even if she ain't my girl, I don't like ter think about what's going on.'

Down in the cellar, Adam put his ear close to the door of room six and eased the key into the lock, listened again, and slowly opened the door. The room was dark and empty.

Lighting the candle, he looked for signs that Meredith had been there. The truth being it looked as though no one had been there. He had put all his hopes into this one dingy room. A deep emotional loss rose up, akin to when he lost his father.

'I'll go back upstairs and ask around,' Woody said.

'Yes. And go out into the streets. Someone may have seen her. I need to think.'

Adam locked the door; he didn't want to be caught unawares by Madame Lightfoot. Holding the candle high he went into the hidden room; he was too late, the paintings were gone. Wherever she had taken them was where Meredith would be. But there was no clue. The only place associated with her was here, in this room. How had she moved such large paintings without anyone seeing? The inn was a very busy establishment and there were other rooms in the cellar. The back yard could be as busy as inside with Woody's carpentry, storage and deliveries. Surely, someone would see.

Where could he go? Madame Lightfoot appeared and faded like a ghost. She had Meredith a prisoner; what did she intend to do with her? The horrors of what a young woman of good circumstances could be sold for ran through his mind. He had to find her! Nothing else mattered. She had come to mean more to him than a tutor for Sarah. He had willingly entered her world of art and crime with the full knowledge of the dangers. Kidnapping her was an act too far. He would find her, even if he had to search every inch of London.

He circled the inner room looking for any clue. But there was nothing. Then the candle flickered. He stooped and waved the candle sideways. It flickered again. Was there another door? He ran his fingers over the bricks and felt another doorway, a similar mechanism and pushed it in. A tunnel appeared.

Meredith waited with Madame Lightfoot. The door opened and Cuba John came into the room. 'They're here; enough men for each painting.'

'Good. Take Miss Sanders to your room.'

Meredith's fear returned. 'No, I won't go with him.

Please, not that, he will …' A sob choked away any other words.

'So, it's down to pleading with me now. Why should I care what happens to Frederick's little innocent girl? Do you really expect me to believe that?'

'Frederick was a father and a friend to me. How can you speak of him so? How did he ever become associated with you?'

'You to wonder, Miss Sanders, and my secret to keep. But Cuba will not have his way. He knows what will happen. The Chinese dens will not supply his need without gold crossing their greedy little palms.'

The reassurance didn't make Meredith feel any better as he led her out into a corridor. The quiet of the hall was shattered by the front door opening and banging against the wall. Suddenly, the space was filled with a hoard of bedraggled sailors. Before they reached her, Cuba John steered her up a flight of stairs onto a landing. Holding his single candle high, he opened the door to his room.

What she saw made her stop. *She couldn't go in there*. The smells that came at her were appalling and there was something else, something unnameable she had never known before. It filled her mouth and went down into her throat. Meredith retched. 'Can we open the window?' There was no way she could hold down the bile. 'Please?'

He pushed her forward. 'No.' His reply was sullen, yet there was pleasure in the way he said it.

Without thinking of the consequences, she was sick. Instead of being angry, Cuba John laughed. All she could do was wipe her mouth with her sleeve.

'Sit down. She won't want you all pale and weak, and I'll get the blame and she won't give me the guineas.' Again he pushed her, and this time she moved forward.

Next to a dirty wall was his unmade bed. There were

no sheets. just a stained blanket and pillow. The only furniture was a tavern table and chair. Meredith sat down, but she didn't look anywhere else, only at Cuba John. 'Please, will you open the window?'

It seemed her plea amused him and he licked his finger and touched the window, circling his nail on the grimy pane. 'Perhaps it would be better. I would find you an awkward bundle to carry.' He splayed his fingers along the frame and pushed the lower part up a few inches.

Meredith got up and went over to breathe in the air and found it no better than the room. She could smell the river, the odious smells of the road, could hear the sound of voices, one louder than the rest, calling heave-ho.

'Where is this house?' She didn't turn to look at him. 'We're near the river, I know that.'

'A know-it-all, ain't yer? We're near to the Tower; it's a pity we can't lock yer in there.'

Meredith closed her eyes; none of this was going to help her escape. She couldn't jump from the window and she would never make it to the door. Her only chance had been when she was moved from the room below, but the arrival of the sailors had barred the way. She had been sure that an escape was possible when they came along the tunnel, but not now with Cuba John watching her every move.

Time passed and outside the window the sky darkened into night.

Meredith sat on the chair. Her fear didn't lessen and she never let her gaze wander away from the dirty little man. The constant watching made her eyes ache; even the foul smells became less choking.

Finally, Madame Lightfoot called from the corridor below. 'It's time to go. Bring her down.'

CHAPTER THIRTEEN

Adam came to a halt at the end of the tunnel. The wooden door looked solid.

Here was another problem, he needed a key – Roseanna Lightfoot would not leave it unsecured. He knelt and looked through the keyhole, but saw nothing. On a hopeless gesture he touched the latch and it lifted soundlessly. Madame Lightfoot was getting over-confident, or careless, but a lucky moment for him. Pushing gently with just his fingers the door opened a few inches. The room beyond was in semi-darkness.

The candle in his hand was almost spent and, with a last flicker, he saw the other door. In a few strides he reached it and turned the knob; this door was not locked either. He opened it a crack and listened. A woman's voice was calling, 'It's time to go. Bring her down.'

Those few words reassured him that he had found Meredith. Or to be more accurate, he now knew where she was. The problem of rescuing her was another matter. Now that he was within yards of her, his fears doubled. Was she all right? Had the woman harmed her in any way? The sound of several pairs of feet coming down from an upper floor made him close the door to within an inch of the frame. The urge to burst out and confront them burned red hot, but if he failed, he would be a prisoner too. He should have gone and found Woody to bring with him. But then he wouldn't be here now, at this vital moment to hear what Lightfoot intended. A glow from a candle lit the corridor and the sounds of those descending changed from tapping feet to striding steps.

'Open the front door, Cuba, and make sure there are no lurking footpads around.'

Adam could only hear her words, for to open the door wider was much too risky, the slightest movement might alert them. A wave of air ran down the corridor and their footsteps died away as the front door slammed shut. He ran along the corridor and out into the road. Fifty yards away he could see three figures: one giant of a woman, Meredith, and a thin man. This could only be the lackey who had invaded her bedchamber. The thought of what he could have done to her surged through his veins like boiling oil. He followed, stepping cautiously on the cobbles, willing any dog not to bark and give those in front cause to turn. At the end of the road he hid in the shadows and watched.

Adam guessed they were making for one of the river quays, which meant a boat was waiting. He increased his pace, and a few moments later saw them being helped into a dinghy. This may have been his chance to rescue Meredith, but without help all he could do was wait and see which ship they boarded anchored mid-stream.

Meredith was almost thrown into a small boat.

'Tie her hands and ankles, Cuba. I don't want any trouble while we are rowed out.'

'Is that the only bit of her I'm going to see?'

'Hold your tongue fool. Sound carries far and wide over water.'

Cuba John sat next to her, trailing his hand in the water and staring at the sailor pulling on the oars. She looked up at the sky, at the moon shining bright and full round. The last time she had seen it like this was just before she left Appleton House. She should be back there now, in the country, snug and safe in her bed, but wishing the impossible was not the answer to her predicament. Right now each oar stroke took her further away from that possibility.

The sailor shipped oars in the shadow of a great sailing ship. Meredith could see the prow and figurehead, and in the moonlight it looked like a black demon. A lantern light swung above her and she saw a rope ladder ending a few inches above the water.

'Make haste, José. The Cap'n wants to heave-ho as soon as the tide turns.'

'I'm sending them up. I'll hold on here to make the return.'

The ropes were untied and Meredith saw her chance to jump and swim for it. But even as this moment presented itself, Madame Lightfoot held a small gun aimed at her.

'I can read your mind, Miss Sanders. Jumping will only send you to the bottom. I am an expert shot, another little thing Mama remembered to teach me.'

There was no escape, no heroic damsel winning over the wicked witch. Live or die was her option. But to live would always give her the chance of escape. 'You win. I will surrender, but not willingly, life is better than death.' She stood up and waited while Cuba John steadied the ladder and she climbed aboard.

Meredith was pushed along the deck, then down below into the captain's cabin; a small cramped space cluttered with charts and other seafaring paraphernalia.

'Welcome, *señorita*, to the *Orlando*. I shall try to make your passage as pleasant as possible.'

The captain was a Spaniard, short in height and with a girth that bulged over his belt. His hair hung in greasy strands, much like his beard. But his dark eyes had a sharp piercing stare that would miss nothing.

Meredith now knew what was planned for her. All the guesses she had been making were nothing compared to this. It would be slavery of the worst kind – a whore!

'Come, *señorita*, I am not an ogre, I wish only to make our journey together ... how does one express it in English? ... profitable.'

The captain smiled, showing a row of broken teeth. He was utterly repulsive. No better than Cuba John, with the same vile mind and ways. She shuddered, physically showing him how disgusting he appeared to her.

Madame Lightfoot threw a leather pouch onto the table. 'There is your fee, Captain Raimunda, in guineas. She brings no baggage and has no family. You are quite safe. I hope you can deliver her untouched. I'm sure one of the governors will be looking for a pure English wife. So if you want a prize purse, see she arrives so.'

She turned to leave.

'Wait, you can't go, you can't leave me here.' Meredith reached out and grasped Lightfoot's arm. 'Please, take me back. There's still time to find the Turner.'

Her fingers were prised away. 'It's too late. Frederick has outwitted us all. I misjudged him. He was nothing more than a doting old man praising his young protégé. If the original is ever found, it will be too late for me.' The venom in her voice filled the cabin. 'I don't care what you do with her. Feed her to the sharks for all I care.'

Lightfoot's retreat from the cabin left a void, all the odorous air dragged out behind her. Meredith was too stunned to move, feel any reaction. She was abandoned to this captain for as long as he wished. Her paid passage was a bribe to keep Madame Lightfoot's secret.

'Ah, so I have a choice, *señorita*; you or gold? It's a long way to Botany Bay ...' His words trailed away, but his eyes never left her as he stroked his beard and smiled.

Meredith trembled as shock and disbelief set in. She

was cold, for she had left that afternoon wearing only a light gown and shawl. Why hadn't she guessed the message was a trap? Oh, why hadn't she waited for Adam? He was so capable, so strong and able to look after her. A sob shuddered through her and she sank to the floor, closed her eyes and waited. Even her father would not have sold her into this.

A hand gripped her arm. 'There is a place for you to sleep. I have kicked my first mate out with the rabble. Soon you will wear the beautiful gown I have for you, *señorita*; a Spanish red gown and a flower for your hair.' He spoke in a soft coaxing voice, but when she looked up at him he was dribbling from his mouth.

A rage, so deep and full of hate, ran through her. 'Take your hand away, sir. I will not be handled by you or anyone else. I don't want your gown or your flower. I will stay wherever you put me, until I reach my journey's end.'

His hand moved and he grasped her hair, pulling her head back. His face lowered slowly until his lips touched hers and he said. 'Eight months is a long time, *señorita*. We shall get to know each other well before then.' He pushed her away and shouted in Spanish. A sailor came in. 'Put her in Diego's cabin and lock the door.'

She prayed Diego's cabin was at the other end of the ship, but she was pushed into the cabin next to the captain. Her life was ruined; she was to become the ship's whore. She would sink below that of a warder's wife. She would become a person that Adam would shun with disgust if he ever saw her again.

The key grated in the lock. This was to be her prison cell for eight months! The cabin was small with little room to move and lit by a lantern hanging from a beam. A narrow mattress lay secured inside a wooden frame and Meredith wrinkled her nose at the smell of stale urine in a chamber pot in the corner without even the courtesy of a cloth cover. And the promised red gown with layers of white petticoat lay on a shelf fixed to the wall. Tears touched her eyelashes; the captain's intentions spoke volumes for the appalling life he had planned for her. The stiffened bodice was cut low, its lace-frilled edge designed to attract the eyes of the suitor.

The floor tilted with a movement of the ship. Any hope of escape was gone.

Adam waited only long enough to see which ship the dinghy moored under. He raced along the quay looking for a small boat with its oars in. The last in the line proved his prize. Untying the rope, he jumped aboard. His strong even strokes pulled him swiftly out into the current and into the darkness.

Coming in close to the ship Adam saw a dinghy bobbing gently in the ship's shadow. A light swung above and Madame Lightfoot descended the rope ladder.

Instantly her plan was clear. To protect herself, she had abandoned Meredith to a fate worse than death. This type of ship had no passenger accommodation. Her captain only wanted to fill his hold and lower decks with a full cargo list.

He could see the current was slack and the tide was about to turn and run out to the sea. He didn't have much time. Minutes later the sailor rowed towards the quay.

Adam reached the rope ladder. He let the dinghy go with the current; he couldn't risk discovery by the returning sailor. Slipping over the gunnel, he saw the deck hatches were battened down, the rigging set and the ropes coiled ready for the run down the estuary. The native tongue of Spanish sailors carried clearly from below. His knowledge of their language was scant; he would have to be careful not to confront one. Adam felt the ship pulling on the anchor. The crew would soon be swarming on to the deck like ants. He had to find

Meredith before the ship reached the wide estuary mouth.

There was one thing he had to thank his father for – know your ships well, my son, business starts from the hold to the topsail. The captain's cabin was aft and the unthinkable of what could be happening to Meredith ran through him like a knife.

He discarded his jacket and shirt to look more like a sailor. Boots and stockings followed, leaving him barefooted. Ruffling his hair, he pulled it forward onto his forehead. What he needed was canvas pants, the fine woollen breeches were too conspicuous indeed, but there was nothing to hand. He threw everything overboard.

He needed something to carry. Wedged between two bundles of canvas he found a tar barrel and hoisted it to his shoulder and sauntered towards the aft deck. The night sky was clear, quiet like the eye of a storm deceiving the unwary of the trauma to come. Unexpectedly, the stench of sweat, tobacco, and garlic wafted before him and a hand gripped his free shoulder like a vice. Spanish words filled the air. '*¿Qué estás haciendo?*' A squat muscular sailor stepped out of the darkness and barred his way.

Adam didn't have time to try and translate and he grunted, '*El capitán y señorita requieren vino ahora.*'

The sailor didn't release him, just stood silent, menacing; then slapped his shoulder and walked past, muttering, '*Señorita, señorita, bah.*'

The crew were stirring; he had less time than he thought. He reached the aft stairs and listened; all was quiet. He put the barrel behind the open door and descended with caution. The creak of the ship made it difficult to hear anything that would lead him to Meredith. There were several doors and he tried the first, which was an empty cabin. The next was a well-stocked storeroom. There were two left and he guessed the one directly in front of him was the captain's cabin.

He put all his hopes into the one on his left. The door was locked and he took a penknife from his breeches pocket and slid the blade between the door and frame. The steel point didn't reach the lock. Adam shaved the door frame to widen the gap. He could hear the shouts of the sailors above readying the ship to sail. Sweat broke out on his forehead; any moment a sailor could come down the stairs and see him. He pushed the knife blade in and under the lock. One swift wrench and it split away from the frame and came open.

Meredith lay on the cot, her face to the wall, curled up like a kitten. Was she asleep or drugged? He moved quietly inside and closed the door. Gently touching her shoulder and stroking her hair, he hoped to awake her gently. Without any warning she turned and became a mad woman, aiming a small weapon at his face, his eyes. He grasped her wrist but she brought up her other hand and clawed at his bare chest with fingers turned into talons. She was terrified and didn't recognise him.

'Meredith! It's me, Adam!'

Her eyes grew wide and he could feel her pulse hammering against his fingers. 'Can you hear me? Meredith, it's me. I've come to get you off this ship and take you home.'

Her fingers slackened and he eased a whale bone from them and threw it on the floor. Lifting her from the cot he cradled her in his arms. 'Oh, Meredith, I thought I had lost you. What have they done?' He kissed the softness of her neck and then her mouth. Her response was hesitant; then she seemed to understand and kissed him back, kissed him with passion.

'Oh, Adam, you came for me. How did you know I was here? I know I should have sent a message, but there wasn't time and then everything was all a trick and …' A sob filled her throat and Adam rocked her. '… She has given me to this captain who is sailing for Botany Bay. He said such awful things about what would become of me.'

He brushed her lips with another kiss. 'Nothing is going to happen to you now, I won't let it. We have to get off this ship before it reaches the estuary. Can you walk, my love?'

Meredith tightened her arms around his neck. 'I want to stay with you, just like this, but yes, I shall be all right.'

Adam set her down and looked round the cabin. In the dim light his gaze stopped at the red gown. There was no doubt as to the purpose of such a garment, but the jewelled bodice was ripped almost to shreds.

'I take it you had no intention of wearing that.' He nodded to the table. 'And I take it that's where the whale bone came from.' A moment of pride ran through him, but in truth, the whale bone would have been useless as a weapon.

'You're a very resourceful lady, Miss Sanders. I think the captain would have had a very interesting time with you.'

'I would sooner die than let him touch me. The bone was either for him or me.'

'Then I thank God I got here before you had to make the choice.' He raised her hands to his lips – he had come that close to losing her.

A rumbling sound ran through the cabin. 'They're raising the anchor. Let's go.' He blew out the lantern candle and listened. 'Can you swim?'

'Of course, I ...'

He placed his finger to her lips; voices were close by, arguing. English sailors; and their words grew louder. '... the cap'n thinks he can keep her locked up forever. Let me tell yer, I want a bit of that. I don't mind second helpings.' The other man laughed. 'I'll have fun watching yer flogging then. He might even toss yer over to the fishes, yer know what a temper he has.' A commanding voice yelled down the stairs and there was a scurry of feet fleeing up to the deck.

The crew were mutinous even before the ship left the river. Without doubt their captain ruled by the whip. The sailors' argument reinforced his own thoughts – the captain would show no mercy if they were caught trying to escape. Each moment they remained on board they were sailing into unbelievable danger. He had to get Meredith overboard and away within the next few minutes.

Adam held Meredith's hand and felt her tremble. 'Don't speak, just follow me and do as I say.' He led her along to the stairs and whispered close to her ear, 'I'm going to the top, tie your skirt around your waist.' The fear in her eyes were more telling than any words and he pulled her to him and kissed her hard. 'Be brave, my love.'

His bare feet made no sound on the wooden treads. He waited below the doorway and could hear orders being shouted. Raising his head he surveyed the deck. He crept out, crouched and looked behind him. On the upper deck the helmsman was standing with another man; Adam guessed it was the captain. Sailors were working everywhere now, pulling ropes, tending the sails. This was their best chance of escape. He beckoned Meredith up.

'It's now, Meredith. Are you sure about swimming?'

'Swim or drown, Adam, I have no choice.'

He took hold of her hand. 'Don't be afraid. I'm with you now.'

They crept across the deck and Adam chose a space between the cleated ropes. The gunnel was too high for Meredith to slip over. He would have to help her, which would give any sailor full view of them. But there was no alternative if they were to escape.

'I'll lift you to the top of the side and then you must jump. Don't hesitate if you hear them raise the alarm. Don't look back. I'll be right behind you.'

'But if they see us, there are so many of them, they'll get you. I won't leave you behind, Adam.'

'You must. I can deal with them if I don't have you to worry about. Please, Meredith, don't wait.' That now familiar rebellious look came into her eyes and he repeated, 'Just jump.'

Then before any more words could be exchanged he pulled her to him, lifted her, and then fate played a damning blow – a voice shouted, and then more voices joined in. Above them, the thunderous voice of Captain Raimunda carried clearly in the night air. 'The woman, get the woman, kill the man.'

Footsteps pounded and Adam balanced Meredith on the side. She looked down at him, her face white, her eyes full of terror. 'Adam, I won't …' He pushed her over.

They were coming for him; the leader with his sword raised ready to cut him down. He heaved himself up, straddled the rail and, as he swung his leg over, pain spread across his shoulder.

CHAPTER FOURTEEN

The shock of the cold water took Adam's breath away as he sank deep. Surfacing, he looked up at the ship. The captain was at the side and in a gesture of farewell he raised his hat in a salute.

Adam trod water and circled, looking for Meredith. He couldn't see her in the dark and the moonlight made the water flash with bursting stars as the rush of the tide ripped towards the widening banks.

'Meredith! Meredith!' Adam could feel the strong current and panic rolled through him as he twisted and turned looking for her. Suddenly, in a patch of flat water, he saw her.

She was floundering, her arms thrashing, and he kicked hard, not taking his eyes from her. Then she was gone. He dived, knowing he had but a moment to find her before she was lost to the murky bottom of the Thames. Instantly he was in a world of demons: shredded clothes passed like wraiths and a dead man slid past, touching his hand. Adam forced more power into his legs. Had he saved her only to let her die? Then he saw her struggling to surface.

Adam grasped her arm and pulled her to him, put his arm round her waist. His lungs were now empty of air and the urge to take a breath and drown was paramount. He gave one fierce stab of his feet and struck out with his free arm upwards. The river was not going to take her life, even if it took his.

He broke the surface gasping for breath and let the

current take them. He heaved Meredith around her middle and water spurted from her mouth, she choked and more water spewed out. She coughed; then opened her eyes.

'Meredith! Can you hear me?'

'Yes.' Her reply was weak, but that was all he needed.

Slowly, using the current, Adam steered them towards the bank and a stretch of beach. The mud sucked at his feet as he pulled Meredith through the shallow water and lifted her into his arms. Her eyes were closed, but her soft breathing caused him no concern. In the moonlight her face was so white. A primitive urge to protect her flowed through him as he waded forward out of the river on to the grass. He twisted round and saw only flat open ground, nothing to offer them shelter.

'Damnation! We have to find somewhere warm or we will die of the cold.'

Adam drew Meredith closer to him. She was either in a faint or something worse. He had to find a place for them to rest. He walked along the bank, carrying her. The darkness hid everything, only the river flowing down to the sea gave him any direction. A breeze strengthened behind him and he shivered. His bare feet were cold and his breeches clung to his legs. Meredith fared no better; he muttered a prayer, 'Please, find us a warm place to rest.'

After all the trauma they had just shared he chuckled as a thought passed through his mind – he had worried about the propriety of taking Meredith to The Grapes Inn, now he was with her almost naked – could things get any worse? He glanced down at her and in the glimmer of the moon her lips looked grey. She was so slight in his arms and he cradled her closer. There had to be *somewhere* to take shelter.

He began to think fate was truly against him, when

out of the night a large shape formed. Seconds later it became a building and then sounds of voices and music grew louder. The solitary dwelling was an inn. He stopped. This wasn't what he had in mind, a public drinking house, but he had found nothing else and there was warmth inside that they both desperately needed.

He pushed the door open with his shoulder. Inside, the clientele were men with pigtails in dark tunics, and burly sailors with beards wearing coarse canvas. They stopped talking and eyed him with interest. Adam decided Dello Murphy was a far better persona as he kicked the door closed.

'Innkeeper, I be needing a room, with yer hottest water and a fire.' The inn was a typical riverfront drinking house. He didn't know how far they had drifted down stream, but with Chinamen present it couldn't be far from Limehouse.

Behind the counter, the innkeeper pointed a finger. 'What's been happening to you?'

'A slight little accident by the river; the colleen slipped.'

The sailors shouted coarse and loud comments; raised their tankards and the innkeeper grinned. 'Got too frisky did yer and tumbled into the river?'

Adam grinned back. 'Summin like that. She wants me coins, but I wants a bit more before I gives it her. The room, man, have yer got a cosy one fer us?'

'Come on through, the back un's me best. Real goose feathers, that should warm yer up and I'll get me girl to do the rest.'

Adam went to pass into the back, but the man put out his arm. 'Let's see yer coins first, me dandy man.'

'Come up after I've got rid of this load, I'll make it worth yer while.'

A Chinaman shuffled over to Adam and bowing, he asked, 'Mister like a little opium, make your woman happy?' A sly smile creased his face. 'Happy man you can be until the dawn.'

Adam gave him a cheeky grin. 'Thank 'ee, but not needed tonight, she'll be blooming rosy once I get her warm.' He winked and looked towards the others. 'Ain't that right, me 'earties?' Without waiting for any more interruptions, Adam went up the stairs.

The room was small, the bed almost the width of one wall, the length leaving just a few feet to the fire. A pot of water hung from a chain and flames flared around several logs. Adam laid Meredith on the bed. He had made a bold promise about paying for the room; he hoped his tailor's sewn-in thief-proof pocket was still intact – it was, tight against his stomach – four guineas and two silver crowns. There was a movement behind him. When he turned the innkeeper's large body filled the doorway with his hand held out.

'Here ye be, me good man. That covers a jug of yer best ale and a plate of ham and bread. Would 'ee have a shirt me size and a shawl for me colleen? Then we'll not be needing yer services 'til morning.'

A satisfied grin spread over the innkeeper's face at the gold guinea placed on his palm. 'I'll send it up straight away.' He pointed at Meredith. 'She looks a bit worse than a tumble in the river. Got a bit out of hand, me thinks. I don't want any trouble here, so keep yer Irish temper tucked well away.' He pulled the door closed.

Meredith stirred and Adam went to her. She was shivering and he pulled the counterpane over her from across the wide bed. At least the room was clean, something he had not expected from the condition of the tavern room. There was a tap on the door and a child came in.

'Thank 'ee,' he said and took the tray she carried. 'Ah, and you have the clothes, please put them on the chair.' He realised, as her cheeks flushed, their situation was very uncomfortable for her, but she obeyed, and curtsied before she left.

Placing the tray on a small table beside a wash bowl, he ran his fingers through his hair. He had to get Meredith out of her wet clothes before she caught a chill that could turn to a fever in a few hours. He looked at her on the bed; she was not shivering anymore, but that didn't change his decision. Picking up the bowl he went over to the fire and swung the iron bar into the room. Taking a padded square from the hearth he tilted the pot over the bowl.

Still he hesitated; if he had to undress her, what would she think of him later? He eased the counterpane away and put his arm under her shoulders and smoothed the tangled locks from her face.

'Meredith, wake up. You need to get out of your wet clothes. Can you hear me?'

She opened her eyes and looked at him. They were glazed, uncomprehending. 'Adam?' Turning her head she looked past him. 'Where are we?'

'In a riverside inn. We have to get dried and warm. There's a fire and I have a bowl of hot water. Can you stand up?'

'Yes, I think so. I feel so cold. Can I get near the fire?'

He helped her off the bed and saw how her eyes looked first round the room, then at the bed.

'Where is your room?'

There was no way he could soften his words, so he simply said, 'Here. I had to use my Dello Murphy role; this isn't the place to be the lord and lady. Especially the way we arrived. The last thing we need are questions and names; I'm the cocky Irish lad with his colleen who had a tumbling romp and fell in the river.'

'Oh.' Her face coloured bright red. 'We are supposed

to be … I mean, be here to …' She glanced again at the bed. 'Oh dear.'

Adam laughed at her shocked expression. So, his outspoken lady wasn't quite so fiery after all. 'Come. Take off your clothes and they can dry by the fire.' He pulled the damp counterpane off and dropped it beside the bed. Stripping the blanket, he handed it to her. 'This will keep you warm, wrap yourself in it. I'll wait outside.'

He could see she was quite perplexed by all that was happening and he took her hands in his. 'Everything will be all right, Meredith, just wash yourself and get warm.'

'Thank you … and Adam, thank you for saving me.' She didn't take her eyes from him. 'I couldn't swim very well in that fast-running river. I owe you my life.'

God, she looked so lovely, her green eyes full of trust, but to touch her now was the worst thing he could do. He stepped back and bowed. 'I am at your service, Miss Sanders.' He went out and left her alone.

Meredith couldn't get the day's terrifying events out of her mind: Madame Lightfoot kidnapping her, Captain Raimunda and his awful ship. He would have forced himself upon her, no matter how hard she had fought.

When she had heard Diego's door open, she had feigned sleep. Her one thought was to use the whale bone, but when she realised Adam had come to rescue her she couldn't believe it. How had he known where to look? What clue had given him the answer? Oh, there was so much she needed to ask him.

Closing her eyes, she was in the river and the current was too strong for her to reach the bank. Yet to have escaped, she couldn't drown. She fought with all her strength, but finally the river was winning. Adam had brought her to the surface, back to life.

She looked at the bed again; there was nowhere else

for him to sleep except on the floor. A sharp shiver ran through her and she unbuttoned her gown, lifted it over her tangled hair. It had torn in several places and the lace on the bodice hung in tatters; but it could be dried and was wearable. She removed her undergarments and folded them into tight squares; they would dry much quicker in front of the fire if she spread them out but the thought of Adam seeing such private pieces! Oh, she didn't need the warmth of the fire, her inner shame did that.

The fire had warmed the room and she stood naked, the steaming bowl of water in front of the blazing logs. She wetted the corner of the towel and rubbed it over her face, round her neck, and then dried with the rest. Slowly she washed her breasts, body and legs until she reached her feet. Her shoes were at the bottom of the river. She stepped into the warm water and stroked each toe, soothing away the cold. When she had finished the water was tinged brown and she tipped it into a pail beside the table. Meredith fingered the thin blanket. Would Adam be able to see her body through it? There was nothing else to use so she wrapped it round her shoulders and sat on the bed. How was she to spend the night? Adam was outside waiting for her to let him in. He needed to wash and dry his clothes, but the room was so small, there was no privacy. All she wanted to do was curl up on the bed and hide under the covers.

There was a tap on the door, then another. Finally she called, 'Come in.'

Adam looked strained and tired as he closed the door and went to the fire. 'Do you feel more comfortable?'

'Yes, thank you, Mr Fox. I have left the bowl ready for you.' She was burning all over; where was she to look?

He reached for the bowl and took the towel from the table. Something in his movement made her look at him closely and she saw a red gash on his shoulder.

'Sir, you have been wounded.' She scrambled off the bed, forgetting her nakedness under the blanket and went to him. 'How did this happen?'

Adam shrugged, not turning to her. 'It's nothing but a scratch, one of the sailors whipped a cat-o'-nine-tails as I jumped overboard.'

Meredith touched the skin around it. 'It's more than a scratch, Adam. Please fill the bowl with hot water and then sit on the bed while I clean it.'

He turned to her, his eyes very dark in the glow of the candlelight. She thought he was about to say something, but he only nodded.

She slipped the blanket under her arms and knotted the ends between her breasts. He filled the bowl and placed it on the table before sitting on the edge of the bed.

Meredith had never seen a man without a shirt. She stared at him, fascinated by his broad shoulders, the dark hair on his chest. Using another towel corner she dipped it into the hot water and turned to face him and gently dabbed at the cut. He uttered not a word, but his muscles tightened. 'I'm sorry; is it very painful?'

'Some, but your touch is light.'

Meredith soaked the towel again and stroked his forehead, his temples, and across his closed eyes. Through the cloth she felt his bristled cheeks, lastly coming to his slightly parted lips. She touched them with her finger and Adam opened his eyes. They were black coals, but with something in them she wasn't sure she understood. A shiver ran through her, but not with cold or fear. The room seemed to dim, the warmth filling every corner. The towel dropped to the floor.

Those strong hands that had saved her drew her down on to his thighs. He kissed her bare skin above the blanket, his lips soft, each little touch sending an unknown sensation running through her until it stopped low, so low it went on down between her thighs, becoming almost a pain that needed something to satisfy it.

A gasp left her lips as his hand slid inside the blanket, touching, stroking her belly, his fingers circling lower until he cupped her with his hand and the sensation grew. She lifted into him, not knowing what was happening, except she didn't want him to stop.

Adam groaned and lifted his head. 'Meredith, this is wrong, yet I can't stop. All I can think of is that I almost lost you; how that vile captain would be taking from you what I hoped you would give me of yourself.'

Meredith then knew what was happening to her. She loved Adam and this was her body telling her how to show that love to him.

'I will willingly give it to you, my love. Here and now, I am yours until the dawn breaks the darkness of this night.'

'And tomorrow, Meredith? What of tomorrow?'

'Is another day; another time. I have survived kidnap, a captain who would have taken me whether I agreed or not. I don't think he would have been able to control his men, either. Death would have been a certainty, had you not come to rescue me. Tonight I love because I want to.'

She lowered her head and kissed those lips she had drawn in her studio, lips she had wanted to touch ever since awakening in this room. She ran her tongue along his lower lip, along the razor edge of his teeth. She opened her lips, kissing him until she was breathless.

A moment of chill ran over her and she knew he had loosened the blanket; then his hand was caressing her back, moving lower. He cradled her and she felt for the first time his warm flesh. The dark hair on his chest rubbed against her and sent even more sensations rippling through her.

He stood up and laid her on the bed, pulled the blanket over her, and spread her tangled hair. It made her feel like a wicked siren from the tales of sensational novels. But Adam, stepping out of his breeches, shocked her. He stood beside the bed, naked as she, looking like one of the marble statues sculptured by Michelangelo she had seen in books.

Adam lay down beside her, placed his hand on her belly, and looked into her eyes. 'This is our night of surrender – given willingly and with love.'

Meredith raised her arms to him and he came into them. This time he took command and kissed her with that same power he had on previous occasions, but this time her surrender was total.

She floated on a cloud. He cupped her breast, touching the nipple with his fingers, his tongue, circling first with the softest of touch, then using his teeth to tease, then his mouth to suck. There was such pleasure she found herself helping him to draw deeper. When he moved to her other breast, the sensation became a torture. She couldn't keep still, her body moved of its own will, teaching and telling her there was more to come.

Adam moved her thighs apart, his fingers stroking the inside flesh until he reached the soft protecting hair that guarded her most private channel.

Meredith gasped, a moment of shock ran through her, then sheer pleasure and wonder. She lifted and moved, felt his hand completely hold her, yet still there was not enough.

'Adam, I don't know what else I need, except for you to …' she faltered, unable to put into words her desire.

'It is time for us to join, to cherish each coming moment, as only man and woman can.' Adam moved from beside her and knelt between her legs. His skin was hot, burning with the same intensity, and if she should be frightened, there was no such sensation. There was only the expectation, the knowing that this was going to be the most wonderful and pleasurable night of her life.

He came down, lifting onto his elbows, taking her nipple once more between his lips. She knew this time what was coming, waited until her desire surged again deep within her belly, swelled to a crescendo only her lover could satisfy. She called his name, 'Adam!'

Then he parted her wide as he moved higher, kissed her so hard that her lips must bruise, but she didn't care. Slowly he touched somewhere in her that was damp and soft. She opened wider and truly felt him as he slid into her.

'Meredith,' he whispered softly into her parted lips, 'you are ready, ready for us to become one.'

She rocked, pulling him deeper. The moment of pain was unexpected, yet even this could not stop her moving with him. It came as a spiralling sensation, her inside was pulsing, waiting for something, waiting … and then it happened … everything exploded through her: desire, delight, stars of emotion that lasted and lasted until it abated into exhaustion. Her body was coated with sweat, her fingers were gripping Adam's shoulders; she had him trapped with her legs entwined round his back and he was lying on her, spent and sweating like she.

He kissed her throat, trailing up to her lips and whispered into her mouth. 'Are you alright, Meredith?'

She slid her legs down across his buttocks, along his thighs and sighed. 'Yes,' a returning whisper, full of love.

He moved from her and lay down, drawing her close. She shivered and he reached for the blanket, tucked it into her back.

'Sleep awhile. We need to be gone before the innkeeper rises from his bed.'

Meredith curled close, warm and cherished. She obeyed without answer and closed her eyes and slept.

Adam didn't sleep. He lay wondering what sort of monster he was to take advantage of Meredith when she was so vulnerable. Yet it had not been lust. His love for her had been growing daily. Then she had gone missing, and he had seen her being taken aboard the ship. Could his fear of what might have been turned him into a demented man? A man who could not control his desire to have her?

All he had done was compromise her completely. He would ask her to marry him and all could be put right within a few weeks. If there was a child it would have his name and no shame would be put on Meredith. This made him feel a little easier, yet he could not quash the memory of his own behaviour.

The fire had burned low; he got up and put on another log. Her clothes were almost dry and he turned them over. His own breeches, which he had flung down, unheeded, were still damp but he ignored that and pulled them on. The shirt brought to him by the child was thick and coarse, but it fitted well enough.

Meredith stirred and he went and lay back on the bed. Shaking her gently he lifted her into the crook of his arm and kissed her softly on the lips. 'It is time to go.'

She opened her eyes and looked into his. He had wondered what would be in them – fear, hate, regret – but they held nothing but sleep.

'There is food before we leave. Would you like it now?'

Meredith pulled the blanket up to her chin. 'Could I have something to drink, please?'

Realisation of what they had done dawned in her eyes; what her position now meant. He wanted to say something positive, but now was not the time. He got up and fetched a tankard of last night's ale.

After the first sip, her nose wrinkled. 'This is awful.'

'There's only water from the pot over the fire and I don't know where that has come from. Would you like bread and ham?'

'If the food is better than the ale, yes please.'

Adam brought over the tray and sat at the foot of the bed, handing her a platter with a little of each. While he ate the stale bread, he tried to read her expression, but she kept her gaze fixed on the blanket. Only the embers of the fire, falling to ash, filled the silence.

When they had finished, he said, 'I'll go and see if the innkeeper locks his tavern door. Hopefully, he won't have taken out the key. Get dressed; the man may be more astute this morning. I don't want a lot of questions.'

The stairs creaked, something he had not noticed last night with all the babble going on. The key was still in the lock. He unlocked it and placed the key behind the counter, just in case the innkeeper decided to trap them here, maybe demand more money, even call the constable.

Adam tapped on the room door and went in. Meredith was standing beside the bed, her gaze fixed on the rumpled sheets and he had no need to wonder why. He wrapped the shawl around her shoulders. 'All is quiet, let us go.' She didn't move. 'Meredith,' he said softly, 'it's time to go. Everything will be all right. We will be married. If we are careful, no one need know.'

She came alive at his words. '*No one need know*! We have been missing all night, together! There can be no hiding what happened. If we explain, then Frederick's secret will be known. That must not happen. Do you hear me! I will accept the consequences.'

He swung her towards him. 'There will be no disgrace. Have you not heard a word I've said? We will be married.'

'No!' She shouted that one word with such force he was completely taken aback.

From somewhere in the inn, voices sounded. 'Now is not the time for this. Come, we must be gone.' He took hold of her hand and pulled her towards the door, stopped and listened for any footsteps. There were none. They descended the stairs and left.

The inn seemed to float in a deep mist that rose from the river and fields in the pale grey dawn. Adam picked Meredith up and moved quickly away from the inn, taking a dirt track that led inland.

'Sir, I am capable of walking, I don't need to be carried like a child. Please, put me down.'

'Shh. Voices carry a long way when all is silent. We shall soon come to more dwellings, mostly lived in by Chinese families. Perhaps we can buy you a pair of shoes.'

'And what about your feet, do you have feet of iron? Really, Adam, I won't break in two.' But she didn't struggle. Perhaps now she was fully awake common sense would prevail.

Soon the light strengthened and he could see the outlines of the wharfs and warehouses of Limehouse, and behind these were the alleys and streets they wanted.

Adam put Meredith down. 'It is wiser for you to be walking now. We should be able to buy you a pair of shoes soon.'

They rounded a corner and Adam saw a wizened Chinaman setting up his stall. Reverting to his Dello Murphy voice he called, 'Good morning. Do ye be having a pair of fine shoes for me colleen here?'

The old man bowed and looked over his shoulder, calling out in his own language. A younger man came from behind the stall pulling a basket. He offered it with a bow. Adam sorted through an assortment of old and battered slippers. 'Do you think these will fit? They're serviceable and will get you home.'

'I hope so. Anything is better than bare feet.' She slipped them on. 'Perfect.'

Indicating they were acceptable he signalled down to his own feet. A smile spread across the young man's face and he pulled another basket forward. The top pair of boots fitted well enough and Adam passed over a silver coin. The Chinaman's smile widened, well pleased with his payment, and they walked on.

Adam followed a twisted route through a number of alleys, always heading away from the river. Warehouse workers began to fill the streets, heading towards the wharfs. They paid them little attention, but he kept a keen lookout for the slightest move that could turn dangerous if someone suspected he had a purse worth taking.

'We should soon be able to find a hackney and then I can have you home to Tallow House.'

Her reaction to his comment turned a calm and tired woman into a ball of fire. 'I cannot, will not, come to Tallow House looking like this. What do you want to do, have Sarah and especially your aunt having the vapours? I am going home to Ludgate Hill.'

'I'm not leaving you alone in that place. Can't you see how unsafe it is? Madame Lightfoot might think you are now miles away at sea, but she still has the original to find. I cannot agree to such an action.'

He stepped before her, seeing her features harden. 'I know I have put us into a position that is unacceptable to you. I don't know how to apologise, except to say that what happened between us last night was not planned. I can only repeat that everything will be attended to as soon as we are safely back.' Adam waited, every muscle in his body tense, waiting for the outburst he knew she had stored up inside her.

It didn't come out in the explosive way he expected, but as a whisper of despair. 'I will not be a burden as your wife. I will not be forced upon you by circumstances not of your making. I thank you for rescuing me from the ship and a life worse than death. I thank you for not letting me drown. But that is as far as my gratitude will allow me.'

'I see. Even though last night should not have happened, you will not allow one moment to be cherished as love?'

Her intake of breath encouraged him to press her further. 'I did not mean to compromise you, Meredith. You know that. You responded with such sweet passion, I cannot believe there wasn't just a little love there from you.'

She raised her chin, an action he now knew as defiance. 'Sir, I am as much to blame for letting the situation continue, but I repeat, you have no obligation to me. So let us now put aside this talk and get home. I would appreciate your attendance until Ludgate Hill. I shall deal with Mrs Clements in my own way, as you will with your household. Miss Fox must be more than anxious about you.'

Adam didn't reply. There was no way he was going to win this fight of words while she was in such an emotional mood.

'Very well, Miss Sanders, we will discuss the matter more fully at a later date. Now, let us make haste to find a hackney carriage.'

CHAPTER FIFTEEN

Cuba John waited in the narrow entrance of the silversmith shop. *She* had sent him to spy on the servant woman.

Always dressed in her finery, she had no thought for his thin, poorly clothed body. Paintings! That's all she loved. There wasn't a scrap of pity in her. That poor wretch of a girl; given to a captain, and a Spaniard at that. He ought to have helped her escape, but the Madame, she would have taken away all his guineas, and flogged him with that whip she sometimes carried hidden in her cloak.

He huddled down on his haunches and blew breath on to his fingers. It didn't help; they were stiff as kindling wood. Suddenly he started to shake. Damnation to Roseanna Lightfoot! If that servant woman didn't go out soon, he'd have to go in and knock her out. *She* had said search every inch of the place – he couldn't go back without her precious painting.

Coach wheels sounded very loud, slowed, and stopped yards from him. He leant forward and peered down Ludgate Hill. A sailor got out. And God Almighty, Meredith Sanders!

Cuba John wasn't cold anymore, he was burning with glee. How she'd done it he didn't know, but he wasn't waiting here any longer. He had a very, very bad piece of news for Roseanna Lightfoot.

The midnight hour chimed from a mantle clock in

Madame Lightfoot's bedchamber. The richly gowned dark woman was now a richly dressed gentleman. The black hair had been cut and was secured at the nape with a ribbon. A silver-thread embroidered waistcoat covered a white shirt with a perfectly tied neck cloth. A red velvet coat, dark trousers and shoes gave full conviction to the disguise under a dark cloak.

Monsieur Clair de Lune, gentleman of wealth, his dark eyes hidden under a broad brimmed hat stepped into a coach. The only sound was the horse's harnesses and hooves as they pulled away.

CHAPTER SIXTEEN

Meredith gave Mrs Clements no time to ask questions when she walked into the parlour.

'Clemmie, I am so sorry to have been a worry to you, but Mr Fox has kindly been my companion since I met him yesterday afternoon. Someone, I do not know who, tried to kidnap me and Mr Fox was my rescuer. I know you must have been terribly worried, you will forgive me, won't you?' Meredith didn't stop for breath as her words tumbled out; anything was better than the truth.

Mrs Clements struggled out of the armchair. Her eyes were red from crying and her voice hoarse with tears. 'Oh, Meredith, my dear, you're safe.' She wrapped her arms around her charge. 'Worry does not express what I have been going through. You left here yesterday afternoon to see a client. Mr Fox went looking for you, and not a word since.' She stepped back, tears running down her cheeks. 'I have been sitting here all night not knowing what to do. I left the front door unlocked, but was terrified some foot pad might come in. And look at you! You look terrible.'

Meredith held the old lady again until she calmed and stopped crying. 'Everything is all right now, Clemmie, I'm home, safe.'

'If we were living at Harlington I could have gone to the Reverend Lyle. But not here! Not in this city of strangers.'

'I'm so sorry, but truly, everything is all right now. I will make us a pot of tea.' Meredith wished she could rub the hours of fear out, like in a pencil sketch.

Clemmie pushed her away, the gesture hurtful and unexpected, until she saw the look of amazement on the woman's face.

Meredith turned and saw Adam standing in the parlour doorway looking like a cross between an Irish rogue and a gypsy tinker.

'My apologies, Mrs Clements, I can assure you it is me, Mr Fox.'

Meredith realised her bland account of a few moments ago was totally inadequate for the bizarre clothing he wore. But matters changed instantly with Adam's next words.

'You will both come to Tallow House.' His voice had that curt tone, authoritive, expecting obedience.

'Sir, I have already told you —' She was cut off by his next words.

'Mrs Clements, will you please inform this obstinate woman that I am only trying to protect her, and yourself, of course; that staying here alone is a foolish gesture.'

Mrs Clements' cheeks coloured. 'Move to your residence, sir? You think Miss Sanders is in that much danger? But from whom?' Amazement turned to confusion. 'Is there something I'm not aware of?'

'Truly, it is nothing for you to worry about. Let us just say that a person, unknown, seems to have a …' She couldn't think of a lie that would protect her reputation and Frederick.

Her knight errant continued the lie. 'The art world is an infamous place of jealousy, Mrs Clements. No doubt one such person resents a woman presenting herself as competition. I'm sure it will all die down if the building is closed for a short period. Please pack a valise for Miss Sanders, and yourself. I would like to be home before the household realise I, too, am missing.'

Meredith should refuse, tell him that she was quite capable of looking after herself, but this would be an absolute contradiction, since without his rescue she would be far out to sea and beyond the help of anyone.

'Very well, Mr Fox, I agree, but just until this … unfortunate incident has been … well, until I have time to think things through.'

'An unfortunate incident; you wish to think things through?' His voice still had that curt tone. 'I will decide when that threat is past. Now, Mrs Clements, will you please hurry with packing your essentials.'

Flustered and obviously bewildered, Clemmie glanced from one to the other. 'Of course, I will go immediately, sir. Meredith, perhaps we should dispense with the tea?'

'Indeed we will, Mrs Clements.' Adam gave an impatient nod. 'Can you be ready within the half hour?'

'Yes, sir.' And she hurried out of the parlour.

Meredith faced him. 'May I go and change, sir? You will allow me those few moments of your time. Arriving at Tallow House bedraggled and dirty is not how I wish to start my enforced visit.'

'Of course, please forgive my lapse of manners, Miss Sanders. You have one half hour.'

She didn't like this Adam Fox. There was no warmth in his tone, no tenderness. Yet last night he had cradled her in his arms and loved her, driven away the horror of what might have been had he not rescued her. Did he regret what had happened; regret that he had offered marriage? Of course he did, he didn't love her as she loved him. Her refusal of his offer in that riverside room had been the right thing to do. She would never hold him to a betrothal, no matter what the outcome of their night together. Better a fallen woman with a bastard child than seeing Adam tied to her in a marriage of convenience.

'Thank you. I shall not keep you waiting.' Meredith held her head high as she walked past him. What a fool she was to love him.

The household servants were up and busy with their duties when Adam Fox entered Tallow House with Meredith and Mrs Clements.

'Simms, will you please show Miss Sanders and her housekeeper into the drawing room; and a tray of tea and toast, they have not breakfasted. I will be down as soon as I have changed.'

Whatever thoughts the sight of his master in a coarse cotton shirt, breeches, and old boots might have raised, the butler merely replied. 'Very well, sir.'

Adam raced up the stairs two at a time and turned left at the top of the staircase. His room was the first door. Inside he went straight to the wash stand. Hell, what was he going to tell Aunt Izzie? She would want to know where he had been since yesterday. There was an easy answer to that – he had been at the warehouse, an unexpected problem with a shipment. But bringing Meredith here was unorthodox and could raise awkward questions.

He stripped off his clothes and poured cold water into the bowl. In his hurry to escape the quizzing eyes of the servants he had forgotten to ask Simms for hot water. However, the cold water made him more alert and his brain started to form a plan to protect Meredith from gossip.

Dressed in his usual attire of breeches and high boots, shirt, neck-cloth, and coat, he entered the drawing room to find the ladies nibbling his ordered breakfast and looking much more relaxed. He banished this thought as they both immediately straightened their backs and primly put the plates onto the tray.

'Please, continue.' He was now as uncomfortable as they. 'Mrs Hooper will arrange your rooms immediately.'

Meredith nodded. 'You are most kind, sir, thank you. I should like to go to my room as soon as possible.'

Before he could reply Simms came in. 'Mrs Hooper has prepared the lady's bedchambers, sir. Shall I ask her to come now?'

'Yes. I have to go to the warehouse. Please inform my aunt that I shall be back at noon.' He bowed to Meredith. 'When you are settled, perhaps I may have a word with you when I return.'

Outside he climbed into the hackney coach he had instructed to wait. Time was of the most urgent. He would conduct only the most important business of the day with his warehouse foreman and return.

Two hours later he paid a generous sum to the coachman and went into Tallow House.

'Simms, has Miss Sanders come down yet?'

'No, sir, she is still in her bedchamber.'

'Please ask Miss Fox's maid to request Miss Sanders to attend me in my study, at once.' God, he was wound up like a spring. Simms would be wondering what was wrong. He didn't speak to his staff like some lord, biting our orders, expecting immediate action. He needed to calm down. Like his father, the study was his haven of privacy, the room where no one would interrupt him.

A knock sounded on the door. He opened it and Meredith stood there like a servant, her eyes lowered, hands clasped together. Had his overbearing manner reduced her to this? That she now looked on him as her jailer? But how else had he been able to bring her to Tallow House and safety? All he wanted to do now was to take her in his arms, kiss away the sadness and make love to her as he had at the inn. Instead, he stepped aside for her to enter.

'Will you take a seat?'

Her eyes were like green gemstones, those soft lips tight together. 'No, thank you, I will stand.'

To distance himself, he went behind his desk.

'Meredith, I have a plan. We will tell Aunt Izzie that I have made an offer to you. As you have no other living relative ...' he paused, but her expression was impassive, '... I have invited you to come here, to be chaperoned by her. I will then make arrangements for us to be married. This will also allow me to continue my enquiries about Madame Lightfoot and the painting. It is possible that she may attempt a second abduction if she discovers you escaped.'

'I see you have it all mapped out for me, Mr Fox. But you have given no consideration to my wishes.'

He came round the desk and stepped close, but didn't touch her. 'Can't you see this is my only option to protect you? I trust we will do well together and in time, when we know each other better, make a good marriage.' Couldn't he have sounded more ... loving ... instead of though he was offering some sort of contract? And kissing her would only fan her pent-up emotions. At this moment, he was sure she didn't know what she wanted.

'Marriage, sir, is something I did not have in mind when I came to London. I wish to continue with my studio and fulfil Frederick's dream.' She was breathing heavily, standing stiff and straight.

'That is something we could discuss. I am not adverse to you continuing your painting. Perhaps, when you have completed Sarah's portrait, commissions could be forthcoming.'

'Are you saying that as my husband you would not object?'

'The studio here would be sufficient, would it not? Sarah's tuition would not be every day. Aunt Izzie is most keen that she learns all the polite elements of society.' Her eyes softened and he continued, 'Well, Meredith, will you agree to my plan?' In the hall, Sarah's voice trilled happily. 'Do we announce our betrothal at lunch? It sounds as though my niece has been for a walk with her maid and we must have appropriate answers for such an inquisitive child.'

He pulled her towards him, touched her lips. She did not yield, nor pull away. For the first time since leaving the inn, she had given up rejecting everything he suggested.

'If you so wish, sir.' That was all she said. It left him unsatisfied and a little angry. Did she now accept, even in the wild bohemian world, unmarried, her reputation would be ruined, if their night together produced a child? He had been sure she had desired him as he had her.

He thought back over the past days. They had shared more than one night's lovemaking. There was Sarah's tuition, the mystery, and detecting at The Grapes. Woody's claim that she could be his daughter slipped in amongst his thoughts.

If there was any truth in that, then the man he had sent searching for her could be … her father?

But she had shown nothing in her manner when he claimed she had no living relative, and berated himself for thinking ill of her

Meredith wasn't a riverfront girl. She was a lady. Her manners were impeccable. Mrs Clements was her employed housekeeper. *Frederick* was her father; she had said so the day he had taken Sarah to the studio.

The agony of yesterday when he couldn't find her rippled through him. He pulled her against him, not giving her time to react, and kissed her with a passion that washed away any anger or doubt. He ran his hand up to her breast and could feel he had sparked her desire in return. She parted those lips that had looked so prim a moment ago and he deepened his kiss.

He didn't want to release her, but he pulled away. 'Oh, Meredith, I would have searched the world for you, no matter how long it took. But I have you here now and

I only want to love you.'

'But how can I be sure it's me and not your sense of duty?'

The sadness in her voice gave him hope. 'What can I do to convince you? Why do you think I came aboard the ship? I was full of dread for you when I saw the sailors. I see these captains every day and I'm fully aware what life at sea is like for them. Your whale bone would have been no defence ...' Adam paused as her face paled. 'I'm sorry, my love, do not think about it. I have you here.' He stroked her hair, ran his fingers down her cheek until he touched her lips.

Unbidden, she kissed each finger, raised her face to him with tears in her eyes. 'I will become betrothed to you, Adam. But marriage is out of the question. Should Frederick's felony implicate me, then you will be free to break our contract.'

'No. You must be under my protection.' Her half-promise was not enough.

'You have known me but a short time. You were not acquainted with Frederick. A magistrate would accuse me of using you. That our marriage was my way of securing your name and protection.' Meredith broke away from him. 'It is just a betrothal or I will return to Ludgate Hill.'

She had him cornered, leaving him no other option but to agree. 'Very well, we will make our announcement.'

As if to seal their bargain, the gong sounded in the hall.

The repast was its usual ritual. Aunt Izzie announcing the soup required more seasoning; and Simms refilling her sherry glass.

Miss Fox's voice filled the silence. 'Well, out with it. Since you did not return to the house last night, Adam, there is something afoot?' The old lady sat upright with her bony hands clasped together in her lap.

Meredith had to give Adam credit for the way he sat at ease, while she was a coiled spring waiting to gain release and flee the room.

'There was a matter to be settled at the warehouse. I'm sorry, I should have sent a message, but it became very late and I did not wish to disturb the household.'

His aunt was not going to let him off lightly, as she said, 'I can assure you, there was little to disturb. I hardly slept a moment after the clock chimed three.'

'Everything is in order now. There is another matter I wish to discuss with you.' He stood up and just for a fleeting second, his eyes locked with hers.

'Miss Sanders and I are betrothed, Aunt Izzie. As she has no known relative, I have asked her to come and stay here, under your chaperonage, until we are married.'

'*Betrothed!* When did this happen? Why wasn't I informed of your intention?' She stared at Adam, the shock paling her face and then she turned to Meredith. 'Betrothed, Miss Sanders? You are going to be mistress of this house?'

Such a thought had not entered Meredith's head, but of course, by marrying Adam she would take over what his aunt had administered. Her face burned hot. What should she say?

Adam went to his aunt and took hold of her hand. 'Izzie, you know you will always have a home here. Miss Sanders is well aware of our household circumstances. I'm sure you will fare well together.' He kissed her on the cheek. 'Life at Tallow House would be a very sad place without you.'

'Thank you, Adam, for your kind words.' The stiffness left her and she clasped his arm. 'Unexpected shocks like this are not good for an old lady of my age.'

Just for a moment, Meredith expected an unpleasant scene. But instead Miss Fox smiled. 'You have my felicitations, Miss Sanders. When do you expect the wedding to take place?'

Meredith had no intention of letting the pretence of marriage go unchecked and firmly replied, 'We have not spoken on this, but it will not be for some time.'

'It must be by the end of the next three months, Miss Sanders. That is the accepted period after a betrothal.' Miss Fox's reply was just as firm.

Adam offered no help as he pulled the bell-cord.

What had seemed a reasonable compromise, his aunt was pushing into a confirmation she couldn't give. Wondering how to answer, Simms saved her replying as he came into the room.

'Simms, please bring a bottle of champagne to the drawing room.'

The butler looked a little surprised and Adam grinned like a schoolboy who had just won the biggest prize. 'Miss Sanders and I are betrothed. We will celebrate the occasion with champagne.'

Simms returning smile gave Meredith a flutter in her stomach. Things were definitely getting out of hand; she was losing control of her life again.

Miss Fox waved her hand at the butler. 'I think I can forgo my nap. I'm sure champagne will settle my nerves far more than the sherry.'

Adam offered his help as she rose from her chair. 'Oh, I'm sure it will,' he replied as they left the dining room.

Entering the drawing room, Meredith hesitated. Did her status of fiancée now permit her to sit without the formality of it being offered? Her dilemma was diverted with the arrival of the champagne.

'I will open it, Simms. Perhaps this evening you would like to serve a bottle of wine at your own dinner table.' Adam's smile was infectious and the butler's eyes sparkled.

'Thank you, sir. On behalf of the staff I would like to offer our sincere blessings to you and Miss Sanders.' And on that note, he left.

Still standing, having not been offered a seat, Meredith wondered if Miss Fox was showing she was still the official mistress of the house. But her betrothal had been too much of a shock for any scheming plans of hierarchy. The popping of the cork and Adam filling three wine glasses banished any other silly ideas. He handed one to his aunt, then picked up the remaining two and came towards her. His brown eyes had taken on that blackness she had captured in her drawing. He was her confidant, rescuer, and lover. To think him her husband was a fantasy she could only dream about.

There was nothing he could do to help her. Madame Lightfoot had been right, without the return of the original painting the law would start probing and could eventually arrive at her door. Without Frederick alive to explain, all she had was the mysterious dark woman to point her finger at.

'Meredith?' Adam's questioning voice brought her back to the drawing room. 'Are you all right?'

'Yes. I'm sorry I was just thinking about yester ...' She stopped, seeing his lips tighten. She took the offered glass. 'Thank you.' The moment of tension passed and he smiled as he took her arm and drew her towards Miss Fox.

He raised his glass, 'A toast to our betrothal, Meredith. And to my aunt, I'm sure she will be of invaluable help to us.'

'To Meredith and Adam,' Miss Fox nodded to each in turn. 'It is time you settled into married life, Adam Fox.' A wide smile creased her cheeks and her sparkling eyes made her seem much younger. 'Now that sign Fox and Son, will become true again.'

The implication was clear and Meredith suspected that she had not been fooled by Adam's carefully planned ploy.

'Thank you, Miss Fox.' Any other reply would only complicate the situation.

She tasted the pale liquid. So this was the famous wine the nobles and gentry drank. She sipped again; yes, this was definitely something she would like to have at her wedding. But a wedding with Adam was something she could not have, because he didn't know her other secret. That she was the daughter of a riverfront man and nothing could change that.

CHAPTER SEVENTEEN

An hour later, Adam made his excuses and Miss Fox went to take a nap. This left Meredith free to find Sarah. She was in the schoolroom busy with a palette of watercolours, her brush stroking carefully along the lines of her drawing.

'Bravo, Miss Weston. You have captured the stonework, door, and kitchen seat in such detail.'

Sarah's face beamed with pleasure. 'It's how you told me to always look carefully at what I wanted to draw. Before you came, I wouldn't have thought to draw in the marks on the wall, or the broken seat. I'm going to save it for Papa and write the day on the back.' Like a puff of smoke, her happiness faded. 'Do you think he will ever come home?'

Meredith stooped beside her chair. 'I'm sure he will. You will continue to improve with each painting and then he will be even more delighted. Shall you stop now? There is something I wish to tell you.'

'Oh, I know all about you being betrothed to Uncle Adam.'

'You do?' She should be annoyed, yet the child's face was so full of delight she laughed instead. 'My, it didn't take your butler long to spread the word.'

'Isn't it wonderful, Miss Sanders? You will be living here and I can have painting lessons every day.'

'That is not what your uncle wants. He wishes for us to continue as before –' Unprepared for Sarah's enthusiasm, she toppled backwards as the girl threw her arms round her neck and they both ended up lying on the floor.

'Please, Miss Sanders, just one extra day?'

'No, Miss Weston, but maybe a little extra tuition before your bedtime?' There she was again, making plans for a fairy-tale future that couldn't be.

Sarah got up and held out her hand. 'May I help you up? I didn't mean to hurt you.'

'I am not harmed, but a little pull would be appreciated. Do you have any work to complete for when Miss Thomson returns?' Her silence told Meredith she had. 'I see. Wash your brushes, and then finish your school work. I must go and see Mrs Clements.'

The stairs to the attic rooms were steep and narrow and Meredith found Clemmie in a small and sparsely furnished room sitting in a chair by the window. The light emphasised the lines on her face and Meredith realised she had missed the signs that her dear friend and companion had aged.

She touched Clemmie's shoulder and her eyes opened. 'Is everything all right with you?'

'It is, Meredith, thank you. Mrs Hooper has been very kind. I have this room and take my meals with the staff, but she has refused any help. She told me to use this as a respite! Idleness is for masters. I have to look after *you*. Will you explain to her I have always seen to your needs? And I'm not stopping now. Apart from visiting my relatives a few times a year, I'd not left Appleton House since becoming Mr Sander's housekeeper.'

Meredith knelt and took her hand. 'Was it selfish of me to bring you to London? I've taken you from everything and everyone you know. I'm so sorry.'

'Goodness me, what are you saying? Where else would I be? When Mr Sanders brought you home that day, you filled an empty space in my life. I wouldn't want to be left somewhere on my own, even at

Harlington. Never have regrets, Meredith.' She picked up a handkerchief from her lap and wiped the tears from her eyes. 'Mr Fox will see that you are well cared for, but I would have liked to hear about your betrothal first. But Miss Sarah couldn't keep it to herself for one more minute. So she whispered in my ear, saying, it would only be a half telling. She is such a lovely child.'

'Yes, and very strong willed, but I have come to adore her very much. I hope to be able to finish her portrait soon.'

Mrs Clements started to get up, but Meredith stayed her move. 'No, sit here and enjoy your rest. I'll go and fetch *you* a pot of tea and speak with Mrs Hooper.'

The dinner gong was to be at six o'clock.

Meredith had deliberately deceived Adam about marrying him. She should have been honest and forbade the announcement. If her life had been as her father planned, Adam would be treating her as he did Sal, the tavern wench. He would never ask a girl like Merry for her hand in marriage. Like a roaring lioness with a thorn in its paw her anger rose – but her thorn lay deep, ten years deep, festering all the time she lived at Appleton House. She had studied extra hard at her schooling and painting to hide her past. But coming to Ludgate Hill, almost within touching distance of Newgate prison, her father was more and more in her mind. She had nurtured a hatred for him that she thought could never be appeased. Yet when she had seen him it hadn't been hate she had felt.

Meredith tried to analyse her feelings, remembering his words of regret that evening, pleading with her to understand. But the horror had driven her to run away. Why hadn't she thought more about her mother? She was being worn close to death working to feed her children. She had depended on her for help. Had it been

185

her running away that killed her?

Her father had found a way out – somehow. That question ran round and round, spiralling until a pain filled its place. What was she to do?

The answer was simple. Tell Adam, break the betrothal and go back to Ludgate Hill. The painting had to be returned to the Royal Academy the day after tomorrow. She had to either solve the crime or face any consequences.

Her mirror reflected a lady with her hair swept away from her temples and held in place by ivory clasps, her gown was muslin over deep green finely woven cotton. This gown belonged to her second life. Would Adam be prepared to accept her first – the ragged urchin? A girl so frightened and hungry that when she saw a man with a knife in his hand she had wanted to run back to Blackfriars.

Tallow House was beautiful. The bedchamber she had been given was part of a suite with a connecting door to a room beyond – Adam's bedchamber – but the door was locked and there was no key. No doubt Mrs Hooper considered such close intimacy quite inappropriate.

Yet she had already given herself to him, wantonly, in a riverside inn. In her imaginative mind she saw him lying naked on a large bed, his dark eyes looking directly at her. A flutter of desire ached low and she ran her tongue along her lower lip, remembering that same action by Adam.

The turmoil of her thoughts was broken by the sound of knocking and then voices from the hall. Meredith hesitated, but her curiosity overcame good manners and she went out on to the landing and looked down the stairs.

Below, a coachman was dragging the last of some baggage inside. A stranger handed him his fare. From along a passage leading off the landing Sarah's door opened and she came running out. 'What is happening? Why is there so much noise?'

'You seem to have a visitor, with a large number of trunks.'

Sarah leant over the landing rail. 'It is Papa, he has come home.' The next moment the child was running down the stairs, calling out, 'Papa?' The man speaking with Simms turned and swept Sarah up into his arms. Meredith was overwhelmed that Sarah's wish had come true and she couldn't stop the tears of joy. From various parts of the house, doors opened: Miss Fox sent her maid to find out what was going on. Adam looked baffled, his brows drawn together and she was extremely self-conscious that he should see her crying.

Then Sarah wriggled out of her father's arms and came running up the stairs shouting, 'Uncle Adam, Papa has come home. Come down, Miss Sanders, come and meet my papa.' She pulled at Meredith's hand and dragged her down the stairs.

'This is my painting tutor and Uncle Adam's going to marry her and she has almost finished my portrait that we were going to keep for you.' It all came out in one breath in her excitement.

From the landing, Adam called to his brother-in-law, 'Victor, why didn't you send word?' He ran down the stairs and took hold of the man by his shoulders. 'It's a surprise, but the best ever. Come into the drawing room.' He looked over at Simms. 'Another setting for dinner and tell Cook to wait until Mr Weston has had time to change. His room, Simms, is it ready?'

'Yes, sir, it is always ready.'

There was such pride in the butler's voice that Meredith couldn't help suffer a moment of regret. This would be a wonderful family to be part of. She waited, holding Sarah's hand and wondering whether she should follow, but the child pulled her forward and they trailed after the two men.

Victor Weston looked tired and travel worn, to the extent that his clothes and boots were filthy and his neck-cloth grey, never to be white again. His face was much lined for a man who was no older than Adam.

Without hesitation, Sarah sat on the sofa next to the father she had not seen for years. Yet there was no shyness, only pure delight.

'Come here, Meredith.' Adam held out his hand. 'We have an official announcement to make. Victor, may I present Miss Sanders, my fiancée.'

'Sarah was the bearer of this good news the moment I arrived.' He stood up and bowed. 'I offer you my most sincere congratulations, Miss Sanders. And you, Adam, have chosen a beautiful lady to be your wife.'

Adam laughed. 'That, I am well aware of.'

Everything was spiralling out of control again. Mr Weston added another layer to her deceit, but she replied easily, 'Thank you.'

Now Meredith had time to assess the tall man, she realised his years in the sun had made his face very brown and his blond hair almost white. He would stand out like Adonis, the Greek god, to the shaded and protected genteel ladies. There was a familiar facial likeness to Sarah, the same colour eyes, the same nose, perhaps even to her hair colour, in a few months' time.

Adam went to the cabinet and poured two glasses of amber liquid and handed one to him. 'Welcome home.'

'Oh, Papa, will you tell me all about your adventures? If you go back, will you take me?'

Victor's features changed and the happy smile he had given to Adam faded. 'No, Sarah. It is no place for a child. I will not promise something I could not do.'

'But, you were going to take Mama, so why –'

Her father raised his hand for silence. 'No more. I

may never go abroad again. I have had my fill of foreign lands. Let us not spoil your Uncle Adam's evening. I must change, but first present myself to Aunt Izzie. Tell Cook I'm famished and have been looking forward to her dinner platter since I decided to come home.'

'I'll go and tell Cook, Papa. You will love her pudding because I saw the apples on the table this morning.'

'My favourite; I hope she has put them in a pie. I'll be down in a half-hour.'

After they left, silence filled the room. Meredith didn't know what to say. She knew what she should be saying – the truth to end this illusion of respectability.

'Is everything all right, Meredith? I would rather you spoke your mind than look at me as though I were some sort of monster.'

He could never be that. She would love him for the rest of her life.

'I'm sorry, I didn't … I mean … pretence is difficult for me. A betrothal which is being played out for appearances' sake will end with a lot of hurt.'

'It is no pretence for me. I fail to see why you repeatedly throw your distaste of a marriage at me? Would you sooner be shamed? If you became an unmarried woman with a child, you would find it very difficult to maintain a position of respectability, even in London. Added to that, you already know competing in the artistic circles is almost impossible for a woman.'

She stood and took his tirade with her head bowed. He was so very right – respectability was paramount in the society he lived in.

'Yes. But I …' Her words were cut off with Adam pulling her to him and stopping her confession with his lips. She should push him away, but her heart overruled her head and she gave in to what she wanted – Adam: his kiss, his love, and his respect. Breathless, she stepped back, determined to tell him. 'I have something I need to say, something that will change what you feel –'

The door burst open and Sarah came in, her face flushed and holding a casket in her hand. 'Look, Miss Sanders, look, Uncle Adam, Papa made this. He carved it out of a tree and then made these patterns. Isn't he clever? And inside I have a necklace of tiny pearls. Mama's are larger, of course, but Papa says I can have those when I'm grown up.'

Meredith wanted to scream. She had to tell him her other secret, but she forced a smile. 'I'd love to see it. Come and sit on the sofa. I'm sure your Uncle Adam has much to organise for your father.' The moment for truth had passed and she gave him a dismissive nod.

Adam acknowledged with a nod of his own. 'Quite, I will see you in a half-hour for dinner.'

After so much mayhem, the quiet of the drawing room eased Meredith's taut nerves and she half-listened to Sarah's babbling words. '… Papa said this is very old wood.'

'It's beautiful. You can keep all your special treasures in it. I'm so pleased for you. Have you been wishing very hard at night when you say your prayers?'

Bright red flushed Sarah's cheeks. 'Oh, yes, every night. But now he's here, I'll have to pray even harder so that he doesn't go away again.'

'We'll both pray very hard.'

What she didn't say was that her prayer was a lot more complicated to achieve.

Cook excelled with her cuisine. What she had been preparing that afternoon came to the table like a banquet. Simms and the footman flourished platters of duck, beef, and salmon; vegetables and fruit; the best wine.

Adam rose from his chair and raised his glass. 'To your return, Victor, and continued good health to us all.'

Meredith gazed round the table at the family, even Sarah had been allowed to join them on this occasion. Miss Fox had been flamboyant all through the meal and she now signalled to Simms and he came forward and helped her to stand.

'Well, Victor, I thought I would be gone by the time you finally decided to return. But here I am, weaker than when you went, but I hope your wandering days are over. There's going to be a wedding shortly and Adam will need you to stand with him.' She picked up her glass and made a toast. 'To all our future dreams.' Everyone repeated her words. 'Well, gentlemen, I shall not sit again, I am retiring to my room; all this excitement has made me quite tired. I'm sure you both have much to talk about over your port and cigars. Sarah and Miss Sanders, will you kindly help me upstairs?'

Meredith saw Sarah was about to protest, and she quickly stood up. 'Of course we will, Miss Fox. Sarah must be very tired, it is long past her normal bedtime.' She went to the old lady's side and nodded to Sarah that they were to leave.

Simms held open the door and followed them out.

Meredith paused in the open doorway of the nursery room. Sarah was sitting in bed with a slate board on her knees.

'Are you doing your school work? It's a little late to be studying. Are you behind with your lessons?' She hoped her portrait sittings had not caused Miss Fox to forgo giving Sarah her planned schedule of lessons.

'Oh, no, Miss Sanders. I just like to draw all the time. It doesn't have to be with charcoal or watercolours. This is fun. Would you like to see it?'

Meredith sat on the side of the bed and took the slate from her. The girl had drawn a reasonable facial picture of her father.

'You have a talent for portraiture. I have noticed when you draw the flowers in the garden, how well you capture each petal and leaf.'

Sarah's smile told a story of absolute pleasure and pride. 'Could you show me how to make it better?'

'Well, it's a little difficult with only white chalk, but shading helps to give depth and contour. Rub your finger along the jaw line and reduce the thickness of the line.' For a child of only eight years, her talent was extraordinary and needed nurturing.

She had been twelve when Frederick had taken her into his care. He became both her school and art tutor; never losing his temper, never criticising when she couldn't master a problem. She thought of the day they had spent in the orchard and used the fallen apples to demonstrate multiplication and division. Mrs Clements had brought a picnic lunch and then afternoon sandwiches. It would always be one of her dearest memories with him.

'Should I show this to Papa?'

Meredith heard the question, but she didn't want to leave her thoughts, but hiding in dreams was not going to solve her problems. 'Yes. I think he will be very pleased to see how well you draw. You can show him tomorrow. Now, it's time to sleep. It's been an exciting day for you.'

Meredith stood up. 'Good night.'

'Good night, Miss Sanders. Thank you for helping me. Can we hurry and finish my portrait?'

'Of course, especially now your father has come home.'

'Could we have it very soon, as a special present for Papa?'

'If we work hard with not too many stops, yes, I think we could.'

'I'll ask Cook to make a special cake. This has been

the best day of my life.'

The portrait would be the right ending to her time at Tallow House. With her commission completed, there was no reason to stay. The missing Turner would either be found or the magistrate would be investigating its disappearance.

She had to tell Adam. Tell him so she could see his face, see his reaction. A letter would be a demeaning way, both for her and him. She would at least depart from him with her head held high.

She kissed Sarah's forehead. 'Sleep well.' Blowing out the candle, the room was touched by moonlight. A breeze lifted the candle smoke out of the open window.

As she reached the door, Sarah called out, 'We'll be a real family now, with Papa home and Uncle Adam bringing you here.'

Meredith didn't reply. Not all dreams could come true.

CHAPTER EIGHTEEN

The alleyway was dark and Adam had again become Dello Murphy, an Irish rogue. Below the tavern room of The Grapes Inn he opened the door to the tunnel, went in and closed it. His candle flickered. As the air stilled he hurried along to the door leading into the house near the Tower. The room was still bare and the key was still in the inner door lock. In the corridor he stopped and listened. The silence was uncanny, like a haunted house where living people feared to stay.

Adam heard a cough and moved to the bottom of the stairs. He left his candlestick on a small table. Each tread creaked but he reached the landing without cries of alarm. His one purpose for returning was to look for the man who lived here.

There were two doors and he chose the right; this room was dark and empty. As he opened the other a faint light split the darkness like a sword stroke. Adam eased the door wider and stepped inside.

The smell hit him like a clenched fist and he stopped breathing; then slowly took shallow breaths. He crossed the room and stopped next to what passed for a bed. A man lay sprawled fully clothed amongst the ragged covers. He coughed but didn't wake up.

Adam prodded him with his boot. 'Wake up, man. I have gold guineas if ye answer me questions.' There was no reply and he used his boot again, this time moving the man onto his side. 'I donna want to hurt yer, but I'm in a hurry.' These words had an effect.

'I don't know anythin', go away.'

'Now that is yer first lie, the next lie and me boot will nudge a bit harder.' What lay in the rags rose up on to its elbow. 'Git up!' The man tried, but fell back.

'Yer 'ave ter help me.'

Adam lifted a breathing skeleton, for the man was no heavier than a child; his almost transparent skin the only thing holding his bones together. For all his anger against him, Adam pitied the poor wretch as he propped him against the wall.

'Have yer anything to drink?'

'There might be a drop of ale.'

Adam picked up the tankard on the table and handed it over. When it was finished the bony hands gave it back.

'Yer have a choice, man, quick answers for me guineas, or pennies if I have to squeeze it out of yer. What's yer called?'

'Cuba John.' His words were slurred and difficult to hear.

It needed little imagination to recognise that Cuba John had used his reward for services rendered in the opium dens. This time he had indulged too far.

Leaning close to his ear, Adam asked, 'Where's Roseanna Lightfoot?' Cuba drew away. 'Gold or pennies, man?' Adam held a guinea coin close so the man could see.

'No! I can't tell. She'll 'ave me done in.'

'Well, an easier question – where does she live?'

Cuba John started to shake. His eyes began to roll, the eyeballs momentarily white. Adam grasped him by the shoulders. 'Where does she live?' The fool had poisoned his body to the point he was going to die. *'Where, I need to know where?'*

Even in the throes of death, Cuba could still ask, 'First, me gold.'

Adam placed a gold guinea in his hand, 'First one now, the other after. Where does she live?'

He had to lean close to hear what the man said, but when he straightened he had what he wanted. 'You've earned yer fee, man.' He placed another guinea into his hand. The pity was he would never spend it. Perhaps whoever found him would at least pay for a coffin in the churchyard.

Adam went into The Grapes tavern room from the street. He sat at a table in a corner and looked round for Woody. The man was serving tonight and he waited.

'What be yer tankard?'

'Woody, I need to talk to yer. Can ye be findin' a few minutes fer me?'

'Not 'til the serving girl gits 'ere.'

'I'll have yer best ale and wait.'

The room filled to capacity and pipe smoke drifted high. Voices grew in volume as game stakes passed from loser to winner. Adam wondered if Woody would have any spare time even when the girl arrived.

An hour later, Woody put two tankards down. 'Thought yer might want a second and one fer me?'

'Why not? Talking is thirsty work. Sit yer down, Woody.'

The man's bulk cut out most of Adam's view of the tavern. He picked up the tankard, only wetting his lips. Woody downed a good half before putting his down.

'So, where's the fine talk and clothes ye had yesterday? A sailor once showed me a foreign animal; it changed colour when danger's around. Are yer in some sort of trouble, Murphy?'

'That's fer me to know. I pay fer information, not questions.'

Woody raised bushy brows. 'Did ye find the girl? I didn't. She ain't my Merry anyhow.'

197

'And what makes yer so sure?'

'Because she's dead.' His words were resigned and held no doubt.

'I'm sorry to 'ear that, Woody. I did find her and she's safe. Have yer seen any visitors downstairs?'

'No. Well, not that I've seen.' He finished off the ale and nodded. 'Would ye be buying another?'

Adam had all the news he needed. Taking a half-crown from his pocket he put it on the table. 'Buy another and keep the rest fer yer help.' He got up and moved out into the tavern room. 'Just keep watchin'. Remember I pay well.'

At the door Adam looked back. Woody was downing his untouched ale. He wouldn't be using his reward money tonight.

One candle flickered as Adam closed the front door of Tallow House. The silence reassured him the household was asleep. Keeping his Dello Murphy clothes in his office at the warehouse made these forays doubly long. The time was now four o'clock; Simms would be having the servants up in another hour.

His foot was on the first tread when the drawing room door opened and he was caught squarely in the light.

'Adam?'

For a moment he was taken by surprise, then realised his brother-in-law was standing in the doorway. He stepped back and turned. 'Victor? What are you doing down here?'

'I couldn't sleep, the bed is too soft. I had forgotten how luxurious a feather mattress could be. Have you had a good night's entertainment?'

Adam took a deep breath and on a released sigh, it struck him that Victor saw nothing strange in his being out nearly all night.

'Lost a few guineas on chance; then made it up on the trumps.' That was as near the truth: a little simile. 'Would you like my company for a while?'

Victor opened the door wider. 'Yes. Perhaps this is the best time for us to talk.'

The drawing room was in shadow. Victor had only one candelabrum lit and this was placed on the mantelshelf above where he was sitting.

'I already have a brandy, would you like the same?'

'Yes, thank you.' Adam sat down opposite Victor's chair. When he was handed a glass, he saw how drawn and tired Victor looked. 'What's wrong?'

His brother-in-law sat down and leant back, 'I don't know.' He looked down at the glass in his hand.

'You've been away four years, Victor. I hoped you were now at peace with yourself. Losing Beatrice was something none of us had foreseen, but the doctor did all he could. Her loss is something we all had to bear. But you have Sarah to consider.'

'That's the reason I'm here. Beatrice would not want me to shun our daughter. I was wrong to go and leave her. How has she been?'

Adam had so much to tell him, but he could sense that Victor was suffering some form of guilt and so he said, 'I suppose you could separate the years into three parts. The first year, when she was only four, the loss of her mother was uppermost in her mind. Beatrice was a dutiful and loving mother and Sarah missed her daily games, her goodnight kiss. But gradually, Aunt Izzie took her place.

'Then she started to ask about her father. Your work at Kew Gardens always came first over wife and child.' Adam stopped. He should not judge Victor. 'I'm sorry. Forgive my outspoken comment.'

'There is no need for an apology. I've had many lonely nights to regret that.'

'Sarah slowly looked to me as the father-figure in her life. But she has never stopped asking after you. I have read parts of your letters to her about how you are and the West Indies. Old William Jacobs has been extremely diligent in looking after your affairs.'

'Thank you, Adam, but what about the third part of Sarah's life?'

'This past year there's been a change in her. She now has a schoolroom tutor, who is expanding her knowledge. But she has become very sad and tearful when she speaks of you. It's the reason I commissioned Miss Sanders. She is a very competent artist.'

Victor's face brightened into a smile. 'Ah, the talented Miss Sanders, do I detect a note of pre-husbandly pride? It is most unusual for a lady to be associated with business. Do you approve?'

This time Adam smiled. 'When you have known her a little longer, Victor, you will see a spark of determination that I or anyone else would find hard to undermine. It is, of course, her father's fault. He seems to have been her guiding light in the world of painting – encouraging her to continue with his studio.'

'You have seen her portfolio?'

'Her gallery work, yes. That is why I am confident her portraiture will be perfection.'

'You have seen how she has portrayed Sarah?'

'No. None of us has, not even the child. But I believe it's almost finished.'

'So, now we go into the fourth part of Sarah's life. You may find this hard to understand, Adam, but one evening I sat and wrote a letter to Beatrice. As the words flowed I was able to cleanse my soul of her loss. See that I was in the wrong part of the world. The following day, I made arrangements to travel home.'

Adam wondered why he had not written, but it didn't matter – he was here, healed and ready to go forward.

'You are welcome, Victor, to stay with us for as long as you like.'

'Thank you. When Sarah is older, I will give her that letter and hope she will forgive me.'

'Have no doubt, she is so thrilled you are home nothing is going to mar her happiness. Come, the household will soon be about and we should be away to our beds and leave them to their tasks.'

Meredith hadn't slept well. She had spent most of the night turning from side to side and plumping up the pillow.

Where was the Turner? That, above all else, was what her future hung on. The Grapes Inn was not the place. That had become evident when she had been kidnapped by Madame Lightfoot. It left only the gallery.

A light knock sounded on the door and Mrs Clements came in. 'Good morning, Meredith.' She placed a tray on a table by the window and pulled back the curtains. 'It's going to be a beautiful day.'

'Yes, Clemmie, and I intend to use it fully. I shall be down shortly. Thank you for my tea.'

'Mr Weston and Miss Sarah are already breakfasting. I believe they are going shopping directly.'

'That will please Sarah. When they return, I can have her for our last sitting.'

'I'm sure the family will be delighted, dear. You have worked so hard on it, Meredith. I know Mr Sanders would be your proudest admirer.' Her voice broke on a sob, 'Oh, what a sentimental old woman I am.'

Meredith felt suddenly torn in two: she had adored Frederick as a father-figure and friend, yet he had left her never knowing what sort of a man he really was under the disguise he showed her. But she would never destroy Clemmie's devotion and respect for him.

'I really am pleased with it, Clemmie. I must confess

I was very mindful of the responsibility of taking on such a commission, but Miss Weston has been the perfect model to study. I kept remembering all of Frederick's special strokes to enhance her face and those fair curls. I'm particularly proud of her fingers, because I have always found it quite difficult to make them look natural.' She picked up the corner of the sheet and dabbed her eyes. 'How silly of me; I suddenly had a thought that maybe Frederick was guiding *my fingers*.'

'Aye, we both miss him very much.'

'Thank you for coming with me, Clemmie. I should be very lonely without you here.'

This time Mrs Clements picked up the corner of her apron and wiped her eyes. 'I'm helping Cook today. Thank you for speaking to her. I'm sure we shall do nicely together now we understand our places.'

Meredith didn't get out of bed when Clemmie left; instead she lay back and thought of those living in Tallow House. She was now part of a large household and this one had grown two-fold in the same number of days, which brought her back to Adam Fox. He had subtly moved into her life: first as a client, then confidant, then lover and now he wanted her as his wife.

She loved him. There was no denying that truth. She tried to hold back the sobs, but they wouldn't obey. She surrendered and fell into the pit of despair.

When Meredith entered the dining-room, only Adam sat at the table. He had eaten; his used plate pushed aside, and was reading *The Times*. A frown creased his forehead and he sighed. 'This French situation with Napoleon is becoming a most serious business. He has Paris in his grip and thousands of troops loyal to him. The aristocrats are becoming nervous again.'

'It is indeed a worrying situation. Clemmie has noticed many more French maids in the markets. It will not disturb you if I have a late breakfast?'

'Hardly late, Meredith. Aunt Izzie always stays in her room and Victor has taken Sarah to High Holborn. Please, sit down; there is something I need to talk to you about.'

Sitting in her now designated place she buttered a piece of toast. 'If it's about the portrait, I shall finish it today. Providing you are satisfied with my work, then our arrangement is finalised.' She spread a blackcurrant preserve, keeping her eyes lowered.

'It isn't about Sarah. It's about Madame Lightfoot. I found out last night where she lives.'

Meredith glanced up at him. 'How?'

'A little idea occurred to me.'

'Does it help us?'

'Not directly. She owns a milliners shop in Bond Street under the name of Madame de Foile. I want to have a look around. We will visit with the pretence that you are about to be married and require a large number of hats for your trousseau. While you keep the madame busy, I shall search the remainder of the premises.'

'What if she's there? She knows me and ...' She trailed off, thinking about the last time she had been in that woman's presence.

'Not if you are wearing a veil, leaning heavily on a walking cane and complaining about your unfortunate riding accident with the hounds in Hertfordshire.'

She stared at him in disbelief. 'Are you mad? Besides, convention depicts that my chaperone, your aunt, would be the one to accompany me.'

'You are quite right. But, as you are so indisposed, it has been decided that you require a gentleman's arm and strength to support you.'

'What do you hope to gain out of this masquerade? I understand the need when we were at the inn, but *Bond Street*?'

'As you said, Madame Lightfoot may be in residence.

But no matter, I shall go, I'm sure my charm will be able to fulfil my quest.'

'*You will not.*' Meredith almost threw her chair back as she stood up. 'This is my problem and I shall come with you.' She took a deep breath, about to tell him he was not in charge when he started to laugh.

'I love to see you in high spirits, Meredith. You become the most desirable of women. If it wasn't that we are running out of time, I could so easily sweep you off your feet and disappear into my bedchamber, flaunt convention and throw both our reputations to the wind.'

He pushed his chair back, and came towards her.

Meredith stepped back. 'No, Adam, please, we must think of –'

Taking her hands he leant forward and lightly kissed her cheek, 'Run along, my dear, time enough for us later. Do you have a veiled hat?'

'Only the one I had for Frederick's funeral.'

'It will have to do, perhaps a little mauve ribbon?'

'I'll see what I have. You will provide the walking cane?'

'Yes. I'll have the coach here in a half-hour.'

He opened the door and followed her out, then went into his study.

Amongst the bustle of maids and footmen laden with boxes and packages and doting mothers ushering their daughters into shops offering the most delicious chocolates to the latest gown designs required to tempt the wealthiest of beaux, Madame de Foile, Milliner Extraordinaire, had an exquisite display of hats in her bow-window.

Adam helped his crippled fiancée from the coach and handed her a walking cane. Then he supported her into the Bond Street modiste's shop.

Madame de Foile, in a gown of deep green silk, her

dark hair coiled soft and loose at the nape of her neck, came towards them smiling. 'Good morning. I received your note, Mr Fox. I have a high chair ready for your fiancée. Perhaps you would like a chair?'

'Thank you.' He looked around and gestured to a dim corner at the back of the room. 'There, if you please. I do not wish to intrude in any way upon Miss Sanders' consultation.'

'Your diligence is most admirable, sir, if you will permit me to say so.'

Adam nodded this acknowledgement, but made no reply as Madame de Foile moved a visitors' chair to accommodate him.

He helped Meredith forward. 'Now, my dear, will this be comfortable for you?'

'Thank you, Mr Fox. Madame and I will have a pleasant morning discussing colours and styles.'

She had practised using the cane for only a few minutes after Adam had given it to her. But she managed to lean on it and walk with a pronounced limp.

'Shall we start with the sombre colours? I see that you are still wearing mourning black. How long is it that you have lost your dear one?'

'Papa has been gone almost a year. Our wedding will be one week after I discard these mourning weeds. Can we look at the pastel shades, pink perhaps?

'Pink is a delightful choice of colour. Do I see dark hair under your veil?'

'Yes. I do not wish to remove my own hat. The accident has, unfortunately, given my neck a most debilitating ache and my constitution has suffered badly. Today I would like to look at colours and patterns. I still find any exertion quite tiring.'

'My patterns are mainly from the Paris collection, but I can create anything you require.'

'That is most generous of you. Let us start with

the collection you have.'

Madame de Foile fluttered her hands; a bright red flush colouring her cheeks. 'First, I must apologise for not having my assistant here to help. The wretched girl announced, quite unexpectedly, that she was marrying a gentleman from Derby. A pottery maker that she met at her aunt's house! She had the ill grace to leave me quite inconvenienced within two days. As yet, I have not been able to find another suitable assistant. I will have to fetch and carry myself.'

'Please, do not feel so distressed, I am quite happy to extend my visit to accommodate you.' This was a most fortunate circumstance. The milliner would be far too busy to notice if Adam disappeared.

'Thank you, Miss Sanders. I could, of course, ask one of my milliner girls from the workroom above to assist, but I fear their appearance and common voice would not be appropriate. Lady Silburn is coming this afternoon and I would be the ridicule of the tea parlour tomorrow.'

With another flutter of her hands, Madame de Foile brought a small table for Meredith and opened a pattern book. 'The ones I would recommend are marked with a ribbon tab.'

'I can sympathise whole heartedly, Madame. I am so sorry that my immobility prevents me from walking far, so I must rely upon your good nature to pander to my whims. I would love to see what you recommend.'

Adam waited as Meredith concentrated on her play-acting, her eyes nervously looking about her. No doubt Madame Lightfoot was uppermost in her mind.

Once he was sure Meredith had Madame de Foile's full attention, he went to a door he had seen when they arrived. He listened for any movement; all was quiet and he opened the door and slipped inside. It was furnished as an office and he searched the desk drawers, but each one was empty. An eight-drawer chest proved the same.

He leant against the chest, pondering how strange there were no bills of sale or ledgers. Then the chest moved to reveal a low locked door. He was not surprised, having seen the secrecy the dark woman lived in. He pushed the chest back into place, but would dearly love to know what lay beyond. He studied a painting hanging on the wall, perhaps this too had something to hide. He lifted the frame and found a small wall safe. Madame Lightfoot trusted no one. Adam walked round the room – it had been deliberately cleared.

There was a second door with a key in the lock and this opened into a passageway.

Adam turned left and went along to a stairway that led to the upper floor. At the landing there were two doors. From the one on his right he could hear women's voices – this must be the milliners' workroom. On his left a metal door was partially open and he went in. The rooms were much the same as at Ludgate Hill except dust sheets covered all the furnishings. A quick search revealed that Lightfoot had left on a permanent or extended basis. The momentous relief that the threat to Meredith was no more faded as he realised Lightfoot's disappearance proved she hadn't found the Turner. With the forged painting somewhere at sea, all trace of Lightfoot's involvement was erased.

Adam returned to the shop and sat on his chair.

Meredith was still plying Madame de Foile with complimentary words.

'I am in complete agreement with you, Madame; pastel shades will be so much more fashionable this summer. I'm sure our choice of styles will delight my chaperone, Miss Fox.'

She turned towards him and smiled. 'Are you getting bored, sir? We are sorry to have been so long. Madame has been so very generous and supplied many samples and patterns for me to take home. I am assured your aunt will give me her valued opinion.'

Meredith picked up a small linen valise. 'Good day, Madame de Foile.'

He stepped forward to help her from the chair, and nodded to the Frenchwoman, 'Au revoir, Madame. Thank you for being so kind to my fiancée. And for allowing me the pleasure of a few peaceful moments, observing the mysteries of a lady choosing her millinery.'

Adam waited to see if there was any reaction from Madame de Foile. There was none. His absence had not been observed.

In the coach, Meredith raised the veil and sighed. 'Where on earth did you go to, Adam? I was running out of colours to ask the woman to show me. And if that is the latest Paris fashion, I don't think I shall be returning. They were not to my liking at all.'

Adam leant forward, untied the mauve ribbon, and removed Meredith's hat. 'That's better, black mourning is not your colour. I do agree with Madame de Foile, pastels are far more suitable for you.'

'Stop deviating, what did you find out?'

'Madame Lightfoot has left. I don't know whether permanently, but most definitely on a long absence. The office has been emptied of all business papers. The rooms above have been stripped of all her personal belongings. It appears that her art dealer business has ended.'

'You don't sound as though this is good news. What does this mean for me?'

He sat quiet for a moment. What he had to say wasn't good news. He stroked his finger over her pale cheek, guessing she had the answer herself.

'The missing Turner has now become a case of theft. Nothing can be proved concerning the forged paintings.

208

They are now just a cargo bound for Australia. I suspect that the captain, when he was asked to transport you, guessed things were going wrong. He will dispose of those packages in such a way no one will ever know where they came from.'

'I see. Then Frederick will never be identified?'

'Probably not. Anyone associated with Lightfoot will vanish from the horizon like the setting sun.'

'You don't look very happy about that. What are you holding back?'

Adam moved and sat next to her. 'If we could only find the original painting and get it back to the Royal Academy by tomorrow, this underhanded business could be finished with.'

'You are saying that if the magistrate traced the painting to the studio, I would be charged with its theft?'

'I don't want to frighten you, Meredith, but it is better that we face the possibility.'

'Then I must find it.'

He would protect her with all his strength and might, but as she had already pointed out, he had no association with Frederick Sanders. He had known her only a short time. Marriage would not be enough to save her.

CHAPTER NINETEEN

Meredith was closing her bedchamber door. Before she took a step away, Adam came out of his room.

'Ah, my fiancée is restored to health. Have you stored away that undesirable black?'

'Yes. I'm surprised Mrs Clements even packed it when we left Harlington and I can't think why she brought it here. But it served us well today.'

'We'll talk in my study this afternoon. Aunt Izzie will be most upset if we are late.' He offered his arm to her and they made their way down the stairs.

Sarah's privilege to be at the dining table had been extended to include today. She was very excited about her morning outing with her father and was telling Miss Fox all the places she had seen.

'Papa took me to a wonderful toy shop. It is called Noah's Ark. Isn't that a funny name? We looked at so many things, but I chose a new doll and she's sitting on my bed. I've named her Daffodil, after the first flower I painted with Miss Sanders in the garden. Then Papa took me to a bookshop. There were lots and lots of shelves and a special part for children. The owner helped me choose; I have *The Tales of Robin Hood*. Papa says it is only a legend, but the drawings are ...' She stopped and looked up at the ceiling. 'I think I would like to draw like that. When I have read the stories, I will think of something different and draw them. Will you help me, Miss Sanders?'

Would she be able to help or would she be in prison? 'That's an excellent suggestion, Sarah, I'm sure we shall

all be extremely impressed.' She had not given a commitment, but she hoped it would encourage Sarah to continue with her paintings.

Victor Weston held up his hand. 'No more talking, Sarah. Eat your food or Simms will be kept waiting for your plate.'

'Yes, Papa. But it has all been so wonderful.'

Victor, not following his own advice, said, 'The city roads are busier than when I left. There was hardly room for all the carriages; are not the gentry going to their country estates?'

'It's not just those that own carriages now. Imports and exports are increasing daily. I am in the process of acquiring another warehouse. Trade with the far side of the world has doubled since my father's day.'

'So you think this is a good business to invest in? Better than botany? I intend to approach Kew Gardens when I have seen old William Jacobs tomorrow. Would you recommend I change my vocation, Adam?'

'No. But when you have acclimatised back to civilisation, you may wish to consider a few shares in shipping.'

'Ah, do I detect a little family investment?'

Adam laughed and picked up his glass of wine. 'May I toast your new future, and our changing England?'

Conversation drifted around the home life of the Fox family, until Aunt Izzie drew the meal to an end.

'Although your company is both challenging and enjoyable, it is time for my nap. I shall be down for tea at four o'clock.'

Adam got up and helped her from the chair. 'Let me see you to your bedchamber, Aunt, and give Simms the extra time for his duties.'

As they left the room, Meredith wanted to go too. But with Victor still seated she considered it only polite to stay.

He kept his gaze on the glass, twisting the stem round and round. 'Sarah tells me her portrait is nearly finished. I have a small miniature of my wife: would you be able to create a full-size portrait to match Sarah's? We will, of course, find our own house in time and I should like to place them side by side.'

Meredith heard the grief in his voice and admired him for the bravado he was putting on for Sarah.

'Oh, Papa, that would be so beautiful. Miss Sanders can do that, I know she can.' The child's blue eyes had absolute confidence in them. 'You will, won't you, Miss Sanders?'

She should have gone when Miss Fox left. They were forcing her, yet again, into promising something she couldn't be sure of. 'I will look at the painting. Then we can decide.' She stood up. 'If you will excuse me, I have an appointment this afternoon.'

Victor Weston only nodded. Then he said to Sarah, 'I think you have schoolroom work.'

Meredith took this as her dismissal and she held out her hand to Sarah. 'Come, Miss Weston, I will take you to your lessons.'

Meredith tapped lightly on Adam's study door and waited for his call. Once inside and without any preamble he said, 'There's only one place left and that's the gallery.' He got up and came round to her, his fingers grasping her upper arms tightly. 'I won't have you charged with a crime you know nothing about. Frederick Sanders should have finished with Lightfoot long ago. He was not a young man, not even middle aged. He risked everything: his reputation, his daughter's good name. With all the evidence gone ...' Adam let the unfinished statement speak for itself.

Meredith held back the tears that had been building since they returned from Madame de Foile's shop.

Everyone connected with the Turner had disappeared. For the hundredth time, she wondered why Frederick had done what he had. But the answer to that was gone forever. She laid her head onto Adam's chest. He felt solid, dependable, and safe.

He pulled her close, saying nothing, just holding her. Finally, Meredith said, 'So we are at a dead end.'

'Not quite. Frederick had been very careful not to be found out. A careful man is often a creature of habit. He must have used the gallery to copy the painting. Room six is much too public. We know others had a key. The original must be *somewhere* in the Ludgate premises.'

Meredith pulled away from him. 'But I have looked. It's not there.' Adam smiled and that protected feeling cloaked her.

'The coach is ready. Go and collect the keys and let us go hunting.'

Meredith opened the street door. Instantly there was the smell of her oils. In the gallery, her paintings were hanging on the walls, nothing had changed – but everything had changed.

'I could never abandon this studio. It will always be part of my life, no matter what happens in the future. It's not because of Frederick, but that painting will always be a necessity in my life. Selling them isn't what matters, although that does help to lighten one's living costs.' She paused as a frown creased Adam's forehead. 'Have I said something untoward? My independent words, perhaps?'

'I would not wish to curb your enthusiasm, Meredith, but marriage means we will both have to compromise a little.'

She bit her lip, holding back the hot words she wanted to say. Instead she replied, 'That is all for another time. We are here to find the Turner. Shall we start in the studio?'

'Very well; you are sure there are no hidden cupboards in this room?'

'No. I had the panels covered with this linen. Mrs Clements and I cleaned every inch. It's not hidden here.'

In the studio, there was little to move or find. The planked floor was sound and the walls were brick from ceiling to floor. She went up to the parlour and ran her fingers around the panelled walls, calling to Adam, 'Each one of these is quite sound. I've tapped them too, there isn't any hollowness.'

Adam came in saying, 'The kitchen is sound too. There are only cupboards and drawers and definitely no loose floorboards.'

They had searched the safe part of the house where they hadn't needed a chaperone – but now they were going up the stairs to her bedchamber. Adam would see where she undressed and slept in the large bed. She sensed a tension in him that matched her own nervousness as she led him out of the parlour. Yet excitement flowed through her the moment they ascended the stairs. She tried to ignore it, but she couldn't. Adam was her lover. There were only two rooms; hers and Mrs Clements. Her cheeks were burning. How stupid to be shy when they had already shared a bed. The distance between them was a bare few inches, and as she reached to open the door, Adam placed his hand over hers.

'Our night was not a mistake, Meredith.'

He stepped even nearer and her breath quickened, he was going to kiss her. Beyond the door her soft, comfortable bed was waiting for them.

'No. But it has caused a complication that I don't know how to deal with ...' His kiss forbade her to finish and she let him open the door and carry her inside.

He laid her down and she sank into the warmth of the

feather mattress. His eyes were very dark, his face taut, but as she touched his cheek with her finger he relaxed.

'I know this is wrong, Meredith, but you are mine and no one, a fraudster or magistrate is going to take you from me.' She wanted to cry, because that was exactly what she was – a fraudster. She had to tell him now, while he still had his self-respect and could walk away without the shame of seducing her.

'Adam, please, you must listen to me.'

He put his finger over her lips. 'Later. Only you can stop my blood racing through me like a stampede of wild horses; cannot you feel it? I can feel your pulse.' His fingers were on her wrist and he smiled. 'It does not tell lies, my sweet.'

She sensed her skirt rising, his fingers sliding along her silk stockings to the fine hair and he stroked her so softly that an involuntary moan left her lips and a wonderful sensation rippled and fanned through her. She closed her eyes, savouring the moment, so different from the first time, because she now knew the pleasure of his touch. He gently kissed her lips and ran his tongue inside. She closed her lips and drew him in, sucking the rough tip.

His breath came in gasps and with his other hand he tore away the fall of his breeches. She felt his hardness against her, then his skin. He slid into her and there was no pain, just his hardness thrusting deeper, sending exquisite sensations spiralling deeper into her belly.

'Meredith!' Adam moaned her name as he arched above her and her throbbing body reached up and moved with him until there was only the descending pleasure back to reality.

His weight moved from her and she opened her eyes and turned to him.

Adam was everything she wanted as a husband. She knew he had far more than lust in his heart, and was sure it would grow into a deep love. His strong fingers brushed a loose strand of hair from her face and he kissed her cheek. 'You are perfection, my love. Just think how wonderful it will be after we are married.'

'I love you, Adam. But I can't marry you.' The pain on his face sent waves of utter despair through her.

'Why?' It was one word of total dejection. 'Am I so unacceptable? I offer you a comfortable home. I have not forbidden you to continue painting. Aunt Izzie is now old and frail; you will be mistress of the house.'

Adam moved off the bed, tidying himself.

Meredith got up and pulled her skirt into order. 'Because I'm not who you think I am.' She had finally said it, but her words were drowned by a crashing, splintering noise, followed by the terrified neighing of horses and the shouting of men above the screams of women.

'What the hell's going on out there?' Adam went to the window. 'My God, a coach has turned over coming out of the Belle Sauvage. The horses are down and trapped in their harnesses. Wait here.' He ran from the room.

She rushed to the window. Adam was pushing his way through the crowd to the lead horse that was screeching in terror and trying to get free of the harness. He caught its reins, straining to calm the beast while stablemen from the inn pulled the travellers free. A quiver ran through her, every nerve screaming, warning her Adam was in danger. The horse was fighting his hold and might kick him any minute; he could be injured, even killed.

Meredith shrieked at him through the window panes. 'Adam, look out, mind its hooves, it's trying to get up. Oh, my dearest, please be careful.'

Out of the mêlée the neighing and shouts lessened, the dishevelled passengers were being helped back into the inn. The stablemen had all but the lead horse untangled and a boy led each animal away. Adam stood stroking the neck of the horse and with each soothing touch the horse stopped quivering and came under control.

She turned to the mirror. Both combs were loose and her hair was a mess of falling curls around her flushed face. *So, this is what a woman in love looks like*. She clipped the stray locks back into place. Panic spread through her like wildfire. She had to get out of her bedchamber. She had become a wanton wench, doing what many got paid to do. But she loved Adam, didn't that make it different? Not in the eyes of the law.

Meredith ran with the devil chasing her up to Frederick's attic room where she had found the receipts and key to room six in The Grapes Inn – the room that had proved his guilt and association with Madame Lightfoot. She sat at the desk and laid her head on her arms. Love and hate mingled like vines twisting tighter and tighter until one had to die.

She had hated her father and loved Frederick. Did she now hate Frederick and … she couldn't love her father, ever. Yet when she had seen him that first moment in room six, there hadn't been that thorn of hate she had been carrying in her heart all these years.

She gazed at a shaft of sunlight shining off one of the wooden panels. Something about it didn't fit in with the ones either side. Its raised central section looked wrong. Was it the light playing tricks, or the different grains of the wood? She went over and ran her fingers along the groove, finding a small metal circle, no bigger than a nail-head. Lightly touching it the panel opened no more than the thickness of a knife blade. She knelt down and eased it wider and saw the edge of a framed picture inside.

Meredith didn't touch it. Her mind was numb, both

with fear and relief. This had to be it, Frederick wouldn't hide away one of his own canvases. She pulled slowly. Was this Turner's own hand, his artistic genius? The canvas which he made minute touches, and flourishing strokes on? Was she going to see what the Master had done? She pulled it free and propped it against the panelling. Her heart beat so fast it muffled her hearing, yet the footsteps racing up the stairs, Adam calling, forced her back to this moment of discovery.

'I'm here,' she called, 'in Frederick's attic.'

He came in, but she didn't move. How *could* she have missed this panel?

'I've found it, Adam. It has been hidden here all the time.' She sensed him behind her. 'I don't know what to say.'

'Nothing, my love, except now everything will be all right.' He pulled her up and wrapped her in his strong arms. 'All we've got to do now is take it back to where it belongs.'

She leant against him and whispered between her sobs, 'Yes.'

Several hours later, a jaunty Dello Murphy went into The Grapes Inn and found Woody sat at a table playing dominos with two sailors.

'When yer finished, Woody, a word? I'll be sittin' over in the corner.'

A few minutes later the man arrived, carrying two tankards. 'Thought yer'd be thirsty.'

Adam nodded and took a long draught of the ale. 'I'm in a hurry, man, 'ave yer any more news for me?'

'Nothing; all is very quiet down below, if yer git me meaning.'

Adam had one last task to finish. Then he hoped never to hear about room six or Madame Lightfoot again. Meredith could be his, happy and free to marry him as soon as possible.

'I've a little bit of a job for yer in the morning. Be at the back gate at six o'clock. There's a package to be delivered.'

'I'm not an erran' boy, Murphy, and I don't git up with the birds.'

Adam ignored his remarks and pressed home his winning hand. 'Not even for ten guineas?'

Woody stopped drinking and put the tankard down. 'Now, what would yer be paying that kind of money fer?'

'Like I've said before, I pay fer no questions, just yer time.' Adam saw the man dither, could see the money was like a gem stone to him.

'Well now, yer asking a lot of me with all this mystery and no answers. How much danger is there?'

Adam wouldn't lie; he had to give him a truthful answer. 'I don't know. We could both be standin' afore the magistrate come noon.'

'That's not good news, *Dello*. But you've not done me wrong so far. I'll trust yer one more time.'

Adam nodded. 'Six o'clock outside the backyard.'

Woody nodded his agreement and went back to his ale.

'Yer can finish mine.' Adam placed a few coins on the table and pushed his half-full tankard over. 'Donna be gettin' drunk. I won't wait if yer not here.'

Adam stood in front of the connecting door to Meredith's bedchamber. He held the key in his hand; he had only to put it in the lock and turn it. But she had accused him once of treating her like the tavern wench, Sal. That she was not, and he returned the key to his desk drawer, left, and made his way down to the drawing room.

'Good evening, Aunt Izzie.'

She was in her usual chair, a glass of her pre-dinner sherry on a small table.

He sat down and his thoughts went back to when there was only Aunt Izzie and him. Sarah ate early and would be ready for bed. It had been a special time for him and his niece – thirty minutes of reading her a poem or a short piece from one of the Greek mythologies. They had a special relationship; not of father or uncle, but friends. He would miss that now Victor was home. It was a father's duty to read the bedtime story.

Where was Meredith? His impatience was irritating. He wanted tomorrow over and Meredith his, to have and to hold until death do them part. When the gong sounded, she came through the door. Her pallor surprised him; he had expected a radiant fiancée, with all her troubles solved.

'Miss Sanders, at last, I was beginning to wonder if something was wrong.' Miss Fox waved for his support as she tried to stand. 'You do look a little peaky, dear. Have you had a busy day?'

Meredith nodded. 'Yes. Miss Weston and I spent the late afternoon finishing her portrait. The extra sitting time has tired us both. But she is most anxious for it to be ready for tomorrow.'

Victor Weston arrived and bowed to Meredith. 'Good evening, Miss Sanders. I hear from Sarah that you have a surprise for me. It will be an honour to be present at the unveiling.' He offered his arm to escort her into dinner, leaving Adam burning with envy.

Dinner had passed socially enough and Aunt Izzie and Victor were battling out a game of backgammon.

Adam touched Meredith's arm. 'Would you like a little evening air? The garden is well sheltered.'

'Thank you, yes. I do have a slight headache; a little fresh air may do it good.'

He led her out along the passage and into the garden. Taking her hand he tucked it into the crook of his arm and she trembled for just a second. 'It's the reaction, Meredith, to everything that has happened. A quiet stroll will ease away your tension.'

She sighed, but made no reply.

'Would you like to sit on your favourite seat? I always seem to find you there with Sarah.'

'I would. How have you managed to achieve a country garden in London?'

'That is Aunt Izzie's doing. She never wed and lived most of her life in the country with her father, who was not partial to town life. She only came here when my sister died to help with my guardianship of Sarah.'

They reached the seat and she sat down. For a few moments Adam remained standing; then he joined her. He took her hand and rubbed his thumb along her wedding finger. 'After tomorrow, will you agree to a marriage date?'

'No, Adam, I will not agree. We have yet to get the painting back to the Royal Academy. You said earlier that you would make the arrangements. Have you?'

'Yes. It will be delivered anonymously early tomorrow morning. You may have no fears tonight and sleep well.'

'That, I think, will be impossible. I should be there when it is put back.'

'No.' Adam's tone was sharp. 'You must be nowhere within the area. You must be here in your bedchamber, asleep or awake, but there you must be.'

'I am to be safe, while you put yourself in danger of being associated with this ...' She struggled for the correct word and he said it for her.

'Theft?'

'Yes, if you must put it so bluntly, Frederick's

222

villainy.' She looked away from him into the dark garden.

He could see she was fighting an inward battle of guilt, but he was determined she would not be implicated should anything go wrong. Beyond that his personal involvement was his to deal with.

He spoke softly, hoping to calm her. 'Everything will go according to my plan. It is a beautiful evening, let us not quarrel. Come, there is more to see beyond this seat, we may even see an owl. I hear its cry sometimes.' He got up and held out his hand and led her to the seat under the cherry tree. Instead of inviting her to sit down, he pointed to the moon, just past its zenith, shining in a starlit sky. The owl hooted somewhere close.

'Did you hear him? I think Mr Owl is welcoming us to his night world. We will take that as a good omen.'

Meredith sighed. 'It is remarkable that a country bird should be in London. I love their soft silent flight and calling voice.'

Adam pulled her back against him and kissed her neck. 'For you, I would fly to that round white orb, if you asked it of me.'

She turned in his arms and looked at him with no shyness, no shame. 'I am yours forever, Adam. I want you to remember that.'

'Those are ominous words, as though you will not be here.' A sense of foreboding came over him. 'I don't understand what you mean?'

Meredith didn't answer, but wound her arms round his neck and kissed him. When she moved away, he caught and pulled her back. 'Tomorrow, we decide a date.'

Meredith had been awake for hours listening for any sound that told her Adam was about. His desire to keep her away from the Royal Academy, and the painting, sprang from his love for her. It also put him in the greatest of dangers. On the other hand, her disobedience could put him in the worst of circumstances.

Into the silence of the house, she heard the closing of Adam's door. She leapt out of bed and opened her door a few inches. A creak came from one of the stair treads and then the sound of the front door being opened.

Meredith closed her eyes and laid her head against the panel. 'Please, God, keep him safe.' She looked back at the bed; there was no use thinking of rest or sleep now. She would dress and check Sarah's portrait. There was nothing needed, but it would occupy her mind while she waited for Adam to return.

Adam left Tallow House in his disguise of Dello Murphy. His coachman, a trusted man who his father had found half-beaten to death in an alley years ago, had proved a loyal and faithful servant. He would not gossip about this strange rendezvous.

The coach turned into Ludgate Hill. To deaden the rumbling sounds of the wheels, Jackson had bandaged them with strips of canvas. Hence they arrived like a phantom as the dawn light tinged the sky.

Adam used no light. He felt his way up the stairs to the top floor and opened the secret panel. He spread a canvas bag and slid the Turner inside. From his jacket pocket he took a threaded sail needle and stitched the bag closed. Just once did he prick his finger and grunted. 'Being a warehouse owner can be useful, my love, this could have been a much harder task.' He had a prepared label and stitched it to the package. It read: The President, Sir Benjamin West.

The journey to The Grapes Inn was uneventful, even the young bucks were now tucked away in their beds or bedding a wench for a shilling. Woody moved from the shadows of a wall and opened the coach door. 'I'm here.

So first me money before I set a foot inside.'

Adam took a purse from his pocket and threw it at Woody. 'There's yer payment in full. I'm puttin' me trust in yer, man.'

He tapped the roof and the coach travelled west, leaving Aldgate, passing the Tower and on into the heart of the city. Daylight was now filling the doorways and alleys. Traders were afoot pushing their barrows to find the best corners to sell from.

He looked at Woody, trying to assess the man's worth. He had proved well with his information; could he go this last step with the same integrity?

'Well, what's to be done that yer're willing to pay me such a handsome sum?'

'We're deliverin' a package to the Royal Academy.'

'So, it's got value then? More than the ten guineas yer've paid me?'

'Like I said before, I pay for yer to ask no questions.'

The man's face was unreadable. Only his eyes moved from the canvas-wrapped painting, around the inside of the coach, and back to the man known as Dello Murphy.

'I'm yer man, Mr Murphy. Anythin' valuable ain't any good to me. Who would I sell it to? More likely I'd 'ave the Bow Street men after me. Bin in Newgate once, so I don't have any wish to go back.'

The coach slowed beside St Mary-le-Strand church. Across the road, a hundred paces away, was Somerset House, the home of the Royal Academy. The building was open and men were sweeping away the previous day's dust within the great archways.

'It's time, Woody. You carry the package. I'll conduct any negotiations or answer any challenges.'

Woody raised his brows, 'Challenges?'

'Just do as I say.'

The man nodded, opened the door and got out.

Adam slid the painting forward and followed.

CHAPTER TWENTY

Within the great stone archway on the west side, a door led into the Royal Academy wing. The vestibule was not overly large and sculptured busts of Reynolds and Gainsborough sat atop pillars of marble.

Adam cursed the sound of their footsteps on the tiled floor. He had hoped the reception desk would be unmanned this early. This was not so. A steward looked up and raised his hand in query.

Approaching, Adam signalled Woody to stay back.

'I have a painting for the exhibition. Where do I take it?'

The man's pale face and dark eyes were definitely not welcoming. 'You're a bit late for selection. Who told you it could be brought in here?'

'I'm under the tutorage of Mr Turner himself; you ain't going to dispute his instructions, are yer?'

Adam held the man's gaze, hoping he had guessed correctly that the great artist would not be here at this hour, but still in his bed.

'I'd better send a message up first, just to make sure.' He'd taken on the stance of importance, adjusting his jacket and stretching his neck above a badly tied neck-cloth.

'Come on, man. He's even put a label on it to Sir Benjamin West. Yer ain't going to waste his time and maybe put yerself in his bad books.' Turning to Woody, Adam cocked his head, 'Ain't that right?'

Woody stood holding the canvas package, hiding his body from chin to knees and was gripping the sides so tight his knuckles were white. 'That's right, sir, urgently needed.'

At the mention of such eminent gentlemen, Adam waited to see if his bluff would frighten the man into letting them pass.

It worked.

'I do 'appens to be very busy right now. So perhaps it best yer take it up. The second floor is where the great room is.'

Adam nodded his thanks and ran up a few steps to where the spiral staircase rose from the basement to the top landing. A round, glass-domed window in the roof let in the early morning light.

'This way.' He beckoned to Woody and started up the stairway. Halfway to the first floor, he leant over the scrolled iron balustrade. He could see Woody was so awe struck he was rooted to the place where he stood. 'Hurry, man, the great masters are waiting. Time is running out.'

Indeed, time was running out. Soon there would be men who knew there should be no delivery of such a painting today. He looked at the steward, busy with his own work. Any more calling could make him suspicious.

Woody came out of his trance and moved forward. 'Aye, sir.'

On the first floor a central door was closed. Moving on, the next flight of stairs wound higher and Adam looked down. The depth was emphasised by the iron spiral and Woody was now only half-a-dozen steps below him.

Suddenly, on the landing above, a side door opened and an aging gentleman came out. Adam froze; waved his hand at Woody to stop. He cursed silently; they were so near, and now were going to be challenged within yards of their mission. But the man did not look down, the papers in his hand occupying his eyes with more important duties than two people delivering a painting. He walked past the exhibition door and through another side door.

Adam wiped a smear of sweat from his forehead. He glanced back at Woody and beckoned him on, but he noticed the man's usually ruddy complexion had paled considerably.

Stopping on the top landing, Adam looked at the closed double doors. He had no idea what to expect when he opened them. For all the urgency that was required to get the Turner back into the room he could be walking into a situation that no amount of bluffing would get him out of. By noon he could be standing before a magistrate accused of theft.

He looked at Woody. The man had nothing to do with this crime and he didn't deserve to be implicated further. 'I'll take the package now, you can go. If the steward speaks to you, just nod and keep walking. Disappear into the alleyways and go to your home.'

The older man seemed to grow in stature and gripped the painting even tighter.

'I don't know what this is about, but I don't take pay fer 'alf a job. When we leave, we go together. Where der yer want this put?'

Adam wanted to argue, but there wasn't time. He nodded to the doors.

'This is where things could go wrong. You've said you don't want to go to prison again, well I can't guarantee that. Once I open these doors, there's no going back.'

In answer, Woody walked up the last few steps and stood beside Adam. 'Open it.'

Taking a deep breath he turned the brass knob and went in.

The room was enormous and the morning rays coming through the roof windows filled it with shadows.

Large covered paintings leant against the walls and small framed portraits were laid on a table. Ladders were scattered on the floor and others propped against a far wall.

Adam stood amazed at the magnitude of the task facing those responsible for displaying these works of art. Some were already in place and almost touched the ceiling line. He had never been to see the exhibition and he couldn't resist giving himself a moment to take in this great setting. Every inch of the walls would be filled with paintings from the humblest newcomer to the great masters. Somewhere the Turner he had would take its place here.

He sensed Woody behind him and turned to look at his accomplice, a man who had given his word for a fee and chose to stay to the end.

'We'll put our package over there beside that landscape. It looks as though they haven't been decided on yet.'

'I'm beginning to wonder what sort of a man yer be. Where's yer Irish tongue gone again? Thieves take, they don't put back. What's it all about?'

'Woody, for the last time, I pay, you ask no questions. Put it over there and let's go.'

Doing as bid, he placed the Turner where instructed. 'No one would believe me if I told 'em about this place and me being inside. It's a right high tale I'd be accused of telling. Them lot at The Grapes would think I was visitin' the opium dens.'

'That's just as well. This is one story you are never to tell, unless you want to go back to a prison cell or worse, Bedlam.'

'Gawd, Murphy, anywhere other than that mad place.'

'It's time to go. Follow me, like before, master and servant.'

Adam listened at the doors, but they were so thick, any sound wouldn't get in. 'Two minutes and we'll be back in the coach. Ready?'

Woody nodded.

The landing was empty and Adam moved out. He quietly closed the doors and with Woody close behind he ran down the spiral stairs to the ground floor.

No more than one minute had passed; the next was the most dangerous – they had to get pass the reception steward.

Relaxing his shoulders and putting on a jaunty step, he started across the vestibule towards the front door. He was within a yard of it when their way of escape was blocked by the entry of a well-dressed gentleman and, from behind, Adam heard the steward scrape his stool to stand up. He and Woody were trapped between a Royal Society Master and the steward.

Could he bluff his way through a second time?

Adam stopped and bowed. 'Good morning, sir. The package has been delivered as requested. Our honoured artist will be arriving soon.' He bowed again and side stepped around the gentleman and went out through the open door, Woody close enough to be his shadow.

The Strand had come alive since they had gone into the building. Adam dodged round a boy pushing a handcart of loaves and a chimney sweep, his brushes balanced on his shoulder, already covered in soot from his first call of the day.

He saw his coachman straighten up in his seat and flick the reins. Adam tumbled inside and reached out to help Woody as the horses set off at a near gallop. Out of the window Adam saw the steward frantically waving his arms and the gentleman swinging his cane. He grinned at his accomplice. Woody grinned back.

Meredith covered the portrait. This was the best work

she had ever done. Sarah's enthusiasm and joy shone in her eyes, her complexion glowed, and the pale curls seemed to create a soft halo. This was the perfect present for Victor Weston, on his homecoming.

Meredith went down the stairs; the only person who could be breakfasting would be Mr Weston. She didn't want to face any of the family yet, didn't want to pretend everything was normal when it wasn't. Until Adam returned she was living in the black abyss of fear. Instead, she went to the kitchen to look for Clemmie.

'Good morning, Cook, I am looking for Mrs Clements?'

'She's taking her tea in the garden.'

'May I have a cup and I'll join her.' She found her sitting on the bench outside the door. 'Good morning, Clemmie.'

'Meredith, you're up early.'

'Yes. It's such a lovely morning.' She sat down and sipped her tea. 'Have you settled down with Cook?'

'In some ways, yes, but it's strange to be treated as a guest, even though I help where needed.'

'You're a good soul, Clemmie. I'm pleased you are able to have a little time for yourself. How was your visit to Mrs Morgan?'

'We fared well together. I like her. And her new dress to wear for her granddaughter's christening is coming along nicely. We were wondering whether to start using our days off to make other dresses, to sell. Often it isn't the money that stops servants like us from having new things, it's do we want to spend our day off in our rooms sewing. I know when I was young I just wanted to be out, away from the Big House.'

Clemmie sounded so wistful that Meredith wondered what her younger life had been like. 'I think that's an excellent idea. Do you remember how I used to hate having to stay in sewing? And I expect London servants have better wages than in the country. If I can help in any way, you will ask, won't you?' Meredith leant over and kissed her cheek. 'It will be one way to repay you for all the years you looked after me.'

The old woman seemed to blossom and smiled. 'Thank you, dear. I shall speak to Mrs Morgan when I see her next.'

Meredith listened to the birds calling and smelt the mixture of scents from the garden. This was a haven to ease away her worries; but Adam was more than a worry, he was her lover and her life.

By mid-day, Meredith was frantic. There was no sign of Adam, for surely he should be back by now. In fact, she had expected him to return immediately from Somerset House. He must have been caught and accused of theft. No one would believe he was *returning* a painting. And there was nothing she could do, any action outside her normal position as Adam's fiancée would raise too many questions.

The clock chimed three and Meredith was imagining anything from Adam locked in a damp and dark prison cell to him lying dead on a table covered with a cloth. Either way, she wasn't going to see him again. She waited in the studio. This was the one place she could hide – until Sarah came running in. Today was the unveiling of her portrait. It was the worst possible day to choose.

'May I go into the drawing room and have just one little look, Miss Sanders? I promise I won't tell the others.'

'You know very well, Sarah, it is to be unveiled at four o'clock.' She spoke sharply but smiled at the child. 'Persistence may be your tactic for a preview, but I won't be swayed. Now, run along and play with Daffodil.'

'Uncle Adam isn't home yet.'

'No, but I'm sure he'll be here soon.'

Meredith sat on the window seat and looked at the garden. She remembered how Adam had come along the path, tall and handsome, and then asked her to stay and meet his aunt. Now he wanted her to stay and marry him. Where was he? What was happening out there in the streets of the city? Her thoughts flipped from one scenario to another: he was hiding in some alleyway fleeing the Bow Street men. Or worse, chained, waiting to be hanged. Not knowing was unbearable. Her body was so tense it might just break in two.

The sound of voices came through the open door and she caught Adam's laugh as Sarah was telling him he was late.

'It's been a busy day, little niece. But I'm hungry and looking forward to your unveiling party. Is your father here?'

'Yes. He's looking at the bottom of the garden. He thinks we have too many weeds.'

He was safe, Adam was here! He had come back to her like he promised – *surely, all had gone according to his plan.*

Her heart was hammering in her chest. She needed something to quench her thirst. There was a little lemonade in a glass and she sipped it slowly, giving herself time to calm down. Now Adam was home, Sarah's portrait could be viewed. The moment of truth had arrived – success or failure. She left to go down to the drawing room.

Adam's study door was ajar when she reached the last tread on the stairs. Was it an invitation to her? She tapped and waited. Then it opened wide and he smiled at her. 'Come in.'

Her depression lifted instantly. 'All is well?'

He closed the door and pulled her into his arms.

'Yes.'

'Are you sure? How do you know?'

'I, Dello Murphy, with his servant, had an urgent delivery for the exhibition. There was, I have to admit, a moment or two of concern, but the painting is restored to its rightful place, to be hung amongst a multitude of others.'

'Truly, Adam, this is the end?'

'Yes, my love. Now you cannot refuse my offer of marriage. You are free of Frederick's legacy. Lightfoot has disappeared and the forgeries are beyond our shores.'

She moved back, out of his warm comforting arms. A look of surprise crossed his face and then he frowned. 'What is it now, Meredith? What more do you want from me?'

She wanted to rejoice with him, wanted to say yes, she would be his forever. But she couldn't, and whispered, 'Not now, Adam. It's time to see Sarah's portrait.' She turned and left, knowing she went leaving him baffled and angry.

Meredith went straight into the drawing room to be greeted by a scene of merriment. Cook had excelled herself with a deep fruit cake. Aunt Izzie was in her chair with the tea-tray set on a table close by. Victor held Sarah's hand, trying to control her excitement as she hopped from foot to foot. The covered easel was beside the fireplace.

It should have been one of the happiest days of her life; instead she had shunned Adam without so much as a thank you for all the risks he had taken to protect her. Not even given him a kiss of gratitude. She pushed away the disgust she felt about herself. Nothing must spoil this moment – this was the family's day.

Adam came in, a smile on his lips, but his eyes

were dark and bleak.

'At last, Adam, I don't think Sarah can contain herself another moment.'

'Please accept my apologies to you all.' Going to Miss Fox, he gave a formal bow. 'Especially to you, Aunt Izzie.'

He turned to Meredith. 'Will Miss Sanders please unveil her masterpiece?'

Did she hear a slight emphasis on the word masterpiece? Her throat had gone dry again and if she spoke, it would break with emotion. She smiled at the room in general, avoiding Adam's penetrating look. Was he trying to look into her soul?

With trembling fingers she lifted the cloth, stood aside, and waited.

She looked at the patterned carpet, afraid to lift her eyes to the room. There was complete silence. It must be unacceptable. As the silence continued, her face burned with shame. All her boasting thoughts of how well the sittings with Sarah had gone were her own conceit. Why had she assumed she could be as good as Frederick? His faith in her abilities had only been a tutor's encouragement.

Then Victor Weston started to clap. 'Bravo, Miss Sanders. It is a truly beautiful likeness of my daughter.' He came forward and bowed to her. 'I shall cherish it always.'

From her chair, Miss Fox called her over. 'My dear, I had no idea a woman could excel to such a high standard. You are surely destined to take a place in the artists' world.' She turned her head to Adam, who had remained close. 'What do you say to this, Adam? You are about to take a wife who will be acclaimed by the mistresses of the houses, if not the masters.'

He came forward and raised Meredith's hand to his lips. 'I don't know if such a union is destined to happen.'

His words hurt, but she deserved his contempt.

Finally, Sarah brought everything back to normal. She stood in front of her portrait and cried, big tears running down her face, and ran to Meredith. 'Oh, Miss Sanders, it is beautiful. Am I really like that?'

Meredith knelt and took a handkerchief from her gown pocket. She wiped away the tears and said very softly, 'Yes, Sarah. You will be even more beautiful when you are grown up. I'm so glad you are pleased with it.'

The child flung her arms round Meredith's neck and kissed her cheek. 'And you did this all for Papa, but he's here now. Shall we have some tea and cake?'

The room erupted into laughter and Simms, who had been standing back, awaiting the moment to proceed with the tea, stepped forward.

Meredith tried to avoid Adam, but he was not allowing it. He waited until Simms removed the tea tray, and Victor with Sarah's help took the portrait back to the studio.

'Would you like a turn round the garden, Meredith? I think Aunt Izzie has had too much excitement and will doze a while.'

She should decline, but she needed to get out of the confines of the room. The garden was the perfect place, but should it be with Adam? He would only wish to press her again about why she would not consent to a marriage date. But she was only putting off what needed to be said. 'Thank you, just for a few moments.'

To her surprise, he mentioned nothing about their relationship as they walked to the end of the garden and sat under the cherry tree. Then he spoke of his brother-in-law.

'Victor says the garden is in need of attention. Would you agree?'

'Perhaps a little weeding needs to be done. Do

you have a gardener?'

'Yes and no. My coachman does a little, but only when he is free from his own duties. I have kept him well occupied of late.'

Again, there was a double meaning, and she made no comment.

'Victor has also complained of the overgrown dog roses. As you have gathered, botany is his passion. Perhaps I will let him loose on it and see what wonders he can achieve.'

'Oh, you aren't going to let him make this into a formal garden, are you? I would hate that.'

'You are planning to be here then?'

She had fallen into her own trap. 'I'm sorry, that was impudent of me. Of course you may do as you wish.'

'That I may, madam.' His manner and tone radiated his anger from earlier.

She didn't want to cause further upset and thought it prudent to return to the house. 'I have a slight headache. If you will excuse me, sir, I will see you later.'

Without giving him time to comment, she hurried back along the path and to her room. She lay on the coverlet. In truth her head did ache, but her heart ached more. If she took a few drops of laudanum she could sleep for an hour.

Adam Fox! He had come back as though it had been nothing more than a worthless trinket he had been forced to deliver to save her. He was the most annoying, arrogant; she couldn't think of one other name to damn him by and then the word love came into her mind. Oh, the man was impossible. Going to the wardrobe she picked up her valise and took a small bottle of laudanum from a side pocket the doctor at Harlington had prescribed when Frederick died. She poured a few drops into a glass of water, swallowed it quickly and lay down under the counterpane.

Meredith was in a woolly world where nothing mattered: there were no problems, no people, no … She opened her eyes. The room was dark and Adam stood beside her bed holding a candlestick, his neck cloth missing and his shirt opened low to his waist.

'Meredith, are you alright? We've tried to wake you several times.'

She struggled up onto her elbow and rubbed her eyes. Everything was strange, as though her head was floating. 'May I have a drink, please?'

Adam put the candlestick down on the bedside cabinet and went back through the connecting door. A moment later he returned and handed her the glass and sat on the side of the bed.

The cool liquid eased her throat and she sipped until the glass was empty. Handing it back, she asked. 'What is the time?'

'Everyone is asleep, it is past midnight. You were in such a deep slumber come dinner, we decided to leave you. But every time someone came in here nothing would wake you. What have you taken, Meredith?'

Her eyes wouldn't open properly and she still had a headache, but she recognised the demand of his words.

'A few drops of laudanum. I just wanted to sleep and not have any dreams.' She whispered the words, ashamed she had sunk to a point where she needed medicine to wipe away the decision she had to make.

'Have I pushed you that far?'

He sounded distraught and she gripped his arm, digging her nails into the flesh under his shirt. 'No, it's not you, Adam. It never has been anything you have done. Without you, where would I be at this moment? You are my knight who has defended me, risked all that you hold dear – your family – for me.'

'Then what is left, Meredith? Are you saying I should

choose my family above you?'

She released her hold on his arm. In that moment she knew what she was going to do.

'Yes.' The hurt in his eyes was like a dagger through her heart.

He picked up the candlestick. 'Go back to sleep. We will discuss this tomorrow.'

He walked through the door and she heard the key turn in the lock.

CHAPTER TWENTY ONE

Meredith left her bedchamber. The only light to guide her to Mrs Clements' room was from a small window halfway up the attic stairs.

Gently shaking the woman, she whispered. 'Clemmie, wake up. It's Meredith.' A snuffled sigh was her answer, 'It's time to get up.' This time, Mrs Clements opened her eyes.

'Meredith? What's wrong?'

'Nothing, we're going home. I've packed my valise. While you dress, I'll pack yours.'

'Going home? Do you mean Harlington?'

'No. We're going to Ludgate Hill.'

'Why? What has happened?'

Meredith didn't want to get into a long conversation, especially as Cook slept next door. 'I'll explain later. Hurry, please.'

Meredith helped Clemmie down the stairs. Outside Adam's room she paused and listened; only the hall clock chiming four filled the silent house. She should have told him she was leaving – she wasn't even sliding a note under his door. Her heartache weighed heavy in her chest as she crept down the stairs into the hall. She pulled the front door bolts and they went out into the street.

To the east the sky had a pencil line of light pushing away the night. She walked as though alone, not glancing or saying anything to Clemmie, yet there was so much to be said. As the dawn filled the alleys and doorways a horse and cart slowed beside them.

'Looking fer a ride? I'm going as far as St Pauls, if yer like to hop on the back.'

'Thank you, sir. That destination will be most acceptable.' Mrs Clements beamed up at the bearded trader. 'Ludgate Hill is only a short walk from there. Come, Meredith, let us not keep our Good Samaritan waiting.'

They pushed their valises between the vegetables and climbed onto the cart, dangling their legs over the back. The wheels rolled and rumbled along the cobbled road, the clip-clop of the horse's hooves rhythmic as the tick of a clock.

'Well, Meredith, we have nothing to do until we reach St Paul's, except watch the beginning of a new day. What is all this about?'

Meredith bit her lip and sighed; there was no way of avoiding the truth. She owed Clemmie that. 'I can't marry Mr Fox. His offer is generous, we get on well together, but …' she paused a moment, 'he doesn't know about where I really come from – Blackfriars – about my real father.'

'Mr Fox loves you, Meredith. You can't just run away.'

'I know.' Her throat clogged with tears. 'But I am what I am, a debtor's daughter from Thames Street. But I do love him so, Clemmie, and I owe him so much.'

Clemmie took her hand and patted it as a mother does a child. 'Rest now, we will talk when we get home.'

The route was a familiar one for Meredith, but this early in the morning it seemed different. Without the bustle of people, their voices, the trundling of cart and carriage wheels she could be back in the country. It didn't soothe her agitation. She could read and write, she wasn't a twelve-year-old illiterate anymore. There was no excuse for her thoughtless behaviour. Each turn of the wheels was taking her away from the man she loved. But this was her decision, the right thing to do.

The cart stopped. They had reached St Paul's Churchyard.

'Thank you for the ride, sir, it did indeed save our legs a long and weary walk.'

Meredith put their valises on the ground and they waved farewell as the cart rumbled on out of sight. As Clemmie had said, it was only a short walk to their home.

The parlour was cold. 'Why does an unlived in house always seem sad? I remember when we first came here, Clemmie, it took me days to make it feel like home.'

'Don't fret, dear; I'll go to the market when we've settled in. I'll buy us something special for breakfast to celebrate your first successful commission. Mr Sanders, God rest his soul, would be so proud of you.'

Yes, he would, and she really was grateful to him for the home he had given her; for his tender ways in helping her achieve a talent that could have lain hidden forever.

'I'm going downstairs. I'll see you after you've been to the market.'

Everything looked the same. She touched the blank space on the wall where the landscape painting was hanging before Adam had bought it. That now seemed a long time ago. So much had happened to her, to them, in less than two weeks. Was she a coward or a fool?

The morning grew lighter and outside the sounds of the traders opening for business brought a sense of normality. Meredith went into the studio. She placed a canvas leaning against the wall on to the easel. Adam's face looked back at her. What would he think when he found her gone? Ungrateful; that she had used him. That thought hurt. She took a charcoal stick and with bold strokes drew his shirt with the deep vee opening. Using her finger she shaded his dark chest, filled in the strong lines of his throat. She touched the lips she had drawn that Sunday afternoon. What was she going to do without him?

Then Thames Street – the basement room – finally found its way into her thoughts. The urge to go back and make peace with her father became the most important thing she had to do. Perhaps, then, she could look to a future.

She had heard Clemmie leave to go to the market. She locked the front door and walked towards St Paul's and Blackfriars.

Adam stood before the connecting door. Did he have the right to walk through? She had said no to his offer, yet he couldn't accept that without talking to her again. He turned the key and went into her bedchamber. The bed was empty, all her toilette gone. He opened the wardrobe. Empty!

His immediate reaction was a blinding anger, then shock. What was she playing at? He went to the studio; she was not there. He ran down the stairs, through the kitchen, and out into the garden. The early morning light cast shadows and the taller plants looked as though they were floating on dark water. He would find her sitting on her favourite seat; it was the only place he could think of. But she was not there.

He went back to his study, hoping she had left him a note, but his desk was just the bare green leather square. She was gone.

Then, let it be. But he couldn't. Whatever real or imagined problem she had, he would solve it with her. Hadn't he risked everything: his life, his reputation, his business; even his family's position in society? Where would she go? The Harlington house would be re-let, she knew very few people in London. It only left Ludgate Hill; the only home she had.

He raced up to his bedchamber and finished dressing. Within fifteen minutes he slammed the front door, no doubt waking those still asleep.

He found a hackney and with the promise of an extra shilling he had the man whipping his horses into a gallop. The street door was locked. He banged the knocker over and over; he was certain this was where she had come. He had no other address, no names. The coachman coughed, 'Me fare, sir, and the extra.'

Adam's mind was blank, not a thought would come into it. As he was about to instruct the coachman to return to Tallow House, Mrs Clements came into view carrying a well-laden bag.

'Wait here; I may have another destination for you.'

He hurried forward and relieved her of her burden. 'Mrs Clements, where is Miss Sanders? The door is locked.' He waved impatiently back along the street.

'Locked? Perhaps she has gone to rest. Come, I have a key.' Mrs Clements hurried forward, her agitation akin to his. When she unlocked the door, he wanted to push past, but held his impatience in check. Manners decreed that he follow her up the stairs.

Waiting in the parlour, the minutes ticked like hammer blows from the mantel clock. Like a caged animal he paced the room until footsteps sounded coming from above. Only Mrs Clements came into the room.

'I don't understand where she has gone. But she wouldn't have locked the premises unless she went out.' Mrs Clements heaved a great sigh. 'Mr Fox, what is happening? I'm far too old for all this ...' She broke off and covered her face with her hands.

Adam guided her to the sofa and sitting down next to her spoke gently. 'Is there anywhere special she might go? Does she have a favourite place, or someone she knows?'

'No one, sir, only …' Mrs Clements looked up at him, 'surely, she wouldn't go back there?'

'Where, Mrs Clements? Tell me where?'

'I can't. It's her secret, not mine to tell.'

'What secret?' His mind rolled the word around. She had mentioned that word to him before. There was something she wanted to tell him? 'Mrs Clements, you have to tell me. I'm the only one who can help her.'

The old woman looked down at her hands, twisted them round and round. 'Why should I tell you, sir?'

'Because, Mrs Clements, without her my life will be nothing. I love her and I know she loves me.'

Her face softened and she smiled. 'Do you love her enough to accept her as she is?'

Her words made no sense, but he would agree with anything to get an address.

'As she is,' he repeated.

'I don't know the number, but there's a house in Thames Street, in Blackfriars. I don't promise she's there, but she might be.'

'What sort of house?'

'I don't know. You will have to search.'

Adam squeezed her hand. 'Thank you.' He raced down the stairs and into the street. 'Coachman, Blackfriars. And another shilling for your speedy horses.'

The coach stopped somewhere in Thames Street and he got out. 'Wait here. I'll pay whatever you need.'

'I'd be getting a fair number of rides back in the city. So it'll cost yer, sir.'

Adam nodded. 'Whatever your charge, man, I promise.'

He waited on the road. Which way? He was familiar with the docks area and this was not any different – poor houses, poor people. Women watched him from windows, others sitting on the front step. He noticed the children had no shoes; their clothes ragged and dirty. He'd never had a need to visit Blackfriars before as his agent dealt with most of the routine work.

What was Meredith doing here?

He walked, looking from side to side. An inn was open and although he thought The Grapes a place of ill repute, it looked better than this one. Leaning against the doorway was a woman, her dark hair streaked with grey. She smiled, but her eyes were as lifeless as a corpse. There was no hiding what she did for a living as she raised her skirt and drew her bare leg in a semi-circle and beckoned him over.

What was Meredith doing in an area like this?

Passing a young girl scrubbing a step, he thought of asking if she had seen Meredith, but the girl's eyes were lowered, watching her hands push backwards and forwards in some kind of rhythmic trance.

Adam walked on. He almost missed her. Only her yellow gown stood out against the dark grey house. She sat on a basement step, her hands clasped in her lap, a blank expression on her face, her eyes staring, like a child forlorn and lost.

He sat on the step next to her. 'Hello, Meredith. May I sit here with you?' She didn't answer, didn't even acknowledge him. 'Are you visiting someone?' He lifted her hand and despite the morning sun her fingers were cold. The movement seemed to bring her back to the present and she looked at him.

'Adam? What are you doing here?' Her glazed stare turned to one of fear. 'You can't be here, no one knows … did Mrs Clements … no, she wouldn't …' She tried to get up, but he held firmly on to her hand.

'Yes, she did, Meredith, but only because I told her my life would be nothing without you. Why are you here?'

She stilled; then she sighed. 'This is where I was

born. This is where I ran away from.'

Adam didn't know what he had expected her secret to be. But not this!

She came from a riverside family, was part of what he had passed earlier walking along this road? It wasn't possible; she was a lady of means. Frederick Sanders had been an artist, a man who belonged amongst respected citizens. His life in the underworld of Madame Lightfoot was a period outside that of his peers.

'You look shocked, sir.' She withdrew her hand from his. 'I am waiting to see someone. I should be obliged if you would leave me to see him on my own.'

There was now a dignity in her manner that reminded him of that first day, when she had proudly announced that she was the artist of the paintings hanging on the gallery walls. He looked towards the basement door and then up at the house. He didn't want to picture her living here, in these appalling conditions. Why hadn't she told him?

His love should be shattered, but it wasn't. Is that what she feared? That she was not equal to him? He loved Meredith for herself, not where she came from.

'No! Whatever you are facing, we will face together.'

A shadow fell across them and he looked up into the face of Woody, his informant and accomplice from The Grapes Inn.

'Well, now. This is a surprise; and yer've brought the girl with yer to.'

Adam stood up, realisation beginning to dawn. What he had thought was play-acting in The Grapes Inn, was real. Her primness in the gallery after their first visit was a reaction to her past. Looking down, he saw her gaze was fixed on Woody.

'Miss Sanders wishes to see you.' Adam held out his hand to help her rise. 'Well, Meredith, is this who you have come to see?'

'Aren't yer the one in room six, who got her skirt burned?'

Her hand trembled. Her lips were almost white and there was an emotion in her eyes he didn't understand.

'Hello, Papa. It's me, Merry.'

The man seemed to age instantly. His shoulders sagged and the lines on his face deepened. His eyes never left Meredith's face and his lips parted, then closed. Words seemed to have become frozen, unutterable as he swallowed and licked his lips. He put out his arms and then let them fall back to his side.

'My Merry? Yer're my girl?'

'Yes.' A whisper, but he heard.

'How can this be? Where've yer been? Yer mother died with yer name on her lips.' Meredith sagged as though she was about to fall.

'I think we should go into your rooms.' Adam's voice broke the tableau.

Woody nodded and indicated the building behind them. Meredith moved towards the basement, but Woody's voice carried loud. 'We don't live down there anymore. Without yer help I got us above the dirt and rats.'

She stopped. 'I'm so glad ...' her voice caught and was full of tears, '... that Mama didn't die in the basement.'

Adam longed to comfort her. Fold her in his arms, soothe away her pain. But she had to do this on her own.

The room Woody lived in was small, but clean, the one window covered with a thin curtain. The heavy wooden table filled most of the floor space and the two carved chairs looked out of place in the sparse brick-walled room. The one comfortable chair was placed by the hearth. A pot hung in readiness from a chain over unlit logs.

'How many rooms do you have?' Adam asked,

seeing no bed or cot alcove.

'We have another room across the hall fer sleeping in and the basement fer a workshop.'

Meredith came alive and her tone was sharp. 'What have you done with my sister? Where's Tilly?'

'Ho! You think I've sold her off like I tried to you. I was desperate all those years ago. Newgate prison was killing me; I had to promise you to Snipes. Marriage was an honourable way fer yer.' He started to pace the room, much as a prisoner in a cell. 'Without yer being wed, I had to stay, but yer ma worked on and the boys helped. Only good thing was one of the other debtors was a carpenter and he showed me how to carve. So, perhaps yer running away was the right thing.' Woody rubbed his hand over his face. 'Tilly's gone to the country, to help yer other sister with her babes. She's just had two at once. She married a God-fearin' man in the Church and the Lord might want us to …' He stopped. 'Sorry. Yer looks to have become a delicate lady, but one at a time was enough fer yer ma to have.'

He sat down in his chair; his eyes never still, darting from door to table, to Adam and then Meredith. Finally he asked, 'Well, what der yer want?'

Adam now knew her secret: the guilt of running away, Woody trying to force her into marriage and Blackfriars where she was born. She thought it would matter to him, being born here in Thames Street? That he would reject her? Did she not realise his love was stronger than where she came from? *Nothing could ever break that love.*

She stood by the table like a statue, the silence broken only by the shouts of men and the clatter of horse carts from the street outside. The impasse between father and daughter was total. One had to give in and take the lead and bring a sorrow carried deep to an end.

He could not intervene, so he waited and watched

two people come to a reconcilable decision.

Meredith spoke first.

'Papa, I'm sorry. I should have thought of Mama, but what you were doing was wrong. I have carried that with me until I saw you that day at The Grapes Inn.'

Woody turned his head and looked at her. 'Aye, and I should have recognised you. But I have believed you dead for so long.' His voice broke and tears ran down his face. 'Oh, Merry, me girl, what are we going to do?'

'I don't know, Papa. But I had to see you.'

Adam was an outsider to the emotions playing across both father and daughter's faces. He wanted to tell her all was well. Wherever she came from she would always be his. But the moment was not yet; she had to deal with this in her own way. He had never been so inapt. But he forced himself to remain silent and still.

Woody tugged a handkerchief from his pocket, wiped his face. 'Can we be a family again? Would yer visit sometimes?'

'Perhaps.'

Adam cleared his throat with a polite cough. 'There is something I should like to ask. What is your given name, Woody?'

'Me name? And why should an Irish rogue turned English gentleman wish to know that? It might be time fer me to ask what game yer be playing, Dello Murphy.'

'Ah. As Dello said, he was paying for no questions asked.' Adam bowed. 'Mr Adam Fox, sir. Our friend Dello has gone.'

'Mr Jack Burrows, sir,' delivered with just a nod.

So Meredith had used her own name to play her role. Adam chided himself for not putting together this and Woody's reaction when she was kidnapped. Her father thought her dead; yet faced with the hope that she could be alive. He had carried the guilt like a destructive instrument for his daughter's desperate need to run away. A kidnapped girl of her age would have brought the guilt to the surface. But in The Grapes Inn, Adam had only one thought in his mind – to find Meredith.

'Well, Mr Burrows, I request the honour of your daughter's hand in marriage. She has been unable to give me an answer until now. Have I your permission to ask?' Adam hoped this was the moment when she would accept he wanted her *and her hidden past.*

Simultaneously, father and daughter looked at him. Meredith's eyes widened and she started to speak but Adam raised his hand. 'Say nothing, Meredith; this is between your father and me.' He raised his brows at Jack Burrows. 'Well, sir?'

'Marriage, be damned. Does she want yer? I've made one mistake, I'll not make another.' He gestured to Meredith, 'Do you want him?'

Adam liked the blunt attitude of the man. It certainly put Meredith in a position of replying in the same manner.

She glanced towards him, her face now calm and beautiful. 'Yes, Papa, I want him.'

'Then it's done, Mr Fox. She's yers with no charge.'

Adam didn't wait for any other comments. Taking Meredith's hand he pulled her to him and lightly kissed her lips. 'Will you be mine?'

She stepped away from him, glancing at her father, including both in her reply. 'I lied about Frederick. But he found me and gave me his name. I was his daughter since the day I was twelve. I abandoned my mother, my brothers and sisters. But I never intended to hurt you, Adam. I tried to tell you, I wanted you to know, really I did. I trust you, with my life and my love. But before I give you my answer I have to know you can forgive me.'

Now she had taken the step to meet him halfway. He had to bring her the other half. 'Yes, Meredith, I forgive you. You have given me a fine chase, but all is now in the open and we can go forward into the future.'

She smiled at him and he could see the love in her eyes. 'Yes, Adam, I will be yours.'

Her father stood up. She went to him, a flush on her cheeks. 'Thank you. I will visit, I promise.'

For the first time in ten years, father and daughter stood together and when Woody took her hand, Adam saw tears glisten in her eyes.

CHAPTER TWENTY TWO

Adam helped Meredith from his coach outside Somerset House, his diamond betrothal ring on her wedding finger.

'Welcome to your first visit to the Royal Academy, Meredith, and a more dignified entrance for me.'

'Yes. I will never know the truth about Frederick. But his reputation remains untarnished. And I owe it all to you.'

Adam led her past the pale-faced steward, up the spiral stairs to the top floor.

Joseph Mallord William Turner's The Great Fall of the Reichenbach, in the Valley of Hasle, Switzerland, hung on the wall in the Inner Room.

'Isn't it magnificent, Adam? Perhaps, one day, I might try to copy it too.'

THE END

AUTHOR'S NOTE

The Marriage Act of 1753 permitted girls of 12 years and boys of 14 years to marry with parental consent.

In 1929, in response to a campaign by the National Union of Societies for Equal Citizenship, Parliament raised the age to 16 (with parental consent) for both sexes in the Ages of Marriage Act. This is still the minimum age in Britain.

Lightning Source UK Ltd.
Milton Keynes UK
UKOW01f0856011116
286601UK00002B/8/P